PUNCTURED

Published by AmazonEncore
P.O. Box 400818
Las Vegas, NV 89140

ISBN-13: 9781935597582
ISBN-10: 1935597582

LAS VEGAS MYSTERY SERIES

PUNCTURED

Rex Kusler

PUBLISHED BY

amazon encore

CHAPTER 1

It was dusk when Bob arrived at the gate to the RV storage lot. He'd been there for twenty minutes, and now it was almost dark. With Halloween a week away, the days had been getting shorter. He was parked in the middle of five spaces outside the fence in front of the entrance, waiting.

His lower back started to ache in the usual spot on the left side, just above his belt. He needed to lose weight, get rid of the paunch. Those fifty-two-year-old muscles needed all the help they could get. He leaned forward, reached down with his left hand, and began to massage it. Turning his head, he watched two young men standing on the side of the road in front of the entrance to a towing company. They wore white T-shirts and blue jeans. Talking and laughing, occasionally they would turn their eyes in his direction. It gave him the willies. This wasn't the safest area of Las Vegas to be sitting alone in his truck, in the dark.

He opened the door of his Chevy Silverado, eased himself out, and walked stiffly over to the keypad. He punched in his password.

As the gate opened, he hobbled back to his truck, climbed in, started it, and drove inside the lot.

He felt safer now.

Twenty minutes later he saw the twin beams of another truck approaching the lot from down the street. It pulled to a stop outside the gate, and he could see clearly now in his side mirror that it was his neighbor Steve's red Tundra. He got out and waved and punched in the code to open the gate. The Tundra followed him, gravel crunching and popping under their tires, past five rows of assorted boats, motor homes, and trailers. They turned and continued on. Halfway down the gravel and dirt lane, he stopped in front of a late-model motor home.

The two men cut their engines, then their lights. The glow from the half-moon above them reflected faintly off the gray, packed dirt and scattered gravel. It was completely quiet now. Two heavy truck doors opened and then slammed shut almost in unison. They walked toward each other and shook hands, neither of them smiling.

"Sorry I'm late," Steve said. He was taller than Bob, leaner, with a full head of black hair. Twelve years younger, he had the rugged good looks that featured a strong jawline. He carried himself like a professional athlete. "I got hung up at the dealership."

"Ah, don't worry about it." Bob reached up and ran his hand backwards over his bald head as though he were trying to smooth out the hair that was no longer there. He pointed his thumb toward his truck. "Let me get something to see with, and I'll give you the ten-cent maintenance tour."

He walked over to the passenger side of his Chevy, opened the door, and pulled a foot-long flashlight out of the glove compartment. Flicking it on, he aimed the beam toward the Aljo travel trailer that stood parked in the space in front of him.

Circling the trailer together, playing the light over the notable features, Bob opened and closed all of the storage compartments and the outside shower, and pointed out the furnace and hot water tank locations. They worked their way around to the door. Leaning over slowly, with a short grunt, Bob lowered the front step. He unlocked the door, and they stepped inside.

They were greeted by a subtle, musky odor. Leaving the door open, Bob moved around the living, dining, and kitchen areas, snapping on lights, the trailer bouncing in rhythm to every step. The interior filled with a flood of light.

He pointed up toward the corner of the ceiling. "That's your antenna connection up there." He demonstrated the breakdown of the table into a tiny, cushioned sleeping surface, and then he spun around and worked the switches on the control panel. "These are your gauges: battery, black water level, gray water level, fresh water level…water heater switch, both electric and gas…"

Steve offered an approving nod. "Nice. Really nice. This is in good shape." His gaze wandered from one end of the interior to the other. He nodded again. "Those little bulbs put out a lot of light."

"Yeah," Bob agreed. "And they're just automotive taillight bulbs. You can pick 'em up at any auto parts store. Number's stamped on the base of the bulbs."

Steve nodded some more. "Alright." He clapped his hands, rubbing them together a couple of times. "Well, let's do this."

"Okay, good." Bob waved a hand toward the bed. "All the manuals, everything is stacked on the bed." He pulled the title out of his back pocket and looked at it. "I'll fill this out and sign it over…"

"While you're doing that," Steve offered, "I'll go get the cash out of the truck. Eight thousand."

"Right. Eight thousand."

Steve hopped down the steps, causing the trailer to bounce some more, and disappeared past the edge of the open door.

A couple minutes later, he returned holding a thick stack of bills, bulging around a thin rubber band. "Let me count this out, just to make sure there's no mistake." He positioned himself in front of the dining room table and started counting.

As Bob stood watching the parade of bills forming into neat stacks on the table, he glanced through the open doorway at the glow of light spilling out onto the gravel beside the trailer. His gaze fixed on it, and it seemed to hypnotize him. It was deathly quiet outside.

Suddenly an eerie feeling washed over him, causing a chill to run up his spine. A moment later it passed, and he felt strangely calm.

An odd thought ran through Bob Williams's mind just then.

He wondered if this was the way it felt—during the last minutes before death.

CHAPTER 2

Four miles into his morning run, the outside of his right knee began to throb. He slowed to a walk.

"Jesus," he muttered. The Las Vegas Marathon would have to wait yet another year—one more opportunity for provoking, and then struggling to recover from, the next running-related injury. At forty-five, Jim Snow was twenty years past the best shape of his life. Six foot three and two hundred and fifteen pounds wasn't the ideal build for a distance runner. Not that he was overweight at all; he was built more like a bodybuilder than a runner. The iron-pumping sessions in his spare bedroom were a direct conflict with the joint-pounding expeditions on the roads. The physique of a titan and the stamina of an Ethiopian mountain runner. That's what he wanted. But you can't have it all.

It was a quarter past eight on a Saturday morning. Not much traffic on this Las Vegas street. But now that he'd given up the pounding of his morning run, he left the asphalt roadway and moved over to the harder cement of the sidewalk.

He walked the remaining half mile to his stucco tract home. It was a three-bedroom, single-story structure, located in a middle-class neighborhood of east Las Vegas.

As he approached the front door, he leaned over to retrieve the morning paper from the raised cement stoop. Stuffing it under his arm, he dug the door key out of the tiny, inner pocket of his running shorts and unlocked the door.

Crossing through the living room and into the kitchen, he stripped the rubber band from the paper and opened it on the counter. He left it there, went to the coffeemaker, and filled it with water and grounds. He pressed the switch. Then he went back to the paper to read the breaking news centered on the front page: Unemployment was now above thirteen percent in the city of sin. According to local economists, the giant swirling mass of residents, their homes, and their jobs were getting drawn downward into the abyss, and it would continue for years. The only jobs that were safe it seemed, according to the article, were those of local economists. They would be needed to continue spending long hours studying the situation, in order to provide further assessments to the citizens of Las Vegas. When you're trudging down the desperate road to despair, it's good to have accurate reports periodically, in order to gauge your degree of misery. Over a period of years, it's easy to lose your frame of reference.

He was nearly finished with the article when the phone rang. He looked over at the old trim-line model where it sat on the counter, next to the answering machine and the microwave. It rang again, and he considered answering it, though he was fairly certain it was just another computerized voice, or a friendly human with a poor command of English, interested in adding an identity theft prevention feature to his credit card account.

Old habits are hard to break. On the third ring he picked up the receiver. "Yeah," he said.

He immediately recognized his sister's voice firing through the line. Her tortured words launched out of the receiver in a rush: "Something terrible has happened!" This was followed by a sharp intake of breath.

Snow stiffened, his jaw tensing. "Karen? What's wrong?"

"Bob is dead!" This was followed by rapid, shallow breathing.

"Your husband Bob?" This sounded like a silly question to him as it popped out of Snow's mouth. But it was all he could think to say.

More rapid breathing. "Yes, Jim!" she cried. "Bob my husband! He's dead! They killed him!"

Snow shifted his gaze to the microwave as though that might have something to do with this. His voice held calm: "Karen, take a breath. Sit down. Are you sitting down?"

She was sobbing now. Her words came slower, her voice lowering an octave to its normal pitch. "I need your help."

"Alright," he said. "Who is 'they'?"

"How would I know? Whoever killed him…" she replied. "The police think it was me—and Steve!"

"Who is Steve?"

"The neighbor."

"The neighbor? Where did this happen?"

"They found him in an RV storage lot, this morning, just after six. Some guy coming to pick up his boat found him, lying in the dirt next to his pickup. Dead."

"What was he doing in an RV storage lot?"

Her voice started to rise again. "It's where we store our travel trailer. Bob was selling it—to Steve. There was a lot of cash involved. Steve must have left…and Bob…Bob…" She began to sob again.

Snow began to sort all of this out in his mind. "Have you talked to the neighbor?"

"No."

"Have the police talked to him? Did they say?"

"No. They were planning to go over there when they left here, just a few minutes ago." She sniffed a couple of times. "But they told me it was a pickaxe, something with a sharp, pointed end, and there's a pickaxe in our garage—a brand-new one. I'm the next of kin and I have a pickaxe in my garage—so I'm the murderer—open-and-shut case."

"I'm sure it's not that simple—"

"It is that simple. The cops are that simple. You know how they are. You used to be one of them."

"Are you there by yourself?"

"Yes. Like I said, they just left."

"The detectives."

"Yes," she said. "Mel Harris and Alice James. Do you know them?"

Snow screwed his face into a frown. Melvin Harris. He remembered him. Twenty years with Metro, nine as a detective. They'd never talked much during Jim Snow's tenure as a homicide detective, which had ended three years ago. But that wasn't uncommon—Las Vegas Metropolitan Robbery/Homicide Bureau was big, with over twenty detectives working under four sergeants in just the homicide section alone. But Mel Harris was the sort who was hard to forget. He had a head of thick black hair that grew like wild grass, and the good looks and swagger of an award-winning car salesman. But he usually walked around with a confused expression on his face, bothering the other detectives with some of the dumbest off-color jokes Snow had ever heard. As for Alice James, that was a name he couldn't place.

"I need your help, Jim," Karen repeated. She sighed. "You're my only brother. You're my only living relative."

"Okay," he said. "Stay calm. I'll be right over."

"Do you still have your gun from your cop days?" she asked.

"I do have a handgun somewhere around here. It's packed away. Why?"

"I think you'd better bring it with you," she said.

"What for?"

"Because I don't have one," she said. "And I may decide to shoot myself."

CHAPTER 3

The home Karen was currently living in was similar to Snow's. In fact, in Snow's opinion, most of the newer homes in Las Vegas were similar to his—and everybody else's. They were nearly all constructed of stucco and painted in various shades of off-white or brown, with an assortment of desert plants poking up out of the gravel that covered the tiny front and side yards. But Karen's house was larger than Snow's, about twelve hundred square feet larger, with an extra bedroom and bathroom. What she needed with all that space and extra plumbing he had no idea.

He drove past an Aljo travel trailer, parked on the street in front of her neighbor's home, turned his blue Hyundai Sonata into the driveway, and brought it to a stop in front of the garage door. Climbing out of the car, he glanced briefly around the neighborhood. He caught a glimpse of a slight opening in the blinds of a front window in the house across the street. No sooner did his eyes focus on it than the gap disappeared.

He walked to the front door and reached toward the doorbell. The door opened before he could press it. In the doorway stood a slender woman of forty-eight. She had green eyes that matched his own and small, even features framed by straight brown hair that stopped just below her ears. Her eyes were red and swollen.

Karen leaned into him, slipped her arms around his back, and buried her face in his chest. "I'm glad you're here," she said.

He wasn't sure what to do with his hands. His sister had never hugged him this way before. It felt good—in a sisterly sort of way. He didn't want to seem cold, so he put one hand in the middle of her back, the other in the back pocket of his jeans. It felt awkward, but they stood that way for a moment without talking, and then she backed away from him, turned, and padded across the hardwood floor of the expansive living room in her bare feet, past a matching sofa, love seat, and stuffed chair combination upholstered in what appeared to be some sort of leafy, jungle flower design. The walls were adorned with elegantly framed paintings of riverside cottages, villages, mansions, and churches—all oozing brilliant light from every window, doorway, and streetlight.

Karen and Snow had grown up in a small two-story, three-bedroom home in a small town in north central Minnesota, with a single bathroom and a front door that opened into the kitchen. It had been built just before the turn of the century, and in those days guests were entertained mostly in the living or dining rooms around a giant table. Karen usually followed that tradition, leading her guests—the ones who were welcome—into the heart of her home, the kitchen. Salesmen and other miscreants were always seated in the living room as close to the front door as possible, in order to hustle them out quickly.

Following her over the brushed travertine tile of her spotless kitchen, Snow pulled a chair out from under the end of the kitchen table and sat down. He watched his sister march toward the stainless steel coffeemaker. She wore a white T-shirt with baggy sleeves down to her elbows and a tail that halfway covered the pockets of her blue jeans. "You want some coffee?"

"Please."

As she busied herself with filling the carafe from the gooseneck faucet that pivoted over a dual stainless steel sink, Snow glanced around the kitchen. The countertops were black granite, the cabinets unblemished cherrywood. The double-door refrigerator, dishwasher, and oven were all constructed of stainless steel.

When the coffeemaker had finished gurgling, hissing, and popping, she filled two mugs from the carafe and carried them to the table. She placed one in front of him, and then she sat down in the chair closest to his. She looked into his eyes and forced a smile. "I can't believe I haven't seen you for—what—two years?"

He nodded and shrugged. "Mom's funeral."

"You live three miles from me, and I have to fly to Minnesota to see you."

Snow took a sip of coffee. "Yeah. That's some irony there, isn't it?"

"So what are you doing now? You still playing poker for a living?"

He took a bigger sip, more of a slurp actually because of the heat. "Yes, but that really hasn't been working out that well for me lately. I haven't played in over a month. I hit a dry spell that lasted about six months. Lost about fifteen thousand."

"You planning to stick with it?"

He shrugged. "These streaks happen. I just need to get my confidence back…"

Karen lifted her cup and took a tiny sip. She held it between her hands, her elbows resting on the table. "You look good. Are you still jogging?"

"Running, actually. Jogging is what normal people do for exercise. Running is what you do when you decide to become a masochist."

She winced. "Why do you say that?"

"Every time I start training for a marathon, some part of me breaks down. And it's never the same body part. I've contracted nearly every running-related injury ever documented: plantar fasciitis, shin splints, tendinitis of every joint below my waist, muscle strains, iliotibial band syndrome...

"I'm beginning to believe humans aren't built to run more than a hundred yards at a time. In fact—think about it—what other animal do you see running for hours at a time for no good reason? The entire animal kingdom—the ones that do run—only do it for short bursts when it's necessary: to chase something to eat, or to keep from getting eaten."

She smiled. "Then why don't you quit?"

He looked into his coffee cup and shook his head. "I've been doing it all my life. I'm an addict."

"I've heard that from a lot of people," she said. "I've tried going to health clubs and getting into a program on the treadmill, elliptical, stationary bicycle, those machines with all the metal plates attached—and I just can't get enthusiastic about it. I always end up quitting. Mostly I just walk, once in awhile, whenever I can get myself to do it."

"I don't think you need to exercise, Karen. You're one of those women who have a naturally trim figure. You always look good."

"Oh, thank you, Jimmy." She smiled. She always called him "Jimmy" whenever she was pleased with him, Snow remembered. The rest of the time it was just "Jim" or "you" or something worse.

13

She put her hand on his arm. "You know, we haven't had a really good talk for a long time. And I think that might be part of the problem with us—the reason we never see each other much anymore. We never sit down and just have a really good heart-to-heart."

He looked up and raised an eyebrow. An uneasy feeling crept up his spine, as though he were seated on the set of *Doctor Phil*, waiting for the insinuations to begin—the prying and digging in an attempt to expose the shortcomings and inadequacies of Snow's character that had inhibited the normal development of a loving relationship between brother and sister, and every other poor bastard who had ever come in contact with Snow during his lifetime. "You think now is a good time for that?"

"I think it's the best time," she said. "I don't think you'll be much help to me if you're angry over something that happened years ago."

He nodded. "Uh-huh. Help to you. That's what it always comes down to." He felt his jaw tightening. "That's why you married a guy old enough to be your grandfather. You were—what—twenty? And he was sixty-five? Jesus, Karen."

"I was twenty-two, and he was sixty-two."

"Big difference. You married him for his money."

She straightened in her chair, her eyes widening. "I did not. Age is not an important factor in a loving relationship between soul mates. I felt safe with him. I loved him. We had fun together, did things together: we went to the ballet, the theater, movies, fishing..."

Snow raised his eyebrows. "If I had a granddaughter, that's where I'd take her!"

She motioned toward him with her hand. "What about you? Your first wife was only nineteen. The second one was only

14

twenty—and you were thirty. You marry women for one reason, and it's not for their poise or grace or depth. Put a nubile young thing in a miniskirt and presto—you're in love."

Staring at the far end of the table, Snow wrapped his fist around the handle of his cup. He shook his head slowly. What was it about this woman that set him off every time? He fought back the words that popped into his mind, slipped down onto his tongue.

Then his mouth opened just enough, and they spilled out: "Both of my ex-wives are alive and well. All of your former husbands have gone on to the hereafter. You've never had to work a day in your life, Karen—thanks to the insurance settlements. Which brings me to my first pertinent question that I need to ask..."

He locked his stare on her. "How much life insurance money are we talking about here for husband number three?"

Matching his stare with hers, Karen dropped her hands into her lap. "That's none of your business."

"It is my business. It will be the district attorney's business. It could be the court's business, if it gets that far. I need to know. How do you expect me to help you get out of this mess?"

"This is what you call helping?" she snapped.

He took in a breath and let it out slowly. "Alright," he said. "Let's try to be civilized and start over."

"I just think this whole problem with us started because you could never beat me at Monopoly."

Snow rolled his eyes.

"And Yahtzee. I should have let you win a few times." Her mouth turned up in a half grin. She took a sip from her coffee cup. "Five hundred thousand."

"The insurance?"

She nodded.

"Oh my God. They're going to be all over that."

"They already are," she said. "They asked to see the policy, and I showed it to them. I have nothing to hide. A lot of married couples have policies that high."

Snow looked at the fist holding the handle of his coffee cup. "Yeah, but…probably not too many of them end up face-down in the dirt with holes in their back from a pickaxe."

Her eyes began to well up. "You sure have a way with words…you…"

"Yeah." He took a swallow of coffee. "Sorry. Eight years of advanced interrogation techniques."

"Don't blame it on that. You talked like that when you were nine," she said.

"What about Bob? How did he talk…?"

"Like a gentleman. Always. Never raised his voice; always measured his words. My feelings were always his first consideration."

"So the two of you were getting along good?"

She nodded. "Yes, of course…under the circumstances."

Snow's eyes narrowed. "What circumstances?"

"We were separated. Bob found himself an apartment. A couple of months ago."

Snow shook his head. "This is starting to not look good in your favor, Sis."

"I know, and that's why I'm worried. Very worried."

"Was there anybody," Snow said as he leaned back in his chair and spread his hands, palms up, "anybody at all who harbored bad feelings toward Bob?"

She shook her head. "Everybody seemed to get along with him. He never had anything negative to say about anyone he worked with at the casino. He was just a lovable sort of guy. And that was the quality that attracted me to him from the beginning of our relationship."

"Then why were you getting a divorce?"

"We weren't in the process of getting a divorce," she corrected. "We hadn't progressed to that stage. It was a trial separation."

"Right. My mistake."

"It had just, I believe, gotten to that point in a relationship where two people who really have loved each other for a long time, but need to step back and reevaluate—"

"Were you having an affair?"

She looked him in the eye, her lips forming a straight line. Her eyes were like fire. "Absolutely not. I would never do anything like that to Bob, or anyone else."

"What about Bob? Was he having an affair?"

"He wasn't that sort of man. He was the giving, nurturing, selfless sort. Not the typical beer-guzzling type most women marry, who sit around watching football all day, passing gas, and demanding continual service from the little woman of the house. Bob would never have cheated on me. Never. He was a devoted husband."

Snow studied her face, looking for any sign of deception. There was nothing obvious in her expression. He continued: "Tell me about this transaction at the RV storage lot. Why was Steve paying in cash? Why not a cashier's check?"

"I don't know. I guess he had the money on hand, didn't want to go to the bank and be bothered with getting a check."

"How much was it?"

"Eight thousand."

"He keeps that kind of money lying around his house?"

"Steve's a big gambler," she said. "He's out shooting craps at least one night a week. He won five thousand in just a few hours one night."

"Wow." Snow rubbed his chin. "Is he well off, financially?"

"Seems to be," she said. "He's never had kids, never been married."

"Guy must be rolling in dough," Snow muttered.

"Do you ever wish you'd had children, Jim?" she asked.

He shrugged. "There were a few times over the years when it crossed my mind. But then I always sobered up. I've heard some pretty harrowing stories. I don't think I have the courage."

She sighed, looking up at the cabinet above the sink. "I sometimes wish I had raised a family. But Doug was too far advanced in years, I guess, to get the job done. And with Gene and Bob, I don't know. I just couldn't get in the mood, after the first marriage, to start the process." She turned her eyes back to Snow. "Jim, do you think I'm selfish?"

"No more than me," Snow replied.

"I don't find that reassuring," she said. "I think part of the reason Mom never made it into her eighties was that we never gave her any grandchildren to enjoy. Not even one. I can't imagine the frustration she must have been feeling."

"I read that people with kids have a shorter life expectancy. Not sure what effect they have on the grandparents. Could be the opposite since all they do mostly is play with them."

"That sounds like something you'd read," she said.

Snow decided not to respond to that. At the moment, she seemed to be more petulant than usual. This was understandable under the circumstances. Sometimes, Snow mused, the smartest thing you can say is nothing. The kitchen filled with silence. Then the refrigerator started up and began a low hum.

Finally Karen spoke: "I shouldn't have said that. I guess I'm a little on edge."

"That's okay," Snow said.

"Isn't there anything else you'd like to ask me?"

Snow studied his sister for a moment, then lowered his gaze to his coffee cup, took a slurp from it, and then lowered it back to the table. He looked back up at her. "No, for the moment that's all I can think of. But I'm just getting started. I'm sure something will come to me later. It always does. I'll need the phone numbers for the detectives you talked to."

She got up, went into the living room, and came back with two business cards. She sat back down and handed them to him. "Will you talk to them before they get too far along?" She leaned forward, clasped her hands tightly together, and rested them on the table in front of her. Her knuckles grew white.

"Of course." He put his hand on hers and patted it a few times. "Don't worry, Sis. Eventually the facts have a way of working their way to the surface."

She sighed. "I sure hope so," she said. "Otherwise, I'll end up working my way to a prison cell for something I had nothing to do with."

CHAPTER 4

In front of the Starbucks on Flamingo Road and Sandhill, Jim Snow pulled into the space next to a white, unmarked Crown Victoria. He found Detective Mel Harris and his partner inside, sitting at one of the small tables. Unlike Snow, Harris still had a full head of hair. It was coal black and stiff, appearing to have been combed back and sprayed down with shoe polish. He was an average-size man, a few years younger than Snow, with a slender build. Gone was the overhanging midsection Snow remembered from the last time he'd seen him. He was sporting a white shirt with thin red and blue stripes in a windowpane pattern, black pleated slacks, and black penny loafers.

Across the table from Harris, wearing a black business suit with a skirt and a red blouse, sat a tall black woman. Snow figured her for around forty, though her face was unlined; her hair was straight and covered her ears. Her long, slender legs were crossed at the ankles and bent back under her chair, her skirt riding up to mid-thigh. She had large eyes, prominent cheekbones, and full lips.

As Snow approached their table, the two turned their eyes to him. Harris grinned and stood up, offering his hand. Snow clutched it, gave it a single, firm pump, and released it.

"Citizen Snow," Harris said. "How goes life in the private sector?"

"Can't complain," Snow said.

Harris pointed his hand toward the black woman. "This is Detective James."

She stood up and smiled. Their eyes met and held. Snow took her hand. It felt warm and dry.

"I'm Alice," she said.

"Jim Snow...I don't remember seeing you around the bureau..."

"Oh, I've only been with Homicide for six months. I was working patrol prior to that. Got moved around quite a bit—different commands. But I've been with Metro for over twelve years."

Still holding her hand and smiling, Snow nodded. "That's a good long while. What were you doing before that?"

"Various things. I moved to Los Angeles after high school, did some modeling for a few years. Then the jobs started to dry up for me, so I moved to Vegas and got on as a cocktail waitress." She laughed. "When that started getting old, I got into casino security, and then Metro."

"Just the opposite of the usual career path," Snow said. "For most it goes from Homicide to casino security. Though I don't think many detectives ever get into modeling." He chuckled.

"Oh, I think you'd make a great model," she said. "You definitely have a look that could fit into a Nordstrom catalog—or Macy's..."

"Maybe Tractor Supply," Snow suggested, grinning. "The overall and rubber boot section."

"Kids!" Harris cut in. "Hey! Get a room already."

They turned their heads toward Harris. He was standing with his arms open, his hands facing up—as though he were preparing to perform a magic act.

Snow let go of her hand, touched her arm lightly, and they sat down.

Lowering himself into his chair, Harris nodded at the tall, white paper cup in front of him. It was filled to the brim with white foam. "You want a cup, Snow? I'm buying."

"I'm pretty well coffeed-up. Thanks."

Harris lifted his cup, took a sip, and licked the foam from his upper lip. Alice followed suit with her black coffee.

"So." Harris cleared his throat and shifted his gaze to Snow. "What have you been doing to generate income, Snow? You pick up a pile of jack from an inheritance, or what? Did you make your twenty?"

Snow shook his head. "I was six years shy of that. My folks never had anything much. My dad drove a dump truck, and my mother worked behind a checkout counter in a grocery store. They died broke. I've been playing poker. Three days a week, when the card rooms are full of tourists. Fridays through Sundays, mostly."

"Wow." Harris took another sip of foam and licked it off his lip. "You play in that big tournament? What do they call it? Major League of Poker, or whatever?"

"No, I don't play in tournaments, and I stay away from no-limit. I stick with limit hold 'em, usually twenty to forty limit. You can't make a fortune, but you can grind out a decent living at that level—enough to overcome the rake and pay the bills."

"The rake?"

22

"That's what the casino takes in. But lately, I have to admit, the game hasn't been going so well for me."

Harris raised his eyebrows. "Negative cash flow?"

Snow gave a solemn nod.

"You can always come back to Homicide," Harris suggested. "You can have my spot on the team. I've entertained thoughts of quitting myself over the years."

Snow shifted his eyes toward Alice and noticed her mouth open slightly, her eyes growing larger. She seemed to take this revelation as good news. She looked like a toddler from Whoville, witnessing the return of all her Grinch-stolen presents under the family Christmas tree.

He turned his eyes back to Harris. "What would be the plan?"

"Charbroiled Giant Burger." Harris slipped his fingers around his cup and studied the foam inside it. "That would be the name of it," he said. "Not just the name, but also that pretty much describes the venture." He looked up at Snow. "Here's the deal: There are a lot of burger joints in Vegas, but nearly all of them are fast-food chains. Some of them offer grilled burgers, but none of them really offer a quality burger. I'm talking about the sort of burgers you grill on your back patio—big-ass burgers…" With this he gave up his hold on his cupful of foam and spread his hands in front of him, as though he were relating a fish story. "Thick and juicy. But lean. I'm talking ground sirloin, something of that quality. You look at the crowds of people that swarm into McDonald's, Burger King, Jack in the Box, Wendy's, Wienerschnitzel…"

"Isn't Wienerschnitzel hot dogs?" Alice interjected.

"Yeah," Harris replied, "but I think they do sell hamburgers there."

"Why would anyone go to a hot dog place to buy a hamburger?" Alice asked.

"Exactly! That's part of it." Harris's face lit up. "Now you're getting it."

Snow couldn't believe two of Las Vegas's finest homicide detectives were having this conversation. "So why don't you go for it?" he asked.

Harris lowered his arms to the table; they landed with a thump. "Bottom line? I guess I don't have the balls," he said. "Opening a restaurant, even one as focused as I have in mind, could be a big risk. If it doesn't work out, not only do I lose everything, but I won't have a job to fall back on. I could bust my hump and wind up with nothing to piss in."

"How about the men's room at McDonald's?" Alice suggested.

Snow covered his emerging grin with his hand.

Harris offered her a pained expression. "That's a good one, Detective. Someday, no doubt, you'll be entertaining an audience much larger than just me and Snow here. Would it be too much to ask, getting a little respect from a junior partner?"

No response from Alice. She offered a smirk instead.

Suddenly Harris's eyes widened as a thought popped into his head. He pointed at Snow. "Hey! You still running marathons? I heard you were into that, when you were in the bureau. You still doing that?"

Snow shrugged. "I've been training for marathons for going on six years, but I've never been able to finish one. For most of them I've never even made it to the starting line, even though I was registered and paid in advance."

"What happened?" Alice said.

"I always got injured. Always something different. Right now I've got ITBS."

To Alice, Harris said, "That's where the tendon on the side of your leg rubs against your hip or your knee." He looked at Snow. "Which is it? Your knee or your hip?"

"My knee."

"You need to try Daniels," Harris said. "You ever use Daniels?"

Snow shook his head. "No, never have."

"I think that may be part of your problem—you could be on the wrong program. What program do you use?"

Snow said, "I use the program where you run most days and gradually increase the mileage every week, and then try to run a marathon."

"Oh, that's too simple," Harris said. "Try Daniels. I swear. I used him last year. Las Vegas Marathon. My first marathon. Finished in three hours, forty-nine minutes. I think, if I can continue to improve, another year or two—I could qualify for Boston." His face lit up.

"That's pretty good," Snow said. "You've never had any problem with injuries?"

"Never." He raised his eyebrows and jabbed his fingertips toward Snow. "Try Daniels. He knows his stuff. Or even Pfitzinger. He's good, too. I've heard a lot of good things about Pfitzinger. Some guys swear by him." He swallowed more foam.

Alice turned to Snow. "How is your sister doing?"

"Under the circumstances, not so good. She's somewhat frantic right now."

"I imagine. This must be a difficult situation for both of you. But she's fortunate to have a brother living here with your background and experience. Are the two of you close?"

"Oh," Snow said. "No. Not really."

"She's older than you?"

"Yes, three years."

"She probably used to babysit you when you were little, I imagine."

"Yes, she did."

"That's probably a contributing factor," she continued. "My brothers are both older than me, so they have a more fatherly, protective relationship with me. While growing up, you probably felt at times that your sister was more like a second mother instead of a sibling."

Looking at Alice now, Snow noticed the serenity in her expression. Her gentle mannerisms, the soothing lilt of her voice, and her unassuming demeanor made Snow feel at ease with her. He felt himself slipping into a trance-like state, where he might suddenly divulge the events of his entire childhood to her and her senior partner. "I guess so," he said.

He turned his head to Harris. "I know it's still early in this investigation, but what have you got so far? You mind bringing me up to speed?" Snow leaned forward and pulled a pocket-size notepad out of his back pocket.

Harris took in a breath and blew it out. "Alright. But you know I can't reveal anything that I've been instructed not to release to the public. I don't want to get my ass in a sling."

"Of course." Snow raised an eyebrow. "Is there anything you've been instructed not to reveal?"

Harris shook his head. "But to be safe, nothing I tell you came from me. I'll deny it. We're just old friends having coffee. Right?"

Snow nodded. "We're on the same page with that. Always."

Harris brought his hands up to the fish-story position again. "Okay," he began. "First off, this is not looking good for your sister, or this Steve guy who lives next door. I'm just telling you this up front, to be square with you, because you're one of us—or used to be. Here are the major points of the case right now, starting with the deceased..." He slipped a small spiral notebook out from his shirt pocket and flipped it open. "Cause of death," he began to read, "were two puncture wounds, three inches apart, in the middle of the upper back, appearing to have been caused by a somewhat-round, sharp object with a lot of force behind it. That's why the coroner investigator thinks it was caused by a pickaxe. The size of the holes is an approximate match to what you would find on that sort of tool. Though, he said, it's difficult to be accurate with an assessment because of the elasticity of the skin. The CI said it tends to compress back over the wound after the object is removed. So the opening will look smaller than the object that caused it. He also said the weapon might have been twisted, or worked back and forth during removal, to get it out—I guess like when you're chopping firewood. That would have enlarged the wounds. Both wounds cleared the ribs and punctured the heart. The first one killed him pretty close to instantly.

"Now, as for the circumstances leading up to the murder, according to Steve Helm the neighbor, Steve decided to buy your brother-in-law's travel trailer and pay him eight thousand in cash for it. The two of them met somewhere around eight o'clock last night inside the RV storage lot and proceeded to the trailer, where the victim showed Steve all of the fine points of the item being sold—the trailer. They went inside the trailer, looked around some more, and agreed on the sale. Steve went out to his pickup to get the cash, came back inside, and counted it out. They shook hands and then went out to hook up the trailer to Steve's truck. After finishing with that, Steve pulled the trailer out of its space and waited for Bob, who got into his truck, fired it up, and drove over what seemed to Bob like a rock or something. So Bob jumps out to see what it was; Steve gets out of his truck and comes over. Steve said there was what looked like a handle of a small screwdriver sticking out of the middle of the tread of the right rear tire, and they could hear the air leaking out of it."

Harris took a moment to scratch his head, and then he continued. "Steve says he offered to help Bob change the tire, but Bob insisted he could handle it by himself and told Steve to go on home. Bob gave Steve his code to the gate, and Steve left, towing the trailer.

"The woman who manages the lot told us that Bob's code shows up on her computer exiting the lot at nine oh-seven p.m. No other codes in the database until this morning at six fifteen, when some guy came in to pick up his boat and discovered the body. He called nine-one-one. Responding officer taped off the scene, Detective James and I arrived, along with the rest of the crew."

He continued to read. "Let's see. No evidence at the scene other than the victim and the puncture in the tire. The screwdriver that caused the puncture was nowhere to be found. Crime scene analyst examined the hole in the tire and indicated it was consistent with a very small screwdriver, or ice pick, maybe.

"Apparently your brother-in-law had gotten the jack and lug wrench out and was squatting in front of the tire, preparing to loosen the lug nuts at the time of death. The coroner investigator says that when he was struck by the first blow, the body of the deceased pitched forward, striking the fender of the truck with his head, and then fell sideways and was struck once more. The perpetrator, apparently, turned the body of the victim onto his stomach and removed something from the right front pocket—presumably the cash. The CI says the pocket was slightly open, indicating this." He paused and flipped a couple of pages in the notebook. "Here is an important point: the CSA and the CI both concur that the victim had to have known the perp, and had to have been aware of the presence of the perp prior to the attack."

"Why is that?" Snow asked.

Harris raised his index finger next to his head. "Because, at the time the first blow was struck, the victim was crouched in front of the tire, with his head facing directly forward. The victim knew he wasn't alone—he would have heard the perp sneaking up behind him on the gravel, because no matter how carefully you try to walk on that stuff, it makes a lot of noise. He would have heard the perp approaching him and had his head turned, at least, to see who it was. But the way the body and head were positioned, it indicates beyond any doubt that the victim knew the perp and was aware that the perp was there. So…there is a strong possibility that Steve Helm was still there. Or that your sister was there. Or both of them were there." Harris lowered his finger, took in a breath, and narrowed his eyes at Snow.

Looking back down at his notebook, Harris exhaled slowly and continued. "Persons of interest: We have your sister, twice married previously. First husband died of natural causes—no problem there. However, the second husband, robbed and shot near an ATM, could look a little suspicious in light of what just happened last night to the newest member to join the list of deceased husbands.

"Your sister stated that she did have a pickaxe in the garage. With her permission, that was gathered as evidence by the CSA and taken to the crime lab.

"On to neighbor Steve. There was no pickaxe found in Steve Helm's possession. He stated that he had never owned one. However, investigation into Mr. Helm's background turned up a five-year stretch in the Arizona State Prison at Tucson for multiple counts of armed robbery, to which he confessed."

Snow felt a sudden lump forming in his throat. "How old was he at the time of the conviction?"

Harris looked up at him. "Twenty-three."

"And now he's…"

"Forty."

Placing the tip of his thumb between his teeth, Snow bit down on it. He looked down at the table and sighed as his mind compiled the information he had just received.

"Now, I—" Harris started. Suddenly George Strait began to sing from the front pocket of his pants. He stood up, pulled a RAZR phone out, and flipped it open. He looked down at it. To Snow, he said, "Oh! Sorry, I gotta take this." He turned away from the table and strode toward the front door, putting the phone to his ear.

After he was outside, Alice turned to Snow. "Must be a new love interest. That's been happening a lot lately. At least six or seven times a day. By the way, who is Daniels?"

"Jack Daniels," Snow replied. "He's an expert on marathon training, has at least one book out that I'm aware of. I never bought it. Also a pretty decent whiskey, which I have purchased on occasion." He nodded in the direction of Harris. "How do you like working with him?"

"To be honest—I don't. The first problem we had, right from square one, he started putting his hand on my shoulder. Now, I don't like being touched by anyone who hasn't been invited. Especially on the first day of a business-type relationship. Then he began putting his hand in the middle of my upper back, occasionally. From there, it moved down to my lower back, and that's when I decided to speak up, because I knew it was only a matter of time before he started putting his hand on my butt."

Snow chuckled. "What did he say?"

Her eyes grew large. "He said he was just being friendly. I told him I don't need that kind of friendly from a senior partner on the police force." She took a sip of her coffee. "So now he pretty much ignores me, just treats me like I'm his pet dog. I'm just supposed to follow him around and keep my mouth shut, let him conduct the investigation, collect all the evidence, while I stand there and smile and nod and say, 'Yassah, boss, it be lookin' good the way you be doin' it.'"

Snow laughed. "So how does he 'be doin' it'?"

She leaned toward him. "He's a man of focus. Just like a dog investigating a pile of poop—goes straight to the body and starts sniffing around it. Nothing else matters with him but that body." She started giggling and put her hand on Snow's arm. "And if he sees me walking around inside the crime scene, with my hands behind my back, looking for anything that might be out of place or suspicious, it's always the same utterance that comes out of his mouth: 'Don't contaminate the crime scene, Detective.' Then he'll go back to waddling around the body, hunched over, like a duck—as though he might be able to see something the technicians could miss."

She turned her head to look out the window at her senior partner.

31

Snow turned to see what she was looking at. Out on the front patio of the coffee shop, Harris stood tall, the cell phone to his ear, the other hand in his pocket. With his head tilted back, his chin jutting out, he grinned happily, talking to the sky.

"You ever talk to the lieutenant or your sergeant about switching partners, or maybe a different team?"

She turned her head back to Snow. "No. I don't want to rock the boat. I'm still new. And then, some days I think maybe it's time to just move on toward a new career. Mel seems to love it, but I really get sick of looking at bodies."

Snow nodded. "That was the main reason I quit. And I've never regretted that decision."

"Well." Alice reached for her purse, put her hand inside, and pulled out a business card. She handed it to Snow. "Since you are back on the job for this one case, if you have any questions, anything I can help you with—I want you to give me a call." She looked him in the eye. "I'm here for you…unless you'd rather call Mel."

This brought another burst of laughter. They laughed so hard their eyes began to water.

CHAPTER 5

Hollywood RV Storage was about two hundred and forty miles from Tinseltown. Located on Hollywood Boulevard on the east side of Las Vegas, it was a short distance south of Vegas Valley Road. On the north side of the property sat a vacant, unfenced lot with a For Sale sign in front. To the north of that, alongside the same road, was a towing company, which included a storage yard for damaged vehicles waiting to be claimed or hauled off to a salvage yard. Bordering the south side of the RV storage lot, and also across the road, was an expanse of open desert covered with sage, creosote, and other assorted plants, flourishing in the arid heat of the Mojave Desert.

But today, as Jim Snow pulled his Hyundai Sonata to a stop in front of the steel gate of Hollywood RV Storage, though warmer than usual for this time of year, it was not too hot. With most of October almost gone, it was a balmy eighty-two degrees. Almost light jacket weather for residents of this southwestern desert city.

He climbed out of the car and walked over to the control pad. Leaning over it, he noticed the push-to-talk button and was reaching for it when the gate began to open. He got back into his car and drove inside the lot.

Just inside the gate to the right, Snow noticed a Dumpster and a green portable toilet. To the left of the entrance was a tiny, wooden, shed-size building, painted white. It had a pitched roof with composite shingles. There was no window in front, only a screened door near the edge of the shed, with a metal payment drop-box mounted next to it. Each side wall of the structure had a screened window built into the middle.

The inside door was open. Snow pulled up to the screen door and killed the engine.

"Good morning," came an old woman's voice from inside the shed.

"Morning." Snow opened his car door and got out. He opened the screen door and stepped inside.

It was cool inside. Both windows were open, and there was a slight breeze blowing through. It was a pleasant little office, with a wooden desk next to the front door. On the paneled wall in front of the desk, a calendar with a forested mountain scene hung from a headless nail. Thumbtacked to the back wall was a large poster of two cats playing with a ball of yarn.

On the desk was a computer with an old-fashioned CRT display. Sitting in front of the computer in a worn office chair was a woman who appeared to be in her early sixties. She had curly gray hair, thin lips, a large nose, and tiny blue eyes. She was dressed in powder-blue pedal pushers, white tennis shoes, and a sleeveless white blouse.

Sitting with her hands in her lap, she trained her eyes on Snow. "What can I do for you?"

"Just a few questions," Snow began, "if you don't mind. It's about what happened here last night."

She wet her lips with the tip of her tongue, pressed them tightly together, and nodded. "Are you with the police? Because they've already been here."

"Well, sort of. Actually I'm working as a consultant to help investigate the case."

"You don't have a badge?"

"No."

She studied his face for a moment. "You have a business card?"

"Yes, of course." Snow reached into his back pocket, pulled out his wallet, and dug through the stack of business cards inside. He slipped one out and presented it to her.

She looked at it and frowned. "This is for a Chinese restaurant," she said.

"Yes," he said. "Ho Chow Ming. Excellent food, reasonable prices. I highly recommend it. You ever eaten there?"

She looked up at him, her eyes narrowing. "No, I haven't. You don't have a business card of your own?"

"I'm on a tight budget," he said. Then he pulled a pen out of his front jeans pocket and took the card from her. He flipped it over and scribbled a number on the back. "That's my cell phone number in case you need to get in touch with me."

She looked at the number he'd penned on the card. "What's your name?" she asked.

"Oh yeah." He scribbled his name and then offered his hand. "Jim Snow. I used to be a homicide detective with Metro. Now I'm on my own."

She shook his hand, looking up at him with a confused expression. "I'm Norma Hecker," she said.

"Happy to meet you." Snow took his hand back, dug through the wallet and produced another card, and showed it to her. It was Alice James's business card. "I work with this lady; you can call her to verify if you like."

She brightened, sitting up straighter in her chair. "Oh. Yes. She was here earlier. Her and her partner, good-looking guy with the black hair."

"Mel Harris."

"Right. Nice man, seemed like."

Snow nodded. He pulled his notepad out of his back pocket and flipped it open. "Now, about the incident that happened here last night. I'm sure you've answered these questions already, and I hate to bother you again, but I'm going to need to ask them for my own benefit, which will help to mold my perspective of the case."

"That's perfectly alright," she said. "I'm not busy anyway. Usually just sit here all day staring at this monitor and answering the phone."

Snow smiled. "So you keep track, on that computer, of people coming and going through the gate? Is that right?"

"Yes," she said. "They enter their codes to get in and out, which opens the gate, and it's recorded in the database, along with the time and date."

"I see. And did anyone come or go…say…from six p.m. on last night?"

"No one until seven oh-five p.m. when Bob Williams entered his code from the outside keypad. He then opened the gate around seven thirty p.m. from the inside keypad. After that, Bob Williams's code was entered again from the inside keypad at eight fifty p.m. And no more entries until just after six a.m. this morning when Jerry Albright came in."

"He discovered the body, I take it."

"Yes," she said. "Apparently so, because after his code, I have an entry of the police code from the outside ten minutes later, and then several more police code entries during the following half hour or so."

Snow's eyes moved up from his notepad, where he had been scribbling, and focused on Norma. "Police code?"

"Yes, that's the code we give to the emergency services, in case there's a fire or a medical emergency...or a murder." Her eyebrows shot up and back down for emphasis. "You know, that way they can get in and out quickly."

"Oh sure, I see."

"I guess you never had to investigate inside a storage facility when you were a detective?"

"This will be my first," he said. "Is there a temporary code you could give me to get in and out of here until this case is wrapped up?"

"Of course," she said. "You can use the police code since you're with them anyway. It's pretty easy to remember. It's nine-one-one-nine-one-one, then press the star key."

CHAPTER 6

Yellow crime scene tape encircled an area consisting of nine assorted motor homes, fifth wheels, and travel trailers. They were all parked in spaces that were part of two rows near the center of the lot. There was one empty space between the recreational vehicles inside the crime scene. Just outside the tape, a black and white Metro squad car occupied the lane directly in front of the vacant slot.

Jim Snow parked behind the patrol unit and gave a sloppy, left-handed salute. The officer behind the wheel returned the greeting with a brief raise of the hand. Then he lowered his head and went back to what Snow assumed to be texting on his cell phone.

Getting out of his car and walking toward the crime scene, Snow did his best to keep his back angled toward the officer. Wearing a gray polo shirt and black Levi's, Snow hoped to be taken for a homicide detective, though he was missing a nine-millimeter and a badge clipped on his belt. As he approached the driver side of the squad car, he glanced over at the patrolman and gave a nod. "How's it going?"

The officer looked over at him and returned the nod. "Good," he replied. Then he lowered his gaze back down to his cell phone.

Turning toward the empty RV space, Snow noticed two square yellow cones, positioned about five feet apart near the center of the lane separating the two rows of RVs. They were numbered one and two, with the number-one cone identifying the head of the body, the other cone near the location of where the feet had been, before the body was wrapped in a sheet and taken off to the crime lab.

Standing there for a moment, his eyes surveying the hard ground adjacent to the cones, Snow could see no footprints or even tire marks that were clearly evident. And if there were any partial footprints, they could belong to anyone.

He slipped his hands into his pockets and walked slowly along the perimeter of the crime scene, taking in every detail of every rig inside the yellow tape strung along their sides. Working his way from the empty space past the backs of the two trailers included in the cordoned-off area, he rounded the corner of the second trailer and made his way to the middle of the lane. He stopped there, glancing around. His gaze came to rest on the front of the trailer to his left. It was an older-model Nomad travel trailer, appearing to be about twenty-five feet in length. It was constructed of thin, white, overlapping strips of aluminum. The black steel channels that made up the frame under the trailer jutted out in front of it, forming an A shape, terminated by a hitch coupler. Inside the external A-frame sat a deep-cycle battery, strapped in place with two rubber straps. Four wires were attached to the terminals of the battery. Two of the thicker wires, one white and the other black, were connected to a black, rectangular box bolted down next to the battery. It appeared to be a junction box that came with the trailer. The other two thinner wires ran upwards above the dual propane cylinders to an electronics box, this one attached to the front of the trailer with duct tape, applied quite liberally across the top of the box in both directions. Two more wires poked out of the duct tape at the top of the box and snaked their way to the roof, where they disappeared behind the top edge.

Somebody was in a hurry, thought Snow, or just lazy.

He continued his inspection of the crime scene, circling the outside of the perimeter of the yellow tape. Then he crossed over to the chain-link fence and followed that around to the far corner of the lot, nearest the road. There was a large cement pad there, with a garden hose wrapped around a metal hose hanger. Next to the cement pad was another garden hose and a sewage dump station.

Resuming his examination of the fence perimeter, he worked his way around to the rear corner of the facility nearest the vacant lot next door. This section of the fence was not visible from anywhere inside the storage lot without walking right up to it. There was a large fifth wheel parked in front it. The fifth wheel was covered with dirt and the tires were sagging, giving the indication no one had used it for more than a year.

It appeared that no one had been back here, with the exception of whoever might be coming and going though the corner section of the fence. The five metal bands used to attach the vertical rod in the edge of the back fence to the pole were gone. In their place were three bungee cords, each wrapped around the vertical rod and the pole enough times to hold the fence upright and tight to the pole. The cords were equally spaced from top to bottom. Just above the top of the chain-link fence, a length of razor wire ran from pole to pole, wired to the posts under the post caps. It was free of the fence, probably to keep it from sagging in sections, and working its way below the top of the fence. It appeared that once the bungee cords were removed, the entire fence could be pulled back, allowing anyone to come and go at will.

Along the outside of the back fence was a gravel fire road, and next to that was a gradually sloping bank leading downward into a dense stand of tamarisk bushes growing up out of the bottom of the Las Vegas Wash. The branches were thick, covered with feathery, needle-like leaves. Many of them looked like trees, with thick trunks and branches reaching as high as fifteen feet. Along with the sage, reeds, and other assorted bushes and plants that had taken root, the entire wash in that area looked like some sort of isolated, urban jungle.

A disconcerting thought crossed through Snow's mind. He wondered if anyone might be living down there. There was certainly no water, very little at least, this time of year. It was a perfect spot for a homeless encampment, if only at night. One or more of them could be wandering up out of that insidious forest in the dark, and into this storage lot.

Scanning the far bank of the wash and beyond, Snow noticed another fire road on the far side, and then a brick fence next to that. On the other side of the fence were homes, two stories high. He made a mental note of their location and then continued on.

Walking back to his car, Snow noticed a dark blue Ford half-ton pickup with an extended cab and a large hitch ball sticking out from under the rear bumper. The paint on the truck was faded, and the all-terrain tires were worn down almost to the tread wear indicators. It was parked in front of the door to the Nomad travel trailer. As he drew near, Snow noticed a red bumper sticker attached to the left half of the rear bumper. It read, *Horn Broken—Watch for Finger.*

A tall man, who looked to be in his late twenties, was standing between the door of his truck and the door to the travel trailer. He had shaggy brown hair hanging down over his ears on the sides, and almost covering his eyebrows in front. He wore faded blue jeans, a yellow T-shirt, and high-top hiking shoes. The squad car had pulled up even with his truck, and the patrol officer appeared to be arguing with him.

"Well, why can't it be moved?" shaggy head was complaining.

"I don't know anything about that," the officer responded. "I'm just here to make sure nobody goes inside that yellow tape, and that's all I know."

"What's the problem?" Snow asked.

Shaggy head turned to look at Snow. "This guy says I can't get into my trailer. He says it's part of the crime scene."

Snow walked past the tailgate of the Ford truck, stopped beside the truck bed, and rested his forearm on the rail of the truck bed. "He's right."

"Well, why is my trailer included in the crime scene? It looks to me like the crime happened clear over there." He waved his hand up over his head, cocking his hand in the direction of the yellow cones.

"The way it happened," Snow explained, "is that the responding officer got here, saw the body, and taped off what he thought to be a reasonably large enough area for investigation. The bigger, the better. That's the guideline when it comes to taping off crime scenes."

He put his hands on his hips. "How the hell am I supposed to get into my trailer?"

"You need something out of there?"

"My tools," he said. "And...other stuff. I keep all my stuff in there."

Snow looked at the trailer. "That sounds like a problem, alright. Tell you what—I can get in touch with one of the detectives assigned to this case and have them come out and escort you into your trailer."

Shaggy hair dropped his hands to his sides. "That sounds like a hassle. Can't they just move the tape? Wrap it around the trailer next to mine?" He waved in the direction of it.

"They could do that. It's their decision. But I don't think it will happen."

"Why?"

"I've never seen it happen. Ever."

"You a cop, too?" shaggy head asked. "You're not assigned to this...?"

Snow threw a sidelong look at the patrol officer. He was watching the conversation with interest.

He looked back at the young man. "I'm assisting in the investigation."

This answer seemed to satisfy him. "How long do think this tape will be here?"

"Could be taken down today; could be a week. Could be a couple weeks. It's hard to say."

Shaggy head took in a lungful of air and blew it out. He looked at his trailer and winced. "Well...I guess I can wait. Actually, I was thinking of taking it out of here."

"Where to?"

"Not sure." He shrugged. "I was thinking about heading up to Wyoming, maybe Montana. Colorado. Boondocking for a while. Maybe pick up a temporary job someplace."

"What's boondocking?" Snow asked.

"Basically it's camping for free. No hookups. You can do it in a parking lot, out in the tulles away from the main roads, or in a national forest. The rangers will let you camp for two weeks at a time wherever you want. When the two weeks are up, you just pull up stakes and head down the road a ways. Stay another two weeks. It's a cheap way to live, and it's fantastic." He grinned.

Snow lifted his arm off the truck and sauntered over toward the trailer, studying it. He walked around to the front of it, looking at the jury-rigged wiring. "You out of work?"

Shaggy head turned and walked over to Snow. He shoved his hands into the back pockets of his jeans. Looking at the ground, he said, "Yeah. I was working at Desert Sands Ford. Got laid off a month ago. I think they might be shutting down."

"Sorry to hear that. I know it's tough around here right now. No prospects, huh?"

He shook his head. "Everybody's cutting back; nobody's hiring. Can't even get a job cleaning toilets. That's why I'm thinking about hitting the road. I'm lucky—at least I got this trailer."

"What were you doing over at the Ford dealership?"

"Mechanic."

"Were you there long?"

"Couple years," he said.

"You originally from Vegas?"

"Naw." He shuffled his foot around in the gravel. "I'm from all over—Oregon, Washington, Colorado, Montana, Wyoming.

I don't like it back East. Too crowded. I like the West—it's spread out."

Snow nodded. "I know what you mean. I've always liked the desert. I like being able to see all the way to the horizon in every direction. You can always see what's coming at you."

"That's what I'm talking about," he said. "I'm not crazy about the desert, though. I prefer mountains, forest, and water." He looked up at the mountains to the west. "Wind through the trees and the tall grass, gurgling mountain streams, the call of wild birds—it settles the soul. The Indians knew how to live. Then the white man came along and screwed it all up for everybody. Now, just about everybody is forced to live like rats."

Snow nodded toward the front of the man's trailer. "I was admiring your setup there."

Shaggy head turned to look at the wiring. "That's my solar," he said. He pointed to the box taped to the front wall of the trailer. "That's the controller there. Solar panel is up on the roof. Wish I'd gotten a bigger one, though. The one that's up there is only eighteen watts. I thought that would be enough—but I've got a portable generator. I can always pull that out if I need to. Can't use DC for everything anyway. Air conditioner, and anything that plugs into an outlet—microwave, vacuum cleaner, toaster—you have to run the generator for that."

"So you just plug the whole trailer into it? The generator?"

"Yep. The trailer has a thirty-amp connector, which is what you hook up with in an RV park, but I have a twenty-amp adaptor that connects to the generator, or any regular one-ten-volt outlet."

Snow looked at the controller. "You think that duct tape will hold? It looks to me like it might vibrate loose while you're going down the road."

"Oh, that's just temporary. I wanted to test it out before I screw everything down. Eventually I'll mount the controller to the frame. Come up with some sort of cover for it."

"What about the solar panel? You have that duct-taped to the roof?"

"Naw. That's just sitting up there for now. That roof is rubber, so it won't slide around, and it's heavy enough the wind won't bother it. But I'm going to have to figure out a way to mount it before I take the trailer out of here. Otherwise the first time I hit the brakes hard, it'll end up in the bed of my truck."

Snow looked at the young man, studied his face for a moment. "Looks like you've got it all figured out."

He shook his head. "It's just standard stuff, really."

Back at Norma Hecker's office shack, Snow asked her if it was possible that anyone might be living in an RV, parked on the lot.

"Oh no," she said. "That's definitely not allowed. We put that in the rental contract in capital letters. If we allowed anyone to do that, before long the whole storage facility would turn into a cheap RV park."

"I imagine so," Snow said. "But how do you prevent it?"

"I do a walk-through of the whole facility every morning when I get here at eight a.m. From midnight every night until six a.m., the gate is non-functional."

"What does that mean?"

"You enter your code, the gate won't open—except for the police code. Also, we monitor the code entries, watch for anything suspicious, anyone who might be going in and out every day. But nobody does. The most often anyone has entered the facility recently has been once or twice a week at the most."

Snow folded his left arm under his right and brought his hand up and rubbed his chin with his thumb and the knuckle of his forefinger. He thought about the section of fence in the back corner of the lot, held in place with bungee cords.

"Have you had any break-ins recently?" he said.

"Not in over six months," she said. "That's one of the things I look for when I do my morning walk-through. But after that last break-in, the owner had razor wire put in along the top of the fence. That seems to have done the trick, keeping the riffraff out."

Snow crossed the office to the window nearest the fence. He looked out at the razor wire strung along the top, above the fence. "When you do your walk-through, Norma, you just walk up and down the lanes between the rows of RVs?"

"Yep," she said. "The entire facility. I sort of enjoy it. It's good to get out and get a little exercise in the morning."

"Yes," Snow muttered. "Yes, it is."

CHAPTER 7

After leaving the RV storage lot, Snow drove north on Hollywood Boulevard, turned left at Vegas Valley Road, and passed the sewage treatment plant and two golf courses. He glanced at his watch. It was almost one thirty in the afternoon. His stomach grumbled, and he considered what to do about it.

He didn't feel like spending an hour at a restaurant or even standing in line at a sandwich shop. He decided to pull in to the 7-Eleven at the corner of Vegas Valley and Nellis. He parked in front, went inside, and settled on two packaged ham-and-cheese sandwiches and a bottle of water.

Sitting in his Hyundai, munching on the first sandwich, Snow's mind wandered over the facts surrounding the stabbing death of Bob Williams. Possibly someone else had been present in that storage lot last night when he was killed, someone other than his sister, or more likely, Steve Helm. But even if that could be discovered and proven—what good would it do? One prominent fact stood out among the rest: Bob Williams had known his attacker. The perpetrator had been standing directly behind him with a pickaxe. Had Bob been there alone changing that tire, anyone approaching from behind—whether walking or rushing at

48

him—would have made a hell of a lot of noise on that gravel. Not only would his head have been turned to the side, but he would have been trying to get up. Maybe it wasn't a pickaxe, maybe it was something smaller. A mini hand tiller? No, he'd seen those at Home Depot. Those had two or three claws on one end and a wide, flat blade on the other. But that didn't matter either. No matter what hand tool was used, when someone you don't know approaches you from behind, your natural reaction is to get up and face them. At the very least you would turn your head.

He ran it through his mind and determined the most likely scenario: Steve Helm offers to help with the tire. Bob tells him he can handle it, go on home. Steve insists. Stands there watching Bob get the jack and lug wrench out of his truck. Bob squats down in front of the tire. Steve decides they need more light. Goes to his truck, comes back holding a pickaxe behind his back. Gets behind Bob. And that's all she wrote.

And what would be Steve's motivation? He keeps his eight thousand, plus a used travel trailer? No way. The only reasonable motivation would be sharing in the half-million-dollar insurance settlement with Karen.

Maybe, Snow thought, Steve was the one who shot Karen's second husband near the ATM. No, she probably got somebody else to do that one.

Jesus! What was he thinking? This was his sister. But then most convicted murderers probably had a sibling. And what would that sibling say when presented with the possibility that their own flesh and blood had committed a gruesome act? No way! He or she would never harm a fly.

This wasn't looking good.

And then, what about the screwdriver sticking out of the tire? How would that get there? Snow pondered this for a moment. If you ran over a screwdriver at speed on the highway, there would be a fair chance of it twirling around and ending up rammed into the tread of your tire. But if someone were to wedge it under the tire at an angle while it was parked, and then you drove forward onto it from a stopped position, even a tiny screwdriver probably wouldn't penetrate. The end of the handle would just slide along the ground. Maybe an ice pick, he thought. Something sharp like an ice pick might have a better chance, especially if you got it started, stabbed it into the tire partway and angled it just right. But Steve Helm had told Harris it was the handle of a small screwdriver sticking out of the bottom of the tire. An ice pick handle looked nothing like the handle of a screwdriver.

But then, thought Snow, what difference does it make what Steve Helm says? He's probably the guy who put it there. If you stick an ice pick in somebody's tire in order to kill them with a pickaxe, what will you tell the detectives? *There was a handle of an ice pick sticking out of the tire?* Of course not. You'd tell them you saw the handle of a screwdriver sticking out of the tire.

Snow's train of thought was interrupted by the rattling of what sounded like a metal cart rolling along the sidewalk behind him. He glanced in his rearview mirror. An elderly homeless man was pushing a grocery cart. It was filled with multiple black garbage bags. Two bags looked like they were stuffed with personal possessions. The larger bag, which took up half the cart, was bulging with cans and bottles. He wore a long-sleeve denim shirt, khaki work pants, a dark blue ball cap, and tan work shoes. He looked fairly clean, though he had a ragged gray and white beard that looked as though it had been trimmed with a cheap pair of scissors and no mirror. His hair was the same color, and it was combed back over his ears and touching the collar of his shirt.

Snow stuffed the remainder of the sandwich he'd been eating back inside the plastic container it had come in and dropped it into the grocery bag. He climbed out of the car and strode purposefully toward the old man.

"Hey," he said.

Still pushing the cart along, the old man turned his head toward Snow. His eyebrows shot up and his eyes got big. He stopped the cart. "I didn't do anything."

"I never said you did." Snow stopped in front of him.

The old man froze, keeping his hands on the handle of the grocery cart.

Snow reached into his back pocket, pulled out his wallet, and slipped a bill out of it. He offered it to the old man. "Here's the twenty I borrowed."

The old man looked at the bill, the corners of his mouth turning up. He reached a hand out and took the bill, stuffing it in the front pocket of his work pants. "Much appreciated. Thank you, sir," he said.

Snow smiled and nodded. "Good luck to you."

His mood lifting slightly, he turned around and walked back to his car.

CHAPTER 8

Steve Helm must have been hovering near his front door when Snow arrived. As he trudged up the walkway, it opened in front of him, and Steve filled the doorway wearing a yellow knit shirt, black jeans, white tennis shoes, and a wide grin on his face.

Helm produced a firm handshake, and as Snow stared into his face, he began to get an uncomfortable feeling about the man. What was he grinning about?

"Your sister told me you'd be stopping by," Helm said. "She gave me the lowdown on you."

"Anything good?" Snow mumbled, stepping into the living room.

"All good. I'm impressed, to say the least." He motioned toward the couch with his hand. It was large, with three cushions, wooden legs, and covered with a dark green fabric that contrasted nicely with the standard beige carpet underneath it.

Snow seated himself near the end of it. Helm plopped down to the right of him in a black Naugahyde recliner. "She said you used to be a homicide detective, and a good one at that."

Settling back on the couch, Snow surveyed the living room. It was what you would expect to find in a typical bachelor pad.

Rounding out the diverse color scheme of his seating ensemble, at the far end of the couch, angled toward the giant flat-panel TV, was a thinly padded, sky-blue easy chair that looked as though no one had ever sat in it. There were no footstools, no coffee table, only a simple wooden end table with a lamp on it next to the end of the couch where Snow sat. The off-white walls were augmented by a scattering of various cheaply framed photos and paintings of wild animals, oceans, lakes, trains, cars, and one of dogs playing poker directly to the right of the TV.

Snow studied the dogs in the painting as he spoke. "I can't speak for my own ability in that profession. But I always assumed I was probably pretty close to average. Most of the cases I investigated solved themselves. Usually when people kill each other, they don't spend a lot of time planning it. And they don't put a lot of effort into covering it up. Typically, you'll find a body, and standing or sitting next to the body will be the person responsible. Or, in a more difficult case, you'll discover a body in one room, and the perpetrator, covered with evidence—usually the victim's blood—in another room of the same building."

Helm stood up. "Oh, I'm sorry. I got so caught up in what you were saying, I forgot my manners. Would you like something? A beer maybe? I don't have a big selection. Heineken, Corona, Foster's, and I believe I still have a couple of Tsingtao left in the fridge."

"I think I'll go with the Tsingtao," Snow said. "I just happened to pick up a six-pack of that stuff a few years ago, on a lark. And I was surprised at the quality of it. Smooth, flavorful, just the right amount of bite."

"I agree," Helm said. "Those Chinese are amazing, aren't they? They've got every market dominated these days."

Helm went into the kitchen and came back with two of the green bottles. He handed one to Snow, took a swallow from the other, and sat back down in the recliner. Leaning toward Snow, he said, "I've watched that crime scene investigation program on television quite a bit, and I'm always impressed with the technical expertise and professionalism of the people who solve those difficult cases."

Snow took a slug of beer and nodded. "Yeah," he said, "but that program is based on fiction. The actors all have expensive suits and work in spacious labs with roomy offices. They get called out to a crime scene, gather up evidence, rush it back to the lab, process it all immediately, and make an arrest in record time. The actual criminalists who work in the lab over on West Charleston Boulevard have so little space to work in, usually they have to wait for hours to get a free table to examine new evidence. DNA results for a top-priority case, like a homicide, can take up to a week. Sometimes longer. They find a decomposed body out in the desert—it could take months to process it."

Helm's mouth formed a circle, as though he were smoking an invisible cigar. He took another swallow of beer. "That's interesting," he said. "How many murder cases, would you say, get solved?"

"A little over half, and that includes the ones where the suspect calls it in himself and confesses over the phone to the operator."

Helm nodded. "Amazing. And how is this one looking?"

There were no coasters on the end table, only a half-dozen rings marking the area of the table that seemed to be acceptable for parking bottles, so Snow placed his directly on one of the rings. He looked up at Helm. "That depends on whose perspective you're using to view it. From the bureau's side, it looks promising. From yours it doesn't look too good."

The color ran out of Helm's face. "Why do you say that?"

Snow gave him a quick summary of Harris's report. Then he asked him to relate his version of what occurred the night before. It matched what Harris had told him.

"You didn't notice anyone inside the storage lot while you were there?"

"No. No one."

"Were there any vehicles parked nearby, indicating someone might have been inside one of the other RVs?"

"I didn't see any."

"Did you tell anybody that you would be paying cash for this RV? Anybody at work?"

"No."

"Why did you pay with cash?" Snow asked.

"I always pay with cash," Helm replied. "For everything."

"But eight thousand dollars seems a little excessive."

"I've had more than that on me when I'm shooting craps. Down on the Strip you're likely to find a lot of people walking around with fifty thousand or more in their pockets."

"What about illegal substances or firearms? None of that involved in the transaction?"

"Just the trailer," he said. "I don't use any drugs in any form, and I don't even own a gun. At least, not right now."

"What about what happened when you were twenty-three?"

Helm looked down at his beer. "Oh, you know about that."

"Of course. It came up in your background check."

He brought his eyes back up. "That was a long time ago. I was young and stupid, just out of the Air Force. The only job I could find was as a security guard at a trucking company. I had to buy a thirty-eight revolver and a Sam Browne gun belt for the job. I was making minimum wage, which wasn't enough to live on. So I thought I'd make some side money with the Smith and Wesson to help pay the rent. The first convenience store I robbed, I got almost two hundred bucks and it was a piece of cake. I produced the gun, the cashier gave me the contents of the cash register, and I drove off. It was so easy, I decided to try it again. But the next time I only got forty-seven bucks, so I stopped by another one on the way home and that was a little better."

"How many robberies did you commit before you got caught?"

"I think it was twenty-three," he said. "After a while it got to the point where it was like going out to pick up a carton of milk and a dozen eggs. The last store I robbed, there was a police car waiting in the parking lot for me when I came out. And the cop was standing there with his gun pointed at my chest." He sighed. "They charged me with seven counts of armed robbery, then reduced it, and gave me five years. I served it in Tucson."

"The whole five?" Snow said.

He leaned back in the recliner without propping up the footrest. "I never made parole. My cellmate got a stash of dope smuggled in to him somehow. I didn't ask about it. That was his business. The guy was crazy. Smoked it right there in the cell in the middle of the night, asked me if I wanted a hit. Well, I didn't want to piss him off, so I took few tokes. Might have been more. Shortly after that I flunked a random drug test, and that was that." He took a swallow of beer. "But I've been on the straight and narrow ever since. Now I enjoy a few brewskies now and then, but that's it. Nothing illegal. I don't even drive over the speed limit anymore."

"And where are you working now?"

"Samurai Nissan over on Sahara. I'm the sales manager. Been with them for seven years."

"What can you tell me about you and Bob Williams? The two of you friends?"

Helm shifted his position in the recliner, causing a series of squeaks to come from the Naugahyde. "Not really. Just neighborly type stuff. You know, waving to each other from our yards, small talk at the mailbox. He and Karen invited me over for a barbeque a couple years ago. I took a date, someone I met at the grocery store, and it was a good time. But I never really buddied up to the guy. The age difference wasn't that great, but he was an Archie Bunker sort of guy, and he made me feel like Meathead."

"You don't seem to me like Meathead," Snow said.

He grinned. "Thanks. I appreciate that."

"What about Karen? What is your relationship with her?"

Helm spread his hands, the beer bottle in his right. His eyebrows arched, and he stared at a spot in front of the couch where a coffee table might stand. "Oh...Karen? We've always been friendly toward each other. Nice lady."

"More so than with Bob?"

He looked at Snow. "Oh sure. She's easy to get along with, really bright, a real pleasure to talk to. We could stand in the driveway and converse for hours."

"You ever converse in each other's homes?"

"Sometimes she'd invite me in for coffee, or some pie, or I'd ask her inside to show her something interesting."

"Uh-huh."

"Like a new appliance, or something like that," he qualified.

"How did you find out about this trailer that Bob had for sale?"

He wiggled around in the chair some more. More squeaking from the Naugahyde. "Karen told me about it. Of course Bob had moved out by then, and so Karen came over and gave me the details. She thought I might be interested because I had heard about their expeditions in it. I had commented several times that I was thinking of getting one—motel rooms cost a fortune, and it's a lot of trouble dealing with luggage. Plus you can get right out there, park near the beach, or wherever, and you always have your own bed to sleep in at night—sounded good to me. So I told her I was interested. And the rest is history."

Snow nodded. "Unfortunately," he said, "so is Bob."

Helm frowned. "Yeah. Poor guy."

"Now, about this screwdriver that was sticking out of the tire…"

"Yes."

"What can you tell me about that?"

"Well," he said, "I had pulled ahead with the trailer hooked up to my truck, ready to go, and Bob had just moved forward maybe five feet or so and stopped. Then he got out, so I got out to find out what was wrong. And he told me he'd had a big whump with his tire."

"A whump."

"That's what he called it. Said it felt like he ran over a rock or something, but it didn't feel right. So we went around to the back of the truck and found the handle of a screwdriver sticking out the back of the right rear tire, right in the middle of the tread. But it was kind of angled upward. Might have been bent a little because the tire ran over it. And the air was coming out of the tire. You could hear it."

"What did the screwdriver look like?"

"All I could see was the handle sticking out; the business part of it was stuck inside the tire. But the handle was made of plastic. It had a band of blue near the blade, and clear over the rest of it. And I'd say it was about three to four inches long."

Snow considered this. He lifted his beer, took a couple of swallows, and then held it on the arm of the sofa. "Do you have much money in the bank?"

Helm shook his head. "Not really. Couple thousand. The interest doesn't pay anything these days. I keep upwards of fifteen thousand hidden around the house for a bankroll—you know, for craps, mostly."

"Any other assets, other than your house? Stocks, bonds?"

"None at all."

"Any heavy debts?"

"I owe some on my credit cards—I guess about forty thousand."

"So the craps table hasn't been paying off."

"For the casino," he said.

Snow smiled. "Mr. Helm, have you consulted with an attorney?"

He shook his head. "I don't have money to waste on that. Besides, I didn't do anything wrong."

Snow nodded. "I guess that's all I can think of for now. I appreciate your help." He looked at Helm. "Are there any questions you have for me?"

"Yes, actually, I was wondering if I might be able to hire you."

"Hire me for what?"

"To do what you're already doing for your sister regarding this…problem…only, include me in it as a primary interest as well."

"You are already included in it."

"But I'm not included in your best interests. You're working on behalf of your sister, but not on my behalf."

"What are you getting at?"

59

Helm sighed. "Simply this: Karen is your sister, so you'll do everything you can to try to clear her, even if it involves incriminating me. Isn't that true?"

Snow shrugged. "I'm just trying to dig up the facts."

"Well," Helm said, "I would like to hire you so that you can dig for me as well."

"You can't hire me. I'm not licensed."

"Then I'll slip you something under the table. Cash."

"I don't work that way."

Helm leaned forward. "Could you make a suggestion that would be acceptable to you?"

Snow sighed and scratched the side of his nose with the back of his thumb. He thought for a moment.

"Alright, here's what you do: I'll do whatever I can for both you and Karen. If I can uncover clear evidence pointing toward someone else, and you're happy with the results of my work, make a check out for two thousand dollars and donate it to the Salvation Army. That way you'll even be able to deduct it for this tax year. And if you're not happy with the results—for whatever reason— you can use that money toward a good criminal defense attorney."

Fifteen minutes later Snow's cell phone began chirping. He pulled it out and flipped it open. It was Karen. He let it ring over to voice mail, pulled into a strip mall, and then called her back.

"Why didn't you answer your phone?" Her words were rushed, tinged with a tone of hostility.

"I was driving. If I remember correctly, you were the one who told me I couldn't walk and chew gum at the same time."

"And which, if any, of those two things were you doing?" she said.

He paused, trying to figure out the logic behind that statement. "What's up, Karen?" he said.

"That's the question I have for you, Jim. Do you have any leads yet?"

"I'm not sure."

"How can you not be sure about a lead? Either you have a lead, or you don't. If you find a lead, you pursue it. Right? If you don't have a lead, then you look for one. So you're saying you don't have a lead, and you're still looking for one?"

Snow sighed. "Alright, I have a lead, but it's pretty thin."

"What is it?" she asked.

"If I sit here and discuss it with you, then I won't be pursuing it—will I?"

"Just tell me what it is."

"Karen, I'm not going to call you and discuss every little detail I happen to run across. If I do that, I'll never make it to square one."

"Well, I'm sitting here worried sick! And Steve just came over here and told me that you interrogated him—and that you're out to get him! And if you're out to get him, and you succeed, then I'll end up going right into the slammer with him!"

"Karen, I think you're overreacting."

"*I am not overreacting!*" she bellowed. "*I just want to get through this terrible mess!*"

"Karen, listen, I'm not out to get Steve. There are questions that have to be asked so that I know which direction to go with this."

"But he said you're asking him the same questions the detectives asked him, only worse. He says you don't like him."

"I don't have an opinion one way or the other about the guy," Snow muttered. "But there is something about him you should know."

"What?"

"He spent five years in an Arizona state prison for multiple counts of armed robbery."

Silence.

"Karen?"

"I have to go," she said. Then she hung up.

CHAPTER 9

There were eight of the two-story homes on Duit Avenue directly across the wash from Hollywood RV Storage that Snow considered to be likely possibilities. The first two doorbells he rang yielded no results; no one answered, or possibly nobody was home. The third and fourth attempts brought a response. However, no one could remember seeing anything suspicious taking place on the other side of the wash. For these people, as expected, their bedrooms were on the second floor. For the most part, the only times they looked out of their upstairs windows were when they were opening or closing blinds or windows. And during those times, they never saw anything other than an occasional jogger chugging along the fire road next to their fence.

The fifth home Snow approached was a different story. The man who came to the door was in his mid-thirties. He was slightly shorter than Snow, with a shaved head, wearing Bermuda shorts and a T-shirt advertising the World Series of Poker. Snow recognized him as soon as he opened the door.

The man's mouth opened and he stared for a second. Then he pointed at Snow. "Treasure Island card room," he said.

Snow smiled and nodded. They shook hands.

"Chuck Sharar," the man said.

Snow introduced himself and went inside.

"So you just mainly stick with limit games?" Sharar asked. "I don't remember ever seeing you at a no-limit table."

"Yeah," Snow said. "I've gotten comfortable with that. Never could handle the possibility of dropping my entire stack in one hand."

Sharar motioned his hand toward an overstuffed chair. "Have a seat. You want a beer?"

Snow hooked his thumbs into his front pockets. "Thanks, but I can't stay long. I just stopped by to ask a few questions. And I'm really sorry to bother you…"

"No problem." He paused. "But how did you find out where I live?"

"Oh, this has nothing to do with poker," Snow said. "I wish it did. Actually it has to do with the RV storage lot on the other side of the wash. There was a murder there last night, and I'm helping to investigate."

Sharar's eyebrows shot up. "A murder? I didn't hear anything about that. Well, I haven't listened to the news yet. How did it happen?"

Snow gave him a short summary of what the police had found and asked him if he'd seen anything.

"I wasn't home last night. Didn't get in until four this morning. I was playing."

Snow nodded. "Treasure Island?"

"No, actually I went to the Bellagio. I've been playing there for a few weeks now."

"You like it better?" Snow asked.

"It's pretty classy," Sharar said. "I've had a good run there so far. You play there?"

"Mostly there. Treasure Island. Wynn. Those three."

"You play full time?" Sharar asked.

"For about three years now. I quit the force to play full time—until about a month ago."

Sharar's eyes narrowed, and his head shifted forward. "What happened?"

Snow looked directly into Sharar's eyes. "Nothing good, I can tell you. Lost my ass for six months straight, practically every session. It was like I hit a brick wall all of a sudden. Every time I've hit pocket kings, I've lost, even after flopping a set. I got to where I dreaded pocket kings—even in late position. Pocket aces have been lousy too. I think I must have somewhere around ten percent win rate with those. All kinds of maniacs betting into me before the flop. I got the best hand pre-flop, right? These lunatics end up with monster hands every time. I flop a flush with a three-card, gut-shot straight flush draw showing on the board, no pairs. Only two cards in the deck can beat me, and my opponent needs them both. He got 'em. That happened to me three times. King high flush—every time the other guy's got the ace. Everybody's got a bad beat story. But when you get to the point where the best you can hope for is to fold pre-flop every hand, it's time to back off."

"That's tough," Sharar said. "I've been pretty lucky, I guess. Been playing part time for over five years, and I've done pretty well. I've heard it's not unusual to have losing years when you're playing full time. But I've never had a bad run last more than a few weeks. I think it's the difference between limit and no-limit. With limit hold 'em you're missing one of your most valuable tools—the ability to bluff."

"Yeah…well…maybe you're right."

"You know," Sharar said, "I've been thinking about quitting work too, getting into it full time, but the wife wouldn't go along with that. We've got two kids. And if I did manage to convince her, I'd probably lose my nerve and end up like you, losing for six months in a row."

"Yeah," Snow agreed. "Don't do anything hasty. What is it you do for a living?"

"I work for RTC," he said. "I drive one of those Deuce buses—the double-deckers. Usually drive the Sahara route, but sometimes I switch around and get the Flamingo Road or Eastern route."

Snow nodded. "You like that sort of work?"

"Beats driving a cab," he said. "And it's pretty stable. My wife is a nurse, and that's even more stable. But I tell you, I don't know how she does it—the hours, all the sick, old people she deals with. Now, homicide detective, that's got to be a tough job…" He paused and folded his arms. "Wait a minute…you said you quit three years ago. What are you doing investigating a murder?"

"I'm assisting in the investigation."

"You mean they call you in from time to time to help out? You must be good."

Snow shook his head. "No, I'm not helping them. It's my sister. It was her husband who was killed last night, so I'm helping on her behalf to find the person who did it."

"I'm sorry to hear that. She must be in a bad way right now."

"She is," Snow said.

Sharar unfolded his arms suddenly and pointed at Snow. His face lit up. "Hey, wait a minute. I don't know where my head is. Listen, I did see something that might help you out."

"What's that?"

"The wife, when she's home, she's always watching these weird programs on television like *Dancing with the Stars* and *American Idol*. We don't have the same interests at all in TV programming. So I put a set up in our room, and I go up there and watch whatever I want. And I'm usually looking out the window when the commercials come on or the program starts to drag. Not that there's much to look at out there, but every so often I'll be looking out at the wash or something and notice the same guy. Usually about the same time every night, right around eight thirty or nine o'clock. He looks like a homeless old guy. I've seen him walking along the fire road, next to the wash. And I've seen him sneaking into that RV lot that you mentioned. It looks like there's something wrapped around the fence at the north corner—"

"Bungee cords," Snow said.

"Right, that's what it looks like. Three of them. He unwraps the top two and pulls the top part of the fence back and goes through and then wraps them up again real tight."

Snow tipped his head to the side and bit his lower lip. "Then what?"

"I don't know," Sharar said. "He disappears behind the trailer nearest the fence. Those RVs are all so high they block the view. You can't see what goes on in there from here. I imagine he must have broken into one of them, and he's using it to sleep in at night."

"Sounds like it," Snow said. "You see anybody else go in there through that opening?"

"No," Sharar said. "Just him. He's probably the one who took the fence apart and put those bungee cords there. Made himself a doorway."

CHAPTER 10

In the second row from the corner of the back fence, Snow found an empty space, fourth from the end. He had noticed quite a few cars parked in the storage lot; he assumed they were left behind when the tenants took their RVs out on the road. So as he backed into the empty space, he wasn't concerned about being noticed. The corner of the fence wasn't visible from his position because of the fifth wheel parked next to it. So he would have to listen for the sound of the fence being pulled back. It was a pleasant evening, just above seventy degrees with no wind. He lowered all four windows and sat staring at the glow cast over the RVs from the partial moon reflecting off the gravel.

At twenty to eight, he heard a jangle coming from the corner of the fence behind the fifth wheel. He straightened in his seat and leaned forward, listening. More jangling from the fence. And then he saw the man, walking along the north fence, behind the first row of RVs, with two half-filled garbage bags slung over his shoulder. He wore a long-sleeve shirt, light-colored work pants, and a dark ball cap. From fifty feet away, Snow could barely make out the beard, but he realized it was the same man he had approached earlier that day in front of the 7-Eleven.

He waited for the man to pass beyond the thin space separating the two RVs in front of him before he quietly eased his car door open and slipped out from behind the wheel. He couldn't hear any sound from the man's footsteps at that distance, so he assumed it would be safe to follow without being heard. Being seen was another problem entirely. But he had no choice—he would have to follow.

At Snow's size, staying light on his feet was impossible, but he kept low, rounding the back of his car, and crept from trailer to trailer, trying to spot the man along the fence in the row across from him. He didn't have to go far; ten spaces from the back fence, he saw the man standing behind a motorboat. It appeared to be eighteen or twenty feet in length, off-white, with a blue nylon cover strapped to the side channels of the trailer that supported the boat. The man was releasing the straps at the cover, one at a time, letting them drop to the ground.

Snow stood behind a motor home across from the boat in the second row, watching as the man lifted the cover from the rear of the boat, threw it forward, and climbed inside. Grunting and cursing, the boat rocking from his effort, he struggled with the cover from underneath it and managed to place the fitted corners over the stern of the boat.

The boat continued to display an occasional spasm of movement for the next few minutes, and then it grew still.

Snow waited a few minutes more, and then he approached the boat, the gravel crunching under his loafers. He stopped at the transom next to the ninety-horse motor and cleared his throat.

No sound from the boat.

Snow rapped his knuckles against the transom four times.

From under the boat cover he heard, "Shit…I don't remember ordering room service."

The boat wiggled around, and then the cover lifted from the corner of the transom, a bony hand holding it up and exposing a white-and-gray-bearded face. The mouth hung open, and loose strands of thin hair dangled over his deep-set, hooded eyes.

The man's eyes narrowed. "You…whuddayuh want your twenty back?"

Snow stepped back a few paces. "Would you mind stepping out of the boat, please?"

"You a cop?"

"No," Snow replied. "But there's one sitting in a squad car, five rows over. I can go get him and bring him over here if you'd like."

The old man's hand maintained its hold on the cover. "You own this boat?"

"No."

"Then why do you care if I'm in it?"

"I don't care that you're in it. But right now, I'd like you to get out of it so I can take a look inside and talk to you for a minute."

"About what?"

Snow sighed. "Alright. I'm going to go get the cop." He started to walk toward the front of the boat.

"No!" The old man scurried to his feet, lifting the cover over his head and letting it go. It fell over the seats behind him. "I'm getting out." He scrambled to the side of the boat, lifted a leg over, stepped onto the trailer frame, and hopped to the ground.

"You're pretty agile for an old homeless guy," Snow said.

The old man reached inside the boat, grabbed the bill of his ball cap, smoothed back his hair, and stretched the cap over it. He glared at Snow from under the brim of the cap, his eyes

narrow. "I'm not homeless," he declared. "And I'm not a bum—
I'm a tramp."

"What's the difference?"

"There's a big difference. A bum is lazy, stays in one place,
and refuses to work. A tramp travels around looking for adven-
ture and works at making money any way he can get it."

Snow nodded. "If you say so. How long have you been at it?"

"Nine years," he said. "Before that I taught history and
coached high school basketball in Buckleman, Iowa."

"What are you doing here?"

"I got laid off. And it's too cold there to sleep outside this
time of year. That's what I'm doing here. They shut down the
school. The whole goddamn thing—kindergarten all the way up.
Not surprising, really—the whole state's been in the dumps since
the seventies. America's heartland—ended up with a massive
coronary." He flipped his hands up in the air. "So I just up and
left. Lost the house, and unemployment—which don't hardly
pay for anything—ran out. I learned the ropes very quickly.
Hell, I taught it in American history. The Great Depression,
millions of able-bodied men riding the rails, living in hobo
jungles, surviving by their wits. Doing whatever it took." He
pointed a finger at Snow. "Whatever you have to do, sleeping
on hard ground, in a boat, whatever…"

"You married? Any kids?"

"I was married," the old man said. "I had kids. Those are
other stories—tales I don't feel like telling."

"You have any identification?"

"I do," he said. "I have an Iowa driver's license. It expired
years ago, but I still carry it around with me so that when my
body's discovered in a gutter someday, they'll know who I
am—like anybody's gonna give a shit."

He reached into the back pocket of his trousers and pulled out a ragged leather billfold, peered inside it, and slipped out his license. He handed it to Snow.

Snow pulled a small LED flashlight out of his front pocket, snapped it on with his thumb, and aimed the beam at the license. "William Dale Hoffman," he read. "Born in forty-eight, so you're sixty-one—getting close to retirement."

The old man nodded. "Yeah. No doubt. In the boneyard."

Snow opened his notebook, jotted down the information from the license, and then handed it back to him. "Were you here last night, Mr. Hoffman?"

"Willie. Call me Willie." He scrunched his lips together in an uneven line and shook his head. "No, I wasn't."

"Didn't come in here at all?"

"No."

"Where did you sleep?"

He waved his hand in the direction of the back fence. "Oh. Down in the wash, in among the bushes. It gets stuffy inside this boat with the cover on it. It's been fairly warm lately. I don't like to flop the same place every night. I like it in the wash—it's peaceful down there. You just need to make a lot of noise so you don't step on a rattlesnake. You just have to stomp around a little, and they'll slither away."

"You sleep there by yourself?"

"No, Cher usually joins me, if she's not doing a show."

"Other than Cher?" Snow's face twisted into a half grin. "There any other tramps or homeless people down in that wash at night?"

"I haven't seen anybody. Most of the homeless stay closer to downtown, near the Sally."

"Sally?"

"Salvation Army."

"How long have you been in Vegas?"

Willie looked up at the sky. "Let's see. I'd say about a little over a month. I was up in the Bay Area for the summer, San Francisco, San Jose, around there. That's a nice time of year to vacation up there. I usually spend the winters around here or Arizona. I've gotten accustomed to the snowbird way of life."

"How did you get down here?"

"Freight." Willie stared into Snow's face. "You sure you're not a cop? You certainly act like one."

Snow nodded. "I was a cop. Now I'm not."

"Why'd you quit? You shoot somebody and feel bad about it? Or they kick you out?"

"No, I never shot anybody. I just decided to take a shot at a different profession."

"Which one?"

"Texas hold 'em. Poker."

Willie arched his brows and nodded. "Nice. How's that working out for you?"

"It's not."

Willie put his hand to his beard and massaged it with his fingertips. "That's the problem with gambling," he said. "It's like a beautiful woman: exhilarating at first, and then she turns on you and takes all your money." He stopped rubbing his beard and crossed his arms. "Why did you want to know if I was here last night? Something happen here?"

Snow explained about the murder, about the possibility of the killer using a pickaxe.

"You don't have a pickaxe handy, do you, Willie?"

He shook his head. "I've never met a tramp who traveled with a pickaxe. It would be extremely difficult to jump a freight

73

train with something like that sticking out of your travel bag."
He paused. "But if you're not a cop anymore, why are you investigating this homicide?"

"The victim was my brother-in-law."

Snow told him about his sister, the insurance money, and the previous marriages. Then he asked about the fence. He asked Willie if he was the one who took the corner section apart and wrapped the bungee cords around it.

"I'm not going to admit to that," Willie said. "I never confess to anything I haven't been caught at."

"Have you ever been caught at anything? Anything illegal?" Snow asked.

"I've got a clean record," Willie replied. "You can check it. Now, let me ask you—are you planning to turn me in for flopping in this boat?"

"Only if I find a pickaxe in it," Snow said.

CHAPTER 11

Sunday morning, six a.m.

Snow usually tried to get out of bed before six when he wasn't playing poker. Poker nights were a different story. Prime poker hours on the Strip in Las Vegas were from eight p.m. until four a.m., Fridays, Saturdays, and holidays. That was when the partying tourists were ripe for picking.

Snapping on his bedside lamp, Snow took in a deep breath and climbed out of bed. He straightened the covers enough to eliminate the prominent ridges, and then he crossed to the small walk-in closet. He flipped the light on and stood in the doorway, studying two racks of running shoes, one on each side of the closet. Twenty-four pairs of shoes in all. Neutral shoes on the left, stability on the right. Snow had vacillated back and forth from one school of thought to the other concerning his gait, degree of pronation, and the need for support to counteract it. A slight inward bending of the ankle was normal, but too much would result in injury. Too much support, on the other hand, could also cause a breakdown.

Some people were lucky. Born with the perfect framework, ideal for running for hours, or even days on end, these anatomical wonders could breeze through a marathon in flip-flops.

Speculating that his current problem had been caused by the dual-density midsoles featured in the stability side of the closet, Snow selected a pair of Asics from the left. He pulled on a pair of running shorts, a sweat-wicking T-shirt, and laced up the shoes.

Stretching produced a tight twinge of pain in the outer side of his right knee. He massaged the right side of his thigh, digging his fingertips in and around the outer tendon that held his knee in place. Snow imagined it must look like a rusty cable from an elevator in an abandoned mine shaft.

Positive thinking. Maybe it was mostly psychological—his lazy side trying to sabotage the accomplishments of his ambitious side. He straightened and strode to the front door, flipped the deadbolt open, and stepped outside. He filled his lungs with the cool, dry air of this October morning and swung his arms wide from side to side. It was not too late. There was still enough time to ramp up his mileage to an adequate level. Fifteen-mile-long run, two weeks out from the marathon, and then the taper. Fifteen miles. That would be the bare acceptable minimum in order to attempt to finish it. Maybe it would be enough. Maybe not. He felt the stiffness building in his iliotibial band.

This was a bad idea.

He went back inside, tossed his running togs in a pile on the floor, and crawled back into bed.

In Snow's mind, small goals were the key to success. On this morning, finishing a cup of coffee seemed like a reasonable goal.

At eight fifteen, he climbed out, slipped on a pair of blue jeans and a T-shirt, and went to the kitchen to make coffee. With that brewing, he collected the morning paper from the front stoop, sat down in his stuffed chair, and opened it. The news story about the murder was buried a few pages deep. In a city with well over one hundred murders per year, the slaying of a pit boss in an RV storage lot was of little importance when compared to the full-page ad on the opposing page featuring coupons for the Boulder Nugget buffet. Snow got his scissors out and removed the coupons.

Then he placed a call to Detective Alice James's cell phone. She answered briskly on the first ring.

"Alice, this is Jim Snow. We met yesterday."

"I remember," she said. "How are you today?"

"I don't know—I haven't had any coffee yet. Can you do me a favor?"

"As long as it's legal." She laughed.

"Well, it's got to be off the record, and don't let Mel know about it. I don't want to cause any trouble for this guy, but I need to check him out. I need you to pull his rap sheet and check for priors."

"Okay," she agreed, "but I can't do that right now."

"Mel is there with you right now?"

"Of course. But give me the information, and I'll get back to you after I have a chance to think about it."

Snow gave her Willie's full name, date of birth, and Iowa driver's license number. He thanked her and hung up.

With a mug of steaming coffee, Snow padded into a spare bedroom, past his weight-lifting machine and dumbbell rack to his desk in the corner. He booted up his computer and brought up the Internet. Multiple searches on Google for William Dale

Hoffman, Willie Hoffman, and various other combinations of additional words and descriptions brought no results. He found the Web site for Buckleman, Iowa, clicked through the menus to the phone number for city hall, and dialed it. The call went to voice mail. He hung up.

He looked at his watch and then did a search for white pages listings for the name *Anderson*, a common German name. Probably ninety percent of the residents of that small town were of that descent. He dialed the number listed for the name at the top of the list. No answer. Probably in church.

He tried the second number. The hoarse voice of an old man came through the line. "Anderson's."

"Yes, I'm trying to get information about a fellow who used to live there by the name of Willie Hoffman. Apparently he taught history in the high school there and coached basketball."

"Never heard of him, and there ain't no high school here anymore. But I've only been living here for five years, so there must be a lot of people from here that I've never heard of."

"Oh," Snow said. "Well, is there someone you know who I could talk to who might have known the man?"

"The principal," the man said. "Former principal. He's retired now, but he still lives here. Nice, friendly sort. Everybody I've met seems to like him. His name is Virgil Wilkie. He can answer your questions—let me go find his phone number." The phone went silent. In the background, Snow could hear the old man, along with the voice of an old woman, discussing something. Snow pictured the old guy thumbing through the slender phone directory, searching for the phone number, with his wife sitting nearby, telling him how to do it.

A minute later his voice came back through the line. "Here it is. I found it. Virgil Wilkie." He read off the number.

Snow thanked him, hung up, and then dialed the number.

After more than ten rings, Snow was almost ready to hang up when a small, timid voice greeted him.

"Mr. Wilkie?"

"That's me."

"My name is Jim Snow, and I'm calling about a man by the name of Willie Hoffman. Do you know anyone by that name?"

"I sure do," Wilkie said. "What would you like to know about him?"

"Anything you can tell me," Snow said.

"Well, I grew up with him," Wilkie began. "We went through school together, played on the same basketball team. Willie was a pretty darn good point guard, though he used to hog the ball a lot. We went on to different colleges. Then Willie came back here after he graduated, and got hired on to teach history. Eventually, they made him the basketball coach. I was living in Waterloo, then Cedar Rapids, and teaching math. Then about ten years down the road from college, I guess it was, I came back here and took the job of principal for the high school."

"So you were his boss," Snow said.

"On paper I was. Nobody could tell that bullheaded lout what to do. Especially not me." He took a breath. "You've seen him, I take it?"

"Yes, he's here in Las Vegas."

"How is he doing?"

"Not too good by my standards. The way he tells it, he's thriving. The fact is—he's homeless. He says he's been that way for nine years."

"Oh boy, I'm really sorry to hear that, but I can't say I'm surprised. That poor guy went through the worst I've ever seen."

"What happened?"

"Well, sir," Wilkie said, "Willie married his high school sweetheart. They started dating when they were sixteen. They attended separate colleges, stayed in touch, and then moved back here after graduation and got married right away. Her name was Janet, and she taught English here at the same high school. They had two boys. Both good kids, but a little rebellious, which is typical considering their parents were both part of the establishment. That usually happens. And no doubt they picked up some of that from Willie. He was the same way, even after he became part of the establishment.

"Well, sir, the youngest one died in a motorcycle accident when he was sixteen. It wasn't even his motorcycle. It belonged to a friend and he wanted to try it out, lost control on a curve, and ran it into a telephone pole.

"The eldest of the two got a job driving a truck. He was robbed and killed while he was stopped on an on-ramp to an interstate, somewhere in Georgia. All of that was pretty terrible, what happened to their two boys, but somehow Willie and Janet pulled through that. Willie's a pretty tough bird. But then the decision came to shut the school down, so they were both out of a job. We all were. The whole town shut down, pretty much. It was bad for everybody. But Willie and Janet got the worst of it."

Snow said nothing.

Wilkie continued: "I tell you, these people around here are an amazing bunch. They get dragged through hell, they all lose their farms, their homes, everything their parents and grandparents worked their whole lives for—all of it gone. But they don't ever blame anybody; they just roll with the punches and keep on rolling, making do the best they can…"

The line went silent for a moment, and then Wilkie came back on.

"Well," he continued, "it didn't take long for Willie and Janet to run through their savings. Unemployment compensation only goes so far. Their home went into foreclosure, and shortly after that Janet gave up. She went out to the garage in the middle of the night, while Willie was asleep, and duct-taped their garden hose to the exhaust pipe of their car, and ran it in through the car window. He found her the next morning; the car was still running. God, that was horrible.

"So after that happened, Willie moved out of the house, sold the car for practically nothing, and rented a room here in town. After his unemployment ran out, so did he. He just disappeared, and nobody ever saw him again.

"He is a good man, Mr. Snow. Even though occasionally he can be a little impetuous. The kids all liked him; he kept them laughing with his antics. You know, history can be a pretty dry subject. I know it was for me. But he had a way of spicing it up. I gave him a wide berth; otherwise, he'd have been in my office every other day. He'd hold class in the gymnasium, out on the football field, up at the Dairy Queen. His coaching ability wasn't so good. We never had a winning season while he was at the helm. But the bleachers were always full..." He paused. "So are you considering hiring him for something?"

"Actually, no...I..." Snow paused, thought for a moment, and then continued. "Well, yes, there is a temporary job I could use him for, I believe."

"Good, that's good," Wilkie said. "Tell him to give me a call. Collect. It'll be good to hear from him again."

"I will. I'll do that, Mr. Wilkie. And you have a good day."

"You too, Mr. Snow. And thank you for calling."

Snow hung up the phone.

He sat there staring at it for several minutes—until it began to ring.

He picked it up. It was Alice.

"I ran the records check you asked for," she said. "It's clean."

"I figured as much," Snow said.

He thanked her and hung up the phone.

CHAPTER 12

The Boulder Strip is home to a handful of small hotel-casinos geared toward the locals of Las Vegas. Featuring inexpensive buffets, giveaways, discounts, lower table limits, and cocktail waitresses working to supplement their social security, many of the regulars from neighboring Southern California never play anywhere else.

Vegas Valley Casino, one of the newer resorts to join the competition on Boulder Highway, was located just south of Sahara Avenue. The exterior of the building appeared to have been designed with economy in mind, resembling an enormous department store.

Entering through one of three sets of double doors in the side entrance, adjacent to the parking lot, Jim Snow walked past banks of slot machines on both sides of the walkway that led to more rows of slot machines as far as the eye could see. Everything around him was lit up, the air charged with what sounded like the electronic mating calls of various species of alien robots. Underneath all of this was a burgundy carpet with a pattern of multicolored, flowered vines crawling all over it. Snow wondered as to the purpose of such a gaudy design. Probably, should one of the guests suddenly vomit, it would blend right in and prevent anyone else from noticing.

Somewhere near the middle of the gambling floor, the slot machines gave way to an open area of tables dedicated to blackjack, craps, roulette, three-card poker, and an assortment of imported games for which Snow had no understanding. He stopped at a table advertising Pai Gow poker and got the attention of one of the suits inside the pit area.

"I'm looking for Craig Peters," Snow said.

The man in the suit, a young Wall Street sort with a buzz cut, pivoted his head both directions and then spun around and pointed to a white-haired man with a goatee, wearing a gray suit. He was standing in the next pit, staring at a monitor, and working his fingers over the keyboard below it.

Snow crossed to the other line of tables and called to him. Peters turned around, and Snow gave his name.

Peters gave him a short wave and then exited the pit and led him to an unoccupied blackjack table in the middle of three vacant tables on the fringe of the table games area. It was covered with green felt and edged with black padding. The rows of chips were locked down by a metal-framed, glass cover. Peters offered a handshake, pointed at one of the high-backed stools, and then seated himself in the one next to it, hooking the heels of his tasseled slip-ons over the lower rung of his chair.

"Sorry, I can't leave the floor right now. And I'm sorry to hear about what happened to your brother-in-law." Peters clasped his hands together in his lap. "Would you like a drink? I can get the cocktail waitress over here…" He perked his head up and looked around for one. "Or maybe not; we're a little shorthanded these days."

Snow raised a palm. "I'm okay. This won't take long." He leaned forward. "So you were Bob's supervisor?"

"Sort of. I'm the floor supervisor for this shift. Bob was a pit boss, responsible for the tables and the play in his assigned pit area. I'm responsible for all of the pit bosses and the whole gaming floor."

"That sounds like a tough job."

"Not really. It can get boring, and there is a lot of standing. But there's really no pressure to speak of, not like other management positions in other industries."

"Sounds like you've been through some of those."

Peters nodded. "I was the service department manager for a large RV dealership in Riverside, California, for quite a few years. I got to a point where the problems and the long hours started to get to me. The money was good, but I couldn't handle the stress anymore. I started dreading going to work. I was here in Vegas for the weekend and saw an ad for limousine drivers. It sounded like a nice change, so I applied for the job. They gave me a driving test that started with getting the limo from the parking garage out onto the street.

"No sooner did we exit the garage than the interviewer told me to pull over and park it. I thought I had done something wrong. Instead he told me I was hired. I was shocked. I said, 'What about the driving test?' And he told me if I could make it out of that parking garage through all those tight turns without hitting anything, I could drive it anywhere."

He looked out over the casino floor. "I did that for a year, and that was a really easy job. I'd take clients to the golf course and sit there for half the day, waiting for them to finish—read the paper, take a nap. But I got bored with it, so I went to dealer school, learned craps and blackjack, and got a job right away at one of the casinos downtown. This place opened and I applied for a dealer position. And they told me they had plenty of applicants for those jobs. They needed pit bosses, so I agreed to that, and when they noticed my background in management, they hired me as a shift supervisor." He laughed. "So I lucked out." He leaned back, raised an elbow, and rested it on the black padding. "How about you? I believe you said that you were a detective and gave it up?"

Snow nodded. "I decided to go for the brass ring, three years ago."

Peters arched his brows and tipped his head back. "Which was?"

"Poker."

"Tournaments?"

"No, just straight limit hold 'em. Twenty-forty. Just high enough limit to overcome the rake."

"You're doing well, I take it."

Snow gave his head a single quick shake to the left and back. "I've overcome the rake easily enough, but lately I can't seem to overcome losing."

Two tables over, came a cry: *Monkey! Monkey!*" A thunderous roar of cheering followed. Snow turned his head to the uproar. A full table of assorted guests, including a small, gray-haired woman on third base, stood up. High fives and fist bumps all around. The old woman raised her arms over her head and wiggled her hips in glee, chanting, "Who's the daddy, who's the daddy now!"

Snow turned his head back around and fixed his eyes on Peters. "So how long had Bob worked here?"

Peters flipped his hands up briefly. "He started when I did, when the place opened for business—five, six years ago."

"Did you know him very well?"

Peters nodded. "He was a good guy. We talked quite a bit when we were on the floor together. The wife and I had him and Karen over for dinner quite often, and vice versa. I have a boat. We used to fish Lake Mead a lot. Until those damn mussels that took over the whole lake clogged up the cooling channels in my outboard. It overheated and seized up. Now I'm going to need a new engine. But why bother? It'll just happen again. It's a damn shame. They can't get rid of them; they just keep multiplying like crazy. It's so bad, a lot of boaters from California won't launch here anymore. If they do, they'll go through hell getting their boat to pass inspection so they can use their boat again back home. The time will come you won't see any boats out on that lake. And there won't be any fish in it."

"Won't be any water in it, either," Snow said. "The water level keeps dropping, the mussels will just dry up and die. Funny how things work out. The result of one problem eliminates another."

Peters grinned. "No doubt. Better stock up on canteens."

Snow smiled and nodded. "What about the other pit bosses and the dealers here? Bob get along pretty good with everybody?"

"Oh sure," Peters said. "Bob was an easygoing sort. He never got anybody riled up over anything...well, except..."

"What?"

He leaned forward and lowered his voice. "He had this thing going with one of the dealers for a while. Linda Maltby. He was still with Karen when it started. She's quite a looker, Linda is. She's only twenty-eight. I told him he was looking for trouble with her, but he wouldn't listen. She was always flirting with him...reeled him right in. So they started fooling around. Bob would sneak over to her apartment after his shift. I think she melted his brain. This all started about a year ago, I think. Then it all blew up. As soon as Bob moved out on Karen, he and Linda started arguing. It got worse—to the point where they couldn't work the same pit together without snapping at each other the whole shift."

"What caused that?"

"I'm not sure. But when Bob suddenly became more available to her, he wanted to be with her all the time. I think once the excitement of sneaking around was gone, so was her attraction for him. I think she got sick of him. And he wouldn't leave her alone. She just seemed to be overwhelmed with frustration dealing with it. Having to be here in the same building with him every day, hovering over her like a chicken hawk after a baby chick."

Snow thought about this for a few moments. "Is she working today?"

Peters looked at his watch. "She starts at one p.m. If you'd like to talk to her, you could probably catch her at home. It would be tough to find a good time while she's working. She gets a twenty-minute break after every hour or two, but that's her own time, and usually the dealers need every minute of that. They don't get lunch breaks."

Snow nodded. "Alright."

Peters got up. "I'll get you her phone number..."

"Maybe it would be better," Snow interjected, "if you call her and see if it's alright if I stop over. Rather than getting a call from a complete stranger."

Peters gave him a pat on the arm. "Good idea. I'll be right back." He walked back to the pit he'd been working in.

Snow spun his stool around to get an update on the action on the hot table. Which now didn't seem so hot. All of the players, including the little old lady, were subdued, quietly watching as the dealer turned over a king to go with her deuce and nine.

None of them seemed happy to see that monkey.

CHAPTER 13

She came to her door dressed in her dealer uniform. Her shirt was white, with a collar and cuffs matching her black trousers. Cut to the middle of her back, her blonde hair spilled over her petite shoulders, framing a small face populated with a round nose, big eyes, full lips, and prominent cheekbones.

Her face formed easily into a smile. "You're Jim Snow?"

"And you're Linda Maltby."

She opened the door fully and stepped to the side, her hand still on the knob.

The apartment was a two-bedroom on the bottom floor of a newer complex located in Henderson. It was about ten minutes' driving time southwest of Sam's Town.

She led Snow into her living room, offered him a seat on the couch, and then lowered herself onto the cushion next to his. As she turned her knees toward him, the smell of her perfume drifted over and filled Snow's head. It was an inexpensive brand, yet subtle and fragrant. Snow looked into her blue eyes, and she seemed to tilt toward him just a hair. How easy and natural it would seem to just slip his arm around her and bring her to him. Suddenly Snow realized how instinctively Bob had fallen into the mess he had spawned with this woman.

"I can't believe what happened to Bob," she said. "It's terrible. I'm still in shock. When I heard about it, all I wanted to do was get back into bed and pull the covers over my head. He was a wonderful man. It's awful. Do the police have any idea who might have done it?"

She didn't appear to be in shock to Snow. Composed and radiant, Linda appeared to have just returned from two weeks in the Caribbean.

Snow shook his head. "They're just getting started. It could take a while."

"Forty-eight hours," she said. "And then that's it, right?"

"That's what?" Snow asked.

"That's the cutoff. If they don't find out who the killer is in forty-eight hours, they never will. Isn't that right? I saw that on TV."

Snow shrugged. "It's not always that way. Sometimes it takes six months. I've worked cases that took six years or more. There's a sense of urgency in the beginning to obtain evidence before it gets hauled off with the garbage and ends up in the landfill. We try to talk to witnesses before they disappear or forget. It just depends. I personally have always thought that most crimes are solved in the first two days because there's nothing to solve. Usually it's obvious who did it. But if the perpetrator isn't someone the victim knew, then there's usually not much that could tie the two together. Those sorts of cases are harder to figure out, and I'm sorry to say they usually don't get solved."

"That's interesting," she said. Her cheeks seemed to glow.

He turned his head down toward the carpet. "I know you need to get to work, so I'll try to get through this quickly."

She put her hands together and rested her elbows on her firm thighs. Snow wondered idly what her legs looked like. He pushed the thought aside and shifted his mind to the purpose of his visit.

He steeled himself and looked back into her eyes. "I understand you and Bob Williams developed a relationship about a year ago. Is that true?"

She nodded, the hair on her shoulders moving with it. "Yes. It started off innocently. We were almost always working the same pit, it seemed. We got to talking quite a bit. It became apparent that we had a lot of the same interests—you know, like talking and listening and laughing."

"What did you talk about?"

She sighed. "Oh, you know, current events, news, the weather, the unusual guests we'd get at the tables." She smiled. "Some of them are so funny they could be doing stand-up comedy down on the Strip. It can be pretty entertaining at times—it's one of the things I love about my job." She paused to gather her thoughts. "I would say that one of the traits I liked most about Bob was his listening ability. You know how some people will interrupt while you're talking, and just like shove your whole train of thought off to the side and bring in their own? Bob never did that. He would mostly just listen to me and occasionally ask pertinent questions that would contribute to the conversation. And he always seemed to make me feel really good about myself. Plus, he was generous. I mustn't forget that."

"Generous."

She nodded.

"What made him generous?"

"Oh, he bought me jewelry—nothing expensive, really, just small things with gold and little diamonds. I love lots of little diamonds in a piece." Her shoulders came up. "They just make me shiver when I look at them."

"What about money? Bob ever give you money?"

"Oh yes. He was always worried about me having enough to get by on. He helped me with the rent quite a bit. And sometimes after he had left I would go into my bedroom and find like a hundred dollars in my dresser drawer, or something like that. He liked to surprise me like that. But that wasn't the quality I liked most in him. It was not only his generosity and ability to listen, but also to understand totally about my feelings and interests."

She wet her lips, causing them to glisten, and then continued. "I have a hobby that I'm really passionate about and that most people, I believe, think is totally stupid. And I could talk to Bob about it for hours on end, and he would never seem to get bored with it. He would just seem to hang on every word and show a genuine interest in what I had to say about it, even though he never really..." She lifted her hands in front of her waist and began to rotate them back and forth like the dual blades of a hand-mixer. "He never really showed an interest in wanting to go with me. And I can't blame him. I mean, I love my hobby, but I think most people would think you're crazy to want to drive for hours on end out into the middle of the desert to dig around in the dirt looking for rocks."

"You're a rock hound," Snow said.

Her face lit up. "Yes! Exactly! Granted, most of the people who are passionate about rocks are older men, which really surprised me to know that Bob couldn't get interested in it, but times are changing. These days women can genuinely get interested in all kinds of things that used to be pursued by men exclusively—like pickup trucks. It used to be that you never saw a woman driving a pickup unless she lived on a ranch or a farm and had to go pick up a couple of hogs or something. Now you see all kinds of young, beautiful women driving giant four-wheelers all over the city."

"Do you own a truck?" Snow asked.

"No, I drive a Hyundai Accent," she said. "It was really cheap. It was like twelve thousand dollars new. And I love it. It never breaks down, just goes all the time—in fact, I've been really frugal, trying to save up to buy a house. And now home prices have dropped to where I could buy something really nice for about a hundred thousand. But I'm so worried about my job that I'm afraid to. They've cut everyone's hours at work, and they keep laying off dealers and waitresses and slot people. It's a very scary time."

Snow waited to see if more would come out of her mouth, but she stopped talking and looked at him with big eyes and her mouth slightly ajar.

"Who do you go rock hounding with?"

"I have a very dear friend," she said, "who I introduced to it shortly after I met him two and a half years ago, and he has taken a profound interest in it and has become as passionate about it as I am. His name is Steve. I met him at the casino while he was shooting craps. That's all he plays is craps, and sometimes I'll be working the same table he's playing at, and we'll get to talking, and we became close friends that way. And what's so cool about it is that it's a platonic relationship. Neither of us has any expectations about romance or marriage or a future life together in any way. We're just really good friends who share a passion for rock hounding, and we go out, sometimes for days at a time, stay in a motel, and travel deep into the desert sharing our passion for rocks."

"You and Steve don't sleep together?"

"Of course we do," she said. "But it's a platonic sort of sex. There aren't any of the encumbrances of love involved. It's more like working out."

"I see."

She reached out and touched Snow on his forearm with her fingers. "It's not just about looking for the rocks, though. That's not even half of it. It's kind of like fishing. First you find the fish and catch them, and then you take them home and clean them and eat them. It's just like that with rocks."

"You grind them up and eat them?"

She giggled. "No, silly. Let me show you."

She took both of Snow's hands in hers and stood up, pulling him up with her. Then she released one hand and led him across the living room, down the hall, and into one of the bedrooms. While they were in the hallway, the thought flashed across Snow's mind that she was taking him to her bed, which he would somehow need to decline in a diplomatic way since Bob was only recently dead and this guy Steve could show up at the door at any time, and there was the matter of dignity. Middle-aged men shouldn't just go around having sex with any blonde-haired bimbo who offers it. That sort of thing was what you did in your twenties.

She opened the door to the spare bedroom, and the sight of a variety of machines filled Snow's eyes. All sorts of powered rock-processing tools sitting on three large wooden tables. There was a sixteen-inch slab saw, a six-inch trim saw, a four-inch faceter's trim saw, a fan-cooled rock tumbler with a removable rubber lining for polishing, a cabochon machine for grinding and polishing flat gemstones, and a faceting machine. There were a few other smaller grinding and polishing machines, and next to those an assortment of polished gems of various colors, patterns, and transparencies. Some opaque and flat, others faceted and transparent. She opened a drawer in one of the tables and brought out a felt-covered tray full of rings, bracelets, necklaces, and earrings, all constructed around attractive gemstones.

Snow was stunned. "This is impressive," he said as he held up a silver cuff bracelet with a single oval of turquoise in the center. "What do you do with all of this jewelry?"

"I sell it on eBay. Some of it I give away for Christmas and stuff."

"And what sort of tools do you use out in the field to pry the rocks loose so you can get them home?"

"Oh, just a rock hammer," she said. "That's all it takes."

She crossed to the sliding closet door, shoved it open, reached up on the shelf, and walked back to Snow with it. She handed it to him. It was the size of a regular claw hammer, but with a flat, square shape to the back of the head. The front of the head came to a sharp point. It appeared to have been worn down through years of use, but filed to a sharp point recently.

"I imagine this gets dull pretty quick when you're out bashing rocks with it on a steady basis."

"It does," she said. "But I just file it down before I use it. That keeps it nice and sharp."

"I bet it does," Snow said. "And what about Steve? Does he have his own hammer, or use one of yours?"

"Oh, he has his own. He went right out and bought his own before we went out the first time. I helped him pick it out." She pointed to the head of it. "This is a twenty-two-ounce Estwing, which is one of the best you can get. Steve's is just like this one, only his hammer has a longer handle. You can get a lot more leverage with it for better penetration."

"I see," Snow said. "Interesting stuff." He handed the hammer back to her. "Well, I better get out of your hair so you can get to work."

"No problem," she said.

"Oh, one other thing…"

"Sure."

"This guy Steve. What's his last name?"

"Helm," she said. "His name is Steve Helm."

CHAPTER 14

Lunch for Snow was at a sandwich shop in a strip mall on South Pecos Road called Sandwich Express. It was a small, clean place. At least in front of the counter. There were three round tables between the entrance and the counter. Behind the counter, hanging from the ceiling, a large white board listed everything on the menu. Along with the usual assortment of sandwiches, there were burgers, fish and chips, spaghetti, fried chicken, chili, Mexican food, and even a few items from the Chinese menu. It seemed like they hardly ever had any customers, yet the Hispanic couple who ran it always seemed cheerful and friendly. The food was good, and Snow felt sorry for them because he doubted they were making enough to meet their expenses, so he ate there whenever he was nearby with an empty stomach.

Today he was having the spaghetti, and he had just started getting the first load of noodles wrapped around his plastic fork when his cell phone rang. He set the fork back on the pile of pasta and flipped the phone open. It was Alice.

"I have news, and it's not good," she said.

"What is it?"

"Detective Jack Flash and I have been interviewing the neighbors on this sunny Sunday, and a few of them believe that your sister Karen has been having an affair with the neighbor Steve for at least four or five months. They've seen her coming and going from his house, a lot. And vice versa. In fact, the old lady who lives directly across the street—she's eighty-five—she's always watching the neighborhood through her blinds practically twenty-four hours a day. And she's seen your sister leaving Steve Helm's home, on numerous occasions, between five and six in the morning. And one morning she saw her running down his sidewalk away from his front door—completely nude."

"Oh Jesus." Snow lowered his head to his fingers and began to rub it.

"Detective Flash, needless to say, is having a field day with this. We checked your sister's phone records. Cell phone and home phone. And, all combined, she has talked to the guy ninety-seven times in just the last thirty days."

Snow released a heavy sigh. He straightened in his chair and stared at the plate of spaghetti and wedge of garlic bread. His appetite was gone. "Well, I'd better talk to her. She told me she hadn't been fooling around on Bob. Told me Bob was on the straight and narrow, too. Now, I've found out both of them were walking on the wild side."

"No kidding," Alice said. "Who was Bob involved with?"

"A dealer at the casino he worked with."

"How long was that going on?"

"A year."

"That's a long time. It's surprising that your sister never knew. What are you doing now?"

"Eating. Spaghetti."

"That sounds good. I wish I were there…and not here."

"Where are you? Where is Mel?"

"We're parked alongside the road on Tropicana. Detective Flash's pocket started singing that song about getting to Amarillo by morning. I'm getting really sick of that. He pulled the car over so fast he drove the tire up on the curb. He's about thirty feet in front of the right fender, sweet-talking that phone. He's got his back to me. I hate to imagine what that's all about. He must get thirty calls a day on his cell from that woman. Hey, he's coming back. I gotta go. Talk to you later."

"Alright," Snow said. "Thanks for calling."

He snapped the phone shut and stared out into the parking lot.

CHAPTER 15

It gave Jim Snow an uneasy feeling parking his Sonata across the street from his sister's home. Maybe the proper thing to do would be to drop in on Karen to see how she was getting along. *Just in the neighborhood investigating a murder implicating you and Steve, thought I'd stop in and say hi.* He didn't have time for that. And he wasn't in the mood. He would talk to her later, after he had more facts. Try to figure out what the real story was—get her to stop lying to him. The problem was, once the truth came out, maybe he couldn't handle the real story. He could imagine it pretty easily: Steve Helm whacking away at poor Bob with that twenty-two-ounce rock hammer, making full use of the leverage from the extra long handle; Karen sitting at home waiting, her calculator out, figuring out how long half a million dollars would last. How long before she'd be forced to begin the search for husband number four.

As he walked up the sidewalk toward the front door of the house across from Karen's, he wondered if he was becoming more cynical in his advancing years—or if it was just reality staring him in the face.

The old lady answered her doorbell in short order. She'd probably seen him drive up through the crack in her blinds. Then went back to her rocker to wait, not wanting to appear too eager. She didn't look to be eighty-five. More like sixty. Her gray hair was cut short, barely touching the tops of her ears. Her face was weathered and tanned like a fine leather. Her clear brown eyes sparkled, and she stood in front of the doorway fully erect with her legs wide, like a boxer ready for the next round.

Snow stuck out his hand. "I'm Jim Snow, Karen's brother. She lives across the street."

He expected a cackling voice full of cracks, but hers was soft and low. Shaking his hand, she said, "Yes, I know. I'm Helen Walton. Please come in."

Snow had been expecting the usual furnishings one would find in an elderly woman's home: a small, flowery sofa and chair, with fleece throw blankets draped neatly over the backs; a creaky wooden rocker with a homemade seat pad; a grandfather clock ticking the passing time. But there was none of that. Instead, the large, overstuffed living room set stood on the hardwood floor, arranged around a Chinese Kashan-style area rug. The living room walls were painted powder blue and adorned with elegantly framed paintings of castles, horses, polar bears, and a large photo of a group of runners with bib numbers pinned to their tank tops, running along the side of a highway in what appeared to be Death Valley.

Snow crossed to the photo and studied it. "Is that the Badwater Ultramarathon in Death Valley?"

Helen stood a few feet behind him, her fingers interlaced in front of her, smiling. "Yes it is. That was in 1994, the last year I ran it. I'm somewhere near the back in that group you see in the picture. That's one hundred thirty-five miles in the middle of summer, with the temperature almost as high as the distance. With a climb of thirteen thousand feet, finishing at the trailhead to Mount Whitney. I'm too old to do that sort of thing anymore. That's for sure."

Snow turned his head to her. "You finished?"

"Of course," she said. "I didn't set any speed record, and I came in last, but I made the sixty-hour cutoff time and got my buckle. I was feeling my oats back then—I was only seventy. Now I can't run anything longer than a marathon, and no more than eight of those a year."

Snow's eyes widened. "Eight marathons a year?"

"Yes," she said. "Pitiful, isn't it? I used to run a marathon every three weeks. It's hell being old."

"You don't ever have any problems with injuries?"

"Not that I remember. My husband Harold only had one injury, but it was a bad one. It sidelined him for good. He was eighty-nine, pushing the pace up a steep hill. Didn't know his limitations."

"What happened?"

"Heart attack," she said. "It killed him."

Snow raised an eyebrow. "I'm sorry to hear that."

"Are you a runner?" she asked. "You look like you're in pretty good shape."

Snow nodded. "Sort of. I run until something breaks, and then I quit until it heals. Start from square one, slowly building my mileage no more than ten percent per week, until something else breaks. It's a continuous cycle with me. I've trained for six marathons in six years. I read that about forty percent of the runners training for a marathon sustain an injury during their training. I've been in that forty percent every year so far. I'm okay until I get up past thirteen miles for my long run, and that's it. The pain starts—always in a different spot. I take a few days off, it gets better, try to get back into the training. It gets worse.

So I take a week off and come back. Then two weeks off. Then two months off. Sometimes my injuries take six months to heal."

Helen stood quietly staring at him.

"So what do you think?" Snow said.

"That's terrible," she said.

"What do you think I should do?"

"Listen to your body."

Snow thought about that for a moment. He spread his hands. "What does that mean?"

"I think it's pretty clear," she said. "Your body is telling you, 'Don't run a marathon.'"

His mouth fell open. "But I want to run a marathon."

"Run a half instead. Those races are actually more popular than the full marathon. Check the results, you'll see. And it's still a pretty respectable distance."

"I guess."

She said, "What if you found you could finish a marathon with no problems whatsoever, so you decided to try a fifty-miler, and that was okay, so you graduated to a one-hundred-mile ultra. And you discovered that you always got injured when you ran that distance?"

"Give up."

"You see," she said, "that's the mistake people make. Instead of staying at the distance they're best at, they want to keep increasing it until they get to the point where they quit, or end up crippled. It's the Peter Principle applied to running."

Snow smiled. "I never thought of it that way."

"So if you can make it to thirteen miles without injury, your body is telling you that you should be running no more than thirteen miles. Therefore the half marathon is your race. If you don't want to run that distance, try another sport—such as cycling." She pointed toward the kitchen. "I was planning to have some peach herb tea. I drink it every afternoon right about now. It's very good. It has hibiscus and rose hips in it, which is excellent for warding off viruses and lowering your blood pressure. Would you like some?"

"That sounds like it might be worth trying."

"Why don't you make yourself comfortable, and I'll be right back." She turned and headed for the kitchen.

Five minutes later, she hustled back into the living room carrying two cups. She handed one to Snow.

He took a sip. "Not bad. It actually has a lot of flavor. I always thought herb tea tasted like boiled oak leaves. But this is actually very tasty."

Helen grinned and tried hers. "I've tried them all, and the peach and the lemon are my favorites. Those are the only two I drink anymore."

"Yes," Snow said. "I'll have to stock up on some of this." He pulled his notepad out of his back pocket and wrote down *peach* and *lemon*. He cleared his throat. "I have to be honest with you, Mrs. Walton. When I was informed by the police that you had witnessed my sister Karen running along the sidewalk at five in the morning, completely naked—well, my sister is forty-eight, so that didn't sound likely. And I was told that you're eighty-five—though, I must say, you look like you're fifty-five. Sixty tops. I saw you yesterday morning, peeping out through your blinds at me—putting it all together, I was expecting to find a crazy old woman living here."

She chuckled. "An eighty-five-year-old woman who runs a marathon eight times a year would be considered crazy in most circles."

"Everyone has their own definition of crazy. That's for sure." Snow took a sip of tea. "But while I'm here, maybe you could just tell me what you told the police about Karen. Sometimes the police make mistakes, and their reports might get skewed—you know, a few words added or left out. Or parts of a statement omitted because they were never written down. The Peter Principal applied to homicide detectives. And I'm not referring to the junior detective that was with him..."

She nodded, smiling. "The handsome gentleman. Yes, I did find him to be a piece of work. Yes, alright...first of all, I should explain why I was looking out though my blinds at you yesterday. And my reason is pretty simple. I could say that I'm concerned about neighborhood security, and that may be a part of it—my own small contribution to the neighborhood watch. But the main reason I like to peek out at the neighbors whenever I get the chance is that I'm nosy." She laughed. "What else can I say? That's the only explanation that really makes sense, and it's the truth."

She lifted her cup, had some tea, and continued: "Now, about Karen. I like your sister very much. She has always been friendly toward me, shows respect, kindness, concern. A few years ago I had a bad flu virus. I took a week off from running, and Karen hadn't seen me during that time, so she came over to make sure I was alright. She even went to the grocery store for me, and the cleaners."

"This is what you told the police?" Snow asked.

"Word for word so far...but..." She paused and looked up toward the ceiling. "The lead detective, the one who did all the talking, this Melvin Purvis—"

"You mean Harris? Melvin Harris?"

"Yes, Harris. He seemed concerned only with your sister's relations with her neighbor Steve. When it became apparent to him that I had nothing but good things to say about Karen's character, he immediately focused on the possibility of their having an affair."

"And what did you tell him?"

"I had to tell him the truth. I can't lie to the police concerning a matter as important as her husband's death."

"Of course," Snow agreed. "What did you tell them?"

She sighed. "I told them that I saw her coming and going from Steve Helm's house at least once or twice per day, including the time that her husband was still living with her—while he was at work, and sometimes while he was home. And Steve paid an equal number of visits to the Williams home.

"I get up and run every morning at four thirty. I'm usually getting back from my runs between five and six, depending on the distance. Ever since Bob moved out, I would see her walking home from Steve's house, nearly every morning during this time. And we would wave at each other, like we always do.

"But one morning a couple of weeks ago, I just happened to be passing in front of Steve's house, finishing my run, when I saw something out of the corner of my eye that looked like a ghost running toward me. I turned my head, and I saw that it was Karen. She was running down the sidewalk away from Steve Helm's front door. And the reason she looked like a ghost was because she was completely nude. Not a stitch on."

"What happened?"

"Well," Helen said, "she turned onto the sidewalk that borders the street and ran along beside me—grinning. She turned her head to me and said, 'Good morning, Helen.' And I returned the greeting. And that was it."

Snow set his jaw and nodded slowly. "I imagine so," he said. "Couldn't see asking her in for tea."

CHAPTER 16

After leaving Helen Walton to finish her herb tea, Jim Snow walked across the street to his sister's front door, casting an idle glance at the Aljo travel trailer, still parked in front of Steve Helm's residence.

Karen came to the door dressed in a pair of sapphire corduroys, white sneakers, and a gold, ribbed tee with a low scoop neck. Her hair was slightly disheveled, and there were bags under her eyes. She looked past Snow's shoulder at his car parked on the far side of the street.

"Why did you park over there?" she asked.

"I was visiting with Mrs. Walton."

Her eyes came back to Snow. "Why?"

"It's part of my investigation," Snow explained.

"What did you ask her?"

"I asked her about you."

Karen tilted her head to the side, her mouth open, her eyes growing large. "What about me?"

"Karen, can I come in?"

She turned and flung the door open. It banged against the wall. She marched toward the kitchen, through the living room, with Snow following.

He seated himself at the kitchen table as the pervasive odor of bleach struck him. "You've been cleaning," he said.

She marched on toward the coffeemaker. "Yes, I've been cleaning. Better write that down in your notebook. You want some coffee?" she snapped.

"No thanks, I'm good."

She stopped in front of the coffeemaker, her back to him. "Fuck!" she said. "I don't want any either." She spun around and stormed to the table, slid a chair out, screeching against the tile floor, and plopped down in it.

With her hands in her lap, she looked into Snow's eyes. Hers were large and round. She appeared somewhat demented, her breathing rapid and shallow.

Might as well jump right in, Snow thought. "Karen, were you having an affair with Steve Helm?"

Her eyes grew even larger, as though they might suddenly pop out. Her mouth opened a crack and formed into a smile. She looked like a pumpkin, carved out for Halloween.

"Of course not," she said. "Don't be ridiculous."

Snow nodded. "I think you're lying."

Her smile faded. "You always think I'm lying, Jim. Why is that?"

"Because a lot of the time you are."

"When did I ever lie to you?"

Snow thought for a moment. "Remember the time you took the nine-volt battery out of my transistor radio? You told me you didn't, and I found it in yours."

"There was no way of proving that was your battery."

"Not the first time," he said. "But after that, I always carved a tiny *J* in the bottom."

"We were just kids then," she said.

"Then there was the time I let you borrow my car for a couple of days while yours was in the shop. You brought it back, and the passenger door had a dent with flat brown paint on it. You told me you had no idea how it happened. You said somebody must have run into it in the parking lot. So I drove over and checked the paint on the doorjamb of your garage, and saw where it had been scraped, right at the exact same height as my car door."

She rolled her eyes.

"You lied to Mom and Dad about practically everything," Snow continued. "And you don't lie worth beans. You always have that look on your face—"

"What look?"

"Like Bette Davis…alright, listen." He placed his hands flat on the table. "I can't help you. I'm going to step out of this and leave you and Steve to handle it. If you want the name of a good criminal defense lawyer, I know a few whom I can recommend."

Snow stood up.

Karen sat looking up at him, her eyes welling with tears. Her mouth turned down, and suddenly she looked like child. "Jimmy, don't go," she said.

"If you're going to lie about everything, there's nothing I can do. You tie my hands."

"I'm sorry," she said. "Alright. It's true. Steve and I did have something between us. But it wasn't anything serious, and it's over now." A tear ran down her cheek.

Snow sat back down. "What does that matter? I'm not your husband. I'm sure Bob doesn't care. He's dead. The problem is, along with a pretty strong motive, this adds a much stronger possibility for collusion. You don't have to be a homicide detective to figure that out. You remember *The Postman Always Rings Twice* and *Double Indemnity*? Your situation is starting to sound like a remake of both those movies."

She leaned forward, her face a mask of agony. "But I didn't do anything!"

"What about Steve?"

She fell back in her chair. "Steve isn't capable of murder."

"What about armed robbery? Did you ever think he was capable of that?"

"No," she admitted. "I was shocked to find out about that."

"Well, you may end up being shocked to find out Steve murdered your husband."

"Why? Why would he do that? I'm the one with the insurance policy."

"You weren't the only one having an affair," Snow said. "Bob was getting it on with one of the dealers at the casino. Her name is Linda Maltby."

She winced. "How long was that going on?"

"About a year. And there's more to it: Steve has been having an affair with Linda Maltby for more than two years. I'm thinking maybe Steve found out about Linda and Bob and got jealous."

"Steve jealous of Bob?" she said. "That would be hard to imagine. What does this Linda Maltby look like? Have you seen her? Is she attractive? She must be if Steve was interested in her."

Snow nodded. "She's a knockout."

"What was she doing with Bob?"

"He was paying her."

"She's a prostitute?"

"I don't think she sees it that way. Sort of an informal offshoot of prostitution."

"A sugar daddy."

"Not completely. More like an added sweetener."

Karen thought about this for a moment. Her eyes had begun to dry. "I think I would like some coffee, after all. You?"

Snow leaned back and flipped up his palms. "Sure, why not."

She got up slowly, her mind working, and crossed to the coffeemaker. She took the lid off the can of coffee and began to spoon it into the basket. "Is Steve paying her?"

"I don't believe so. I think he has been using her as his private Playboy Bunny. Did you know that Steve has a rock hammer?"

She stopped spooning coffee and turned her head. "What is Steve doing with a rock hammer?"

"Hammering rocks. He and Linda Maltby are rock hounds together."

Her eyes narrowed. "Steve? A rock hound? That doesn't sound like him."

Snow nodded. "You'd be amazed at what most men will do to get in the sack with a nubile young female. A few hours of splitting rocks would be a small price to pay."

Karen turned her head back around and finished with the coffee. She came back to the table and sat down. They listened to the gurgling and popping of the coffeemaker for a moment.

"Did Steve know about the insurance policy?" Snow asked.

"Yes. It came up in a conversation we had."

"When?"

"I guess it was shortly after Bob moved out. He was joking around and asked if there was a policy on Bob, and I said yes. And he asked how much, and I told him. And he said I should hire a hit man before the divorce. Then he laughed. So, of course, I knew he was joking."

Snow leaned forward and put his arm on the table. "Now, here is a scenario that I've been tossing around in my head. Tell me what you think of this: Let's say that Steve feels pretty confident in his relationship with you. He figures there is no motive strong enough to arouse more than the usual initial suspicion inherent with the last person to see the victim alive. So he seizes on the opportunity for you to collect on the insurance money by agreeing to purchase the travel trailer, and he insists on cash so that he can make it look like a robbery. Takes his rock hammer along. It's the perfect murder weapon. It's small. Easily disposed of. No rifling evidence like with a bullet. Less of a chance of blood traces on his person, as is more likely with a knife.

"So most likely nothing could be proven. The case goes into the file, and you get your insurance settlement. The romance continues. Steve proposes. You accept. And you are the next victim—or maybe he just enjoys a marriage that's enhanced by the addition of half a million dollars."

She considered this for a moment and shrugged. "I guess it sounds plausible."

"Who initiated the relationship?"

"I don't know. It just happened."

"Mutual attraction?"

"I guess," she said. "I just always thought of Steve as a boy toy. I would never be interested in marrying someone like him. He was exciting. I never knew what he would do next. I mean, obviously he's a hunk, but the way his mind worked was most titillating. One night we were sitting at his kitchen table enjoying a nice steak dinner that he had prepared. And he gave me this look. It was like he was undressing me with his eyes. And he got up and came over to me, and bent over me, and took the top button of my blouse into his mouth and bit it off. And spit it across the kitchen. Then he unbuttoned the rest of them with his fingers—shoved everything that was on the table onto the floor. And we did it right there on the kitchen table." She finished this with a devilish grin on her face.

Snow stared at his sister, his eyes unblinking. Now it made sense: how his sister, at the age of forty-eight, could have been seen grinning like an idiot and running naked from Steve Helm's front door.

He cleared the frog out of his throat. "I appreciate your being honest with me, but this is information that goes beyond the scope of what I need to know."

Getting up from the table, he leaned over and kissed her on the cheek.

Outside on the sidewalk, walking back to his car, Snow glanced over at the blinds covering Helen Walton's living room window. He noticed the opening in the middle of them. Suddenly the blinds pulled back a little, and a hand went up through the opening. The hand waved to Snow.

Snow smiled, nodded—and waved back.

CHAPTER 17

Steve Helm had a football game playing on his flat-screen television. The Sunday paper was spread out over the couch. And the end table next to it was occupied by a half-empty bottle of Heineken. He had on a pair of denim shorts and a T-shirt with a picture a baseball cap and a caption that read *Las Vegas 51s*.

Snow gave Helm's hand the obligatory single pump, and then he pointed at the T-shirt. "You go to the games much?"

Helm looked down at it, then back up at Snow and grinned. "Couple times a month at least," he said. "Love it. It's cheap entertainment, and they play almost as well as the majors. It's astonishing—the number of talented players that are only a few extra home runs away from making it to the big time, but can't quite get there. You ever play the game?"

"For a while. I was pretty good when I was nine. But it was all downhill from there. I couldn't handle the pitching in high school. My eye-to-hand coordination is so slow I needed to start my swing during the windup. I finally gave it up when I was fifteen. I was standing in left field during practice one day. It was a hundred and two degrees, and eighty percent humidity.

Somebody hit one over my head so far that it rolled into the playground, under a swing. I picked it up and threw it as hard as I could, and my hand was so wet with sweat, the ball slipped and almost hit a parked car. So I just decided right then and there that I'd had enough; turned around and walked home. Never showed up for another practice. The coach didn't even bother to call and find out why I quit. What about you? You play?"

Helm nodded. "High school All-American. Played third base. Hit .456 my junior year. Senior year I did something to my rotator cuff, and that was it."

"Did you have surgery?"

"No. I gave it a rest for a couple of weeks and it got better, so I came back, and it got worse really fast. I went to the family doctor and explained the injury to him and all the trouble it was causing. He told me to quit. So I did. That cured my shoulder. These days it's different. They won't let you quit. They'll do everything medically possible for you—until you're broke." He turned sideways and looked at the couch. "This living room is a mess. Why don't we go in the kitchen and sit at the table?"

Snow's eyebrows shot up. "No, this is fine. Don't worry about it."

Helm offered him a beer. Went to the kitchen and came back with a Heineken for Snow and an extra for himself. He gathered the newspaper up off the couch and folded and stacked it in a crumpled mass on the easy chair.

Snow seated himself in the stuffed chair, and Helm sat down next to his beer, setting the fresh one down beside it. He hoisted it and took a long swallow.

"So how goes the investigation? You got any leads?"

Yeah, Snow thought, *and they all point to you.* "Nothing substantial," he said. Then he took a pull on his beer. He swallowed it and started in: "I talked to a young lady this morning by the name of Linda Maltby. You know her?"

Helm's eyes popped wide. He looked as though someone had jabbed him in the chest with a cattle prod. "Sure," he said. "She works the crap table at Vegas Valley Casino. I play there quite a bit."

"That's it?"

He shrugged. "We're pretty good friends. She introduced me to rock hunting. Interesting stuff. You ever done any of that?"

Snow shook his head. "It does sound like a good time; I'll have to leave myself open to it one day when I'm considering new hobbies." He took another chug of beer. "Are you and she romantically involved?"

"I wouldn't call it that," he said. "I've spent the night over there, now and then."

"What about my sister Karen?"

"Uh." He looked at his beer, then at Snow. "So you know. Who let the cat out of the bag about that?"

"Everybody in the neighborhood."

Helm put his hand around the beer bottle and began rubbing his thumbnail over it. "My intentions are completely honorable, Jim. I have a lot of respect for Karen. She's a very special person."

"We all have our moments," Snow said. "Some more than others. When did you find out about Bob's life insurance policy?"

Helm turned his gaze back to Snow. "After they split up."

"Whose idea was it for you to buy the travel trailer?"

"Mine. Well, actually, Karen talked me into it. She likes that trailer. In fact, she was the one who talked Bob into buying it in the first place, and since they were splitting up, she wanted to keep it. And it was half hers. After I bought it, Bob was planning to give her half the money. So in the end, it was a good deal for her."

"Now she has an even better deal."

Helm's eyes narrowed. "What kind of a thing is that to say?"

He had him up the against the ropes now. Suddenly defensive. A good sign. Snow decided to throw it out there. "Did you and my sister conspire to kill Bob Williams?"

Helm's face turned down in a scowl. "Hell no! Why are you asking me that? You're supposed to be helping Karen—and me. Not the cops."

Snow studied Helm's face for a moment. "I can't just investigate the area of the case that's outside the boundary of the two of you. Everything must be looked at. I nced to eliminate you and Karen as suspects—at least in my own mind—before I can focus the whole of my efforts in other directions. And at this point, I can't be sure either one of you is innocent."

"What will it take to convince you?" he snapped.

Snow held his beer with the tips of his fingers and rotated it slowly, studying the label. "Do you own any handheld tools with a sharp point that could have been used as a weapon?"

"The police already asked me that. I told them no. I've never owned a pickaxe. I understand Bob had one in his garage, and they took it as evidence. But I don't have anything like that."

"You don't have anything smaller, say the size of a hammer, that might have a pointed head?"

"No."

"What about a rock hammer?"

Helm stared at Snow without speaking. His mouth hung open, and the blood drained out of his face.

"Linda Maltby told me you have a rock hammer."

"That's true. I'm sorry. I hadn't considered that."

"Do you still have it?"

He nodded. "Pretty sure."

"Can I see it?"

"Sure." Helm got up and crossed to the laundry room door, which led to the garage.

He came back a minute later, holding it loosely with his hand around the grip. He offered it to Snow.

Standing, Snow pulled a pair of disposable rubber gloves out of his pocket. He turned one of them inside out and stretched it over his right hand. Clamping the end of the handle between his thumb and first two fingers, Snow let it hang in front of his face and studied the head of it. The point had been sharpened, similar to the hammer Linda Maltby had shown him. But the rest of the hammer was crusted with bits of gray dirt.

"Did you sharpen this?" Snow asked.

"Linda did. She's really into that. She's a perfectionist. If it were up to me, I'd just let it go dull. What's the difference? But Linda is really fixated on this rock hunting stuff. I don't even really care if we find anything. I just go with her because it's what she likes to do. You know?"

Sure, Snow thought. *Linda's into rocks; you're into Linda's pants.* "Can I borrow this hammer?"

"No problem," Helm said. "What are you gonna do with it?"

He looked at Helm. "You didn't use this on Bob, did you?"

"Of course not."

"I want to give this to the detectives and have it sent to the crime lab, get it checked for Bob's DNA. If they don't find any of Bob's DNA on the head of this thing, then that will help in your favor. Oh, and there's something else I need from you."

"What's that?"

"Plastic wrap. I don't think this will fit in a freezer bag."

"Alright." Helm turned and started for the kitchen. Then he stopped suddenly and turned back around. "I just thought of something," he said.

"What's that?"

"What if somebody took that out of my garage, used it to kill Bob, and then wiped the blood off it and put it back?"

Snow looked incredulous. "Who could have done that?"

"Karen," Helm said. "She's the only one who's been in my garage. She has a key to my front door. She can come and go whenever she wants." He paused for a moment. "There is something you should know about your sister. I don't want to criticize her, but she's been acting kind of weird lately."

Snow frowned. "In what way?"

"Like she's slowly losing her mind. I started to notice it about six weeks ago, I guess, and it's probably the main reason Bob finally moved out. She has these wild mood swings now. Anything might set her off. She'll be going along calm and content—and then suddenly start screaming at me for no good reason. I never saw her like that before. Sometimes she'd come over here and start complaining about something trivial that happened to her, and before she would leave she'd end up complaining about *me*. Yelling at me. If I didn't respond at all, she'd accuse me of not listening. If I tried to tell her it was no big deal, she'd tell me I didn't care about her. If I agreed with her, she'd blame me for patronizing her. No matter what I would say or do, she would attack me!"

Snow's eyebrows went up. "Did she ever hit you?"

"No. It was just verbal. But she could holler loud enough to make my ears ring." He took a few steps back toward Snow.

"One time, a few weeks ago, we were in my car, stopped at a light. She was throwing a fit. She suddenly jumped out of the car, stomped over to the sidewalk, and just stood there with her arms folded, glaring at me. I kept hollering at her to get back in the car, but she ignored me. The light changed, and I drove around the block continually, begging her to get back in the car. After the third time around, she finally got back in, but wouldn't talk to me all the way home—which, in a way, was sort of a relief.

"A week later, she did it again. Jumped out of the car, ran over to the curb, and stood there. So I just drove home. She showed up in a taxi an hour later—and you can't imagine the rage that had gotten pent up in her during that taxi ride..." He looked down at his feet and shook his head.

"Jesus," Snow muttered. "I wonder what's wrong with her."

Helm brought his gaze back up and fixed it on the flat-panel TV. "I don't know," he said. "But I'm getting my locks changed."

CHAPTER 18

They were southbound, inching along on the northbound shoulder of Hollywood Boulevard, a quarter mile north of Hollywood RV Storage. The splash of white from the unmarked squad car's floodlight played over the dirt, rocks, and bushes of the East Las Vegas desert.

Detective Mel Harris was at the wheel. "You see anything, Detective?"

"If I saw anything, I would have said something," responded Junior Detective Alice James.

"We may have to park and comb the area on foot."

"I don't think so," Alice said.

"Why do you say that?"

"Because the caller said they saw it from the side of the road, while driving by—isn't that correct? And if they could catch a glimpse of it while driving at the speed limit, when they weren't even looking for it, then we should be able to spot it easily."

"It was probably still light out when they saw it," Harris suggested. "Plus the sun may have reflected off of it and caught their eye."

"If that's the case, then guess what? That floodlight will do the same thing."

Harris shot an ugly look toward Alice. "You know, Detective, I'm getting really tired of your mouth. You need to start showing more respect for a senior member of this team."

"You start showing me some respect, bub, and you'll get it back."

"My name is not 'bub,'" Harris snapped. "I told you before. You address me as Detective Harris or Mel."

"You start calling me by my name, and I'll call you by yours. You treat me like I'm your secretary. You ask all the questions at the interviews; if I open my mouth to say anything, you give me that look like you're about to beat me. I'm always the one to get the coffee—and you never let me drive."

Harris shook his head in disgust. "Jesus Christ," he muttered. "Women."

"You may want to back up some there, Detective Bub."

"Why?"

"Because you were so busy criticizing me, you missed that metal object out there behind that creosote bush."

Harris snapped his head around to the beam from the floodlight. "Where?"

"Back up. You'll see it."

Braking suddenly, Harris popped the shift lever in reverse and stepped on the gas. The car lurched backward, veering toward the shallow ditch, throwing up a small cloud of dust. He corrected the steering and held the floodlight steady. Fifteen feet back, the light reflected off of the silver finish of the tool, the head of it sticking out from behind the bush.

Harris brightened. "Alright!" he yelped. He pumped his fist in the air with a single jab, stopped the car, and rammed the shifter into park.

The detectives climbed out of the car, their Mag flashlights held above their left shoulders as they advanced.

"Be careful, Detective," Harris instructed. "Watch for footprints. We don't want to step on anything that could be gathered as evidence."

"Yeah," Alice said. "Watch out for snakes, too. Don't want to step on any of them either. They like to come out at night and hunt."

"There aren't any rattlesnakes out this time of year," Harris argued. "It's almost November. They're all in their dens huddled up together for the winter."

"Yeah," Alice said. "Well, if you get bit by one, you better let me drive you to the hospital. Either that or wait for the ambulance. I'm not riding in that squad car with you driving snakebit. You're liable to pass out and kill us both."

"Detective," Harris said, "would you please shut up and keep your mind on your job?"

She said nothing. They advanced a few more steps before Harris's pocket began to sing. He stopped abruptly and pulled out his phone, flipped it open, and grinned.

Putting it to his ear, his voice up an octave, he said, "Well hi, sweetheart." He made a quarter turn to the northeast and ambled away from Alice toward the darkness of the open desert, listening intently and emitting an occasional "uh-huh" every few steps.

Alice shook her head and continued on toward the object behind the creosote bush. She stopped a few feet short of the bush, leaned over, and focused the beam of light over it.

It was the size of a nail hammer, with a plastic grip and a steel head. One end of the head formed a sharp point, and the other end was square and flat. It looked new. She leaned a little closer and noticed the smell.

Holding the flashlight against her side under her arm, she opened the handbag that hung by its strap from her shoulder. She dug through it and brought out a small camera. She turned it on, waited for it to boot up, and then snapped two photos of the pointed hammer. With that done, straightening up, she put the camera away and pulled out her phone.

She pressed a few keys and then held it to her ear.

"Hey, Mary, this is Alice…yeah, I'm out here on the job, working my butt off as usual. How is your sister's new baby getting along?" She paused and listened, chuckling. "She is? Well that's a good sign…I know…no doubt…I bet she is…" She listened some more. "Yes…yes…definitely…well, listen, Mary, I'm going to have to keep this short because we have a new development here. We found some kind of a pointy-looking hammer out here in the dirt about thirty feet from the road. And we're going to need a CSA out here to bag and tag this thing…"

Standing at his stove, frying a grilled ham-and-cheese sandwich, Jim Snow mulled the facts over in his head. It was apparent to Snow that Steve Helm hadn't used his rock hammer to murder the victim. The hammer was covered with dirt. Had it been the murder weapon used by Helm, he would have ditched it somewhere, or at least cleaned it. A good scrubbing would remove any trace of DNA. Now it was back to Karen. If she wanted to put the finger of suspicion on Steve Helm, she could have easily taken the rock hammer out of his garage and then sneaked it back in during the night while Helm was sleeping. Should the DNA show up on the hammer, that would cover her tracks, and it would be enough to convict Helm. Jealousy over a woman, with the added bonus of the eight thousand dollars, would be sufficient motive to convince a jury. Or maybe she just purchased her own rock hammer with cash, killed Bob, and then drove out to Lake Mead and tossed it. It would be covered with quagga mussels in no time.

But the fly in that ointment was that, even though Karen must have had the code to open the gate to get in and out, Norma Hecker said that no entry codes appeared in her database after six p.m. Only Bob's code when he entered at seven thirty-five, and then again when Steve left with the trailer around nine. How could Karen have gotten in and out without using the keypad?

Possibly she knew about the makeshift gate in the back corner of the fence. But how could she, unless she'd been back there? And what would she be doing there? Unless she was the one who took the fence apart and wrapped the bungee cords around it. Not likely. Karen wasn't mechanically inclined. She wouldn't know which direction to turn the nuts, and she might damage a fingernail. It was out of the question.

But what about Norma Hecker? Snow had left her completely out of the picture. This was the problem when operating without a partner. There was no one to cover your blind spots.

Norma Hecker. Now there was a person with opportunity. Having full access to any code she wished to use, and the database that recorded them, she could come and go as she wished and just delete the entry codes. If Steve Helm wasn't in on it, maybe it had been Norma working with Karen. Norma's only task would be to delete Karen's entry codes. Nobody would know.

No matter from which angle Snow looked at it, this wasn't looking good for Karen.

He had just finished flipping his sandwich over to blacken the other side when his cell phone chirped. It was Alice.

"We found the murder weapon," she said.

"You're kidding. What is it?"

"It's a brick hammer, used by bricklayers to scrape the mortar between bricks. It's the size of a regular hammer, but with a sharp, pointed end and a square, blunt end, I guess for beating on things."

"How did you find that out?"

She said, "I took a couple of pictures of it, and we went to Home Depot and showed it to one of the sales guys on the floor. He showed us where they were located in the tool bin. They have the exact same model as this one."

"You think it was purchased at one of their stores?"

"Not necessarily. The sales guy said it's a common brand, and they sell them in any hardware store, plus a lot of other places. Or it could have been purchased over the Internet."

"Where was it?"

"Thirty feet from the edge of Hollywood Boulevard, on the east side, behind a creosote bush."

"You and Mel were just driving by and saw it?"

"No. A citizen called into the station, said he'd heard about the murder on the news, just happened to be driving down the road and saw it. So he called it in."

Snow's sandwich began to smoke. He shoveled it onto the spatula and dropped it onto his plate. "Do you know where the call originated?"

"A pay phone from a gas station. Corner of Vegas Valley Road and Nellis."

"That's odd," Snow said. "Why not from his cell phone?"

"I know a lot of people who don't own cell phones yet," Alice said.

"But how do you know it's the murder weapon? Maybe it dropped out of the back of a bricklayer's truck and a coyote dragged it over behind the bush."

Alice giggled. "You are so funny, Jim, but I don't think it belonged to a bricklayer."

"Why not."

"It had been soaked in bleach," Alice said. "I could smell it. I don't think bricklayers clean their tools in bleach."

CHAPTER 19

It was nine thirty on a warm Sunday evening when Jim Snow parked his Hyundai Sonata in front of the eighteen-foot motorboat. No wind, a clear sky, and seventy-eight degrees. Perfect weather to investigate a murder.

He got out of the car, sauntered over to the transom of the boat, and rapped his fist against it three times.

"Hey, Willie, you in there?" he said.

No answer, no movement. He pounded again. "Willie."

He fished the LED flashlight out of his pocket, released two tie-down straps, and raised the corner of the cover. Lighting up the inside of the small boat with the bright glow from nine LEDs, Snow could see there was no one inside.

He pulled the cover back over the corner, reattached the straps, and sighed. He considered getting back in his car and calling it a night. For all he knew the old tramp could be long gone on a freight train, headed for anywhere. But then he thought about the wash. Sometimes Willie slept in the wash, he had told him.

He hopped back into the car, drove to the gate, and entered the police code. He drove through and parked it outside the gate in one of the visitor spaces. He walked along the outside of the fence through the empty lot to the fire road, crossed it, and made his way carefully down the gravel slope into the Las Vegas Wash.

It was cooler down there near the water, what little of it there was. It only stood a few inches deep in spots. But in most areas that he could see with his flashlight, there was no water. In this part of the wash, which fed runoff water from the city of Las Vegas all the way to Lake Mead, it was quickly absorbed by the invasive tamarisk bushes, leaving little for the reeds and other bushes and plants that had taken root in a desperate attempt to survive in this arid climate.

And the tamarisk was everywhere; spreading out in a thick forest of branches, it made the wash look like a small urban swamp. He'd read in the paper that they had tried burning it, but it just grew back again, sometimes as much as twelve feet in a year.

To the left, near the bottom of the inclined bank he had just descended, he found an opening in the giant bushes, with a small path formed in the reeds. It led inward to the densest part of the jungle, and he followed it, keeping his beam of light in front of him.

Forty feet in, the trail ended in a small clearing, about fifteen feet in diameter. In the middle of the clearing, spread out on the dirt, was a section of cardboard, four feet wide by eight feet long. On top of the cardboard was a sleeping bag, opened up. And stretched out on the sleeping bag, his legs crossed at the ankles, Willie lay with his fingers interlocked behind his head. To his left sat his two garbage bags of possessions. Rolled up under his head was a heavy gray coat.

Snow trained his light on him.

"You have any trouble finding the place?" Willie said.

"Not at all," Snow said. "There was only one entrance, so I took it." He held his arms out. "Here I am."

Willie sat up and wrapped his arms around his knees. "Did you see the snake near the foot of the trail?"

Snow's jaw fell open. "No, I didn't. What was it, a rattler?"

Willie shook his head. "Python. Big one. Must have been fifteen foot." He watched Snow's face, smiling.

Snow took in a shallow breath and held it. "You're kidding."

"No, I'm not. He was lying right there, sticking partway out of the reeds. Just a few feet over from where the path starts."

Standing with his feet planted, Snow raised the beam of the flashlight and played it along the edge of the clearing, under the bushes as far as the light would penetrate, working it around in a circle.

"He's probably still out there," Willie said. "Why don't you go have a look?"

"No, that's okay," Snow said, still looking around with the light.

Willie chuckled. "You afraid of snakes, Jim?"

Pointing the beam from the flashlight straight down, Snow fixed his gaze on Willie. "I'm concerned with anything I can't see."

"What if you can see it?" Willie asked.

"Then I'm scared shitless," Snow said.

The tiny clearing filled with laughter. It lasted close to a minute.

Regaining his composure, Snow wiped his eyes with the back of his hand. "But seriously. What would a python be doing in this wash?"

"It's pretty common these days. I heard the Everglades are full of them. They're reproducing like crazy and giving the gators a tough time of it. I read about two incidents in the last year right here in Vegas where pythons had wrapped themselves around children. Their relatives came running outside with knives and cut the snakes to pieces."

Snow's eyebrows arched. He swallowed hard. "Where did you read about that?"

"The library," Willie said. "I Googled it after the first time I saw Arnold."

"Who is Arnold?"

"The python. I named him Arnold because he made me think of that pet pig on that TV show…"

"Arnold Ziffel."

Willie cackled. "Yeah, that's him. That was some funny shit. But what made me think of Arnold the pig was that my Arnold could eat that pig, no problem."

Snow began to move the beam of light around for a second time. "But how did he get here?"

"Don't worry, he won't harm you. You're too big for him to mess with. He's pretty docile. Probably somebody's pet, and they got tired of him—he got too big and ate too much. Or they got scared of him. Somebody probably brought him down here and let him go."

Snow wiped the sweat from his forehead with the back of his hand. "Jesus. We better call animal control."

"What good will that do? They won't find him. They'll just wonder what we're doing down here and call the cops to roust us. Well…I was just pulling your leg anyway. There's no snake down here."

Snow turned the light back to the ground and sat down on a patch of wild grass.

"Why'd you come looking for me?" Willie asked.

"I called Virgil Wilkie in Buckleman, Iowa."

"Virgil Wilkie." He looked at his hands. "Boy, that takes me back a ways. How's he doing?"

"Good. He's retired now, was wondering about you since he hadn't seen you in nine years. Said he wants you to call him, collect, if you want. He's anxious to talk to you."

"Uh-huh. He's a good egg, old Virgil. I knew him since we were kids."

"That's what he said."

"He was just the opposite of me, though. I used to be a little wild, growing up. He was ultra-conservative. I used to call him Wally because he reminded me of that Wally Cleaver—you know, Beaver's brother. In fact, I think he modeled himself after that character. I was more like James Dean. A rebel. Of course, I think most guys back then wanted to think of themselves as a James Dean, even after they might have gone into a life working in accounting. Not many would want to be thought of as a Wally Cleaver.

"When we were in high school, I remember, on Halloween, a bunch of us on the basketball team would tip over an outhouse that belonged to an old woman in town. We did that three years in a row. The following year, she figured she'd outsmart us. She was waiting for us. She went out and sat in it. So when we came up to it, she could hear us and started yelling to get away. We tipped it over with her in it." He laughed. "Boy, she really started screeching at us then.

"Well, Virgil was standing across the street watching all of this. We ran off. He went over and opened the door and helped her out. She was so grateful, he told me, she took him inside and gave him cookies and milk."

"You weren't concerned she might have been hurt?"

"Nah, she wasn't hurt. We didn't just flip it. We tipped it slowly and set it down gently. We might have behaved like animals, but we were gentlemanly about it." He laughed again. "Yeah, Virgil Wilkie. I ended up working for him, teaching history, if you can believe it. Me, a member of the establishment." He picked a tiny piece of a twig out of his sock. "Why did you call him?"

"I wanted to check you out, make sure you're dependable. I'd like to offer you a temporary job."

"Doing what?"

"Assisting me with this investigation I'm working on."

"Your dead brother-in-law?"

Snow nodded. "Yeah."

"Cops think your sister had him killed?"

"That's about the size of it."

"Damn," Willie said. "I'm sorry to hear that. I'd like to help, if I can. What kind of stuff would you need me to do?"

Snow looked at his shoes, then back at Willie, and shrugged. "Various things. Errands. Whatever needs to be done."

"I don't have a car."

"That's alright. I have one. You can ride with me most of the time, unless I need you to go do something else. Then I can drop you off, or you can take a taxi or a bus. Or walk."

Willie straightened a little. "So I'd be, like, your associate?"

Snow nodded. "Something like that."

"What'll it pay?"

Snow looked up at one of the tamarisk branches. It hung out like a shrouded arm, pointing the direction to the Strip. "How about two hundred per day, cash, paid at the end of each day, and I'll put you up for a week at decent motel. Meals are on me. I'll give you your first day's pay in advance so you can pick up some new clothes and anything else you might need. There's a motel called the Sunrise Inn on Boulder Highway across the street from a Walmart. There's a Laundromat in the strip mall down the street."

"Four hundred in advance, and I'll do it," Willie said.

"Why so much?"

"I'll need some decent clothes. I can't be riding around Las Vegas investigating a murder dressed like a tramp."

"Alright," Snow agreed.

"But why me?"

"I think you can do the job. You seem to be pretty bright for an old guy."

"No, but I'm just a tramp. You could get somebody to work with you who hasn't been living in the bushes…" He paused. "By the way, why did you give me that twenty?"

"I've been pretty lucky, so far," Snow said. "One bad break, I realize, I could end up out on the street. It doesn't add up to much, handing out a twenty every now and then. That's my charitable contribution to society. Can't really write it off, though."

Willie stood up and dusted off his pants, even though they didn't seem to need it. "I'll let you in on something I've observed over my nine years tramping around…"

Snow got up. "What's that?"

"It's never the people with the most money that will hand you a buck. They usually won't give you dime. They look at people out on the street, and they see them as lazy and worthless—tell them to get a job, and sneer at them as they pass.

"It's the people who have the least who'll dig down and find a little something to give you, because they can see where you came from. And it's the same place they are now—one paycheck away from the street."

"Yeah," Snow said. "That's what I just said."

"Right," Willie agreed. "Well, let's get the hell out of this snake-infested hobo jungle and get to work. We've got to find out who killed your brother-in-law so we can clear your sister. I'm ready to roll up my sleeves."

Snow pointed his flashlight at the trail leading out of the clearing. Hunkered down and alert, he moved slowly along the trail, listening for movement, looking for any sign of a giant reptile that might be lying in wait.

From behind him, he heard Willie speak up. "Jim," he said, "you look just like that Indiana Jones character. All you need is the hat." And then he laughed like a madman.

Snow wondered if, perhaps, he'd made a mistake with this guy.

CHAPTER 20

The neon vacancy sign was lit at the Sunrise Inn. Not much of a surprise on a Sunday evening in late October.

Snow pulled up next to the office and looked at Willie. "I think it might be best if you stay in the car. I don't want to create any confusion."

"You mean because I look like an old bum?"

"That's most of it," Snow said.

"How many occupants are you planning to register for?"

Snow considered this. "I guess two. If I get a single and they see you go in there, it could cause a problem, especially since your driver's license is expired. It's probably only another ten bucks or so for a double. Which floor do you want?"

"Upper," Willie said. "I hate it when you're trying to sleep and the assholes above you stomp around all night, yelling and screaming at each other because they lost all their money. And make sure you get a room with two separate beds."

"What difference does it make?"

"Because," Willie said, "two occupants, one bed—and you've got an old man waiting in the car for you?" He raised an eyebrow.

Snow shook his head in disgust and went inside. The clerk told him it was three fifty for one full week.

"Jesus," Snow muttered. "It's only thirty bucks a night at the Cannery, and that place is brand new. Plus it's got a casino and restaurants."

The clerk was an old woman with frizzy gray hair, bulging eyes, crooked teeth, and a yellow and blue striped top that held her torso together like an elastic bandage. "That's probably for a single room," she said. "Sunday through Thursday. If you'd rather stay there, that's your decision." Then she stood staring at Snow with her mouth open. She looked like a large-mouth bass, left in the sun for two days.

"Alright, I'll take it."

He filled out the form and listened patiently while she told him where the room was located and how to get to the ice machine.

Back in the car, Willie said, "They're not triple-A rated by the motor club are they?"

"It can't be that bad. They've got ice machines," Snow said. He could feel the beginning signs of a headache. He just wanted to drop the tramp off at his room and get home. He started the car and pulled ahead. They drove around the end of the complex, which was shaped like a capital *I*. Driving down the opposite side, Snow passed a familiar Ford pickup. It was dark blue with a one and five-sixteenths travel trailer hitch ball and a red bumper sticker. It was the truck that belonged to the tall, shaggy-headed fellow Snow had seen at the storage lot.

He slowed to look at it.

"What's the matter?" Willie asked.

Snow stopped the car. "Have you ever seen that truck before?"

"I don't think so," Willie said. "Why?"

"The owner of that truck has a trailer, a couple of spaces over from where Bob had his RV parked in that storage lot. Have you ever seen him in there at night?"

"I never saw anybody in there at night. I always went straight to my boat and climbed in it as fast as I could."

Snow turned his head to Willie. "You never got out at night to walk around and look for stuff to steal?"

"Never," Willie insisted. "That's a good way to end up in the slammer. I always went straight to that boat and went to sleep. I was out of there every morning before the sun came up. So why are you so curious about that fellow?"

Snow looked back at the truck. He got his notebook out of his back pocket. "I don't know. The guy said he got laid off not long ago. I just wonder—looks like he's living here."

"Maybe he got evicted."

"Yeah…but the thing is, he's got an RV. He could be living in an RV park right down the street for a little more than three hundred a month. Here, he's paying more than three times that."

"Maybe he's only been here a few nights, and he's making preparations to do that," Willie suggested.

"Yeah, that's possible," Snow said. "He mentioned something to that effect. His trailer is taped inside the crime scene, and he can't move it until they clear it. He said he keeps all of his stuff in the trailer…"

"Maybe after he got evicted, if that's what happened, he moved all of his stuff into his trailer," Willie said. "And he got a room here, planning to stay here until he was ready to go."

"Which would have been probably only a few days or a week at most. And then the murder happened, and he got stuck." He turned his head back to Willie. "That's somewhat of a coincidence."

"It is at that," Willie said. "Maybe we should think further about that."

Snow placed the notebook on the center console and glanced up at the room number directly above the truck, on the second floor. Then the room below it. He wrote the numbers down: 238 and 138. Then he wrote down the description and license plate number of the truck.

"That's some good detective work," Willie said. "It's a good start."

"Not really," Snow said. "A case like this, you could fill two or three notebooks. And then, when you go back through it, usually you can't remember the reasons why you wrote most of it down." He sighed. "But, of course, you never know."

CHAPTER 21

Monday morning. Snow thought it a might be a good idea to sleep in and recharge somewhat. But he couldn't. He'd spent a fitful night, waking every hour or two, then tossing and turning until he could manage to drift off again.

Terrible dreams. The last one he could remember clearly, he had been in a small room alone. A voice above him told him he'd had a good life, and now he was dead. Out of curiosity, Snow looked around the room. All that was there was a small bed and a nightstand with a lamp. And on the bottom shelf of the nightstand, there was an old yellow newspaper. He picked up the newspaper, glanced at it, and then tossed it back onto the nightstand. "Damn," he said. "This is really gonna suck."

Now, fully awake, he got out of bed, dressed, and padded into the kitchen to make coffee. He thought about getting the paper off the front stoop, but with the dream still fresh in his mind, that didn't seem to be appealing.

When the coffee was ready, he poured a cup and sat in his overstuffed chair, put his feet up on the footstool, and stared out through the glass patio door into his back yard. His eyes didn't seem to focus on anything specific. Sometimes it was nice just to stare into nothing—and wait for the coffee to take effect.

The phone rang. He set his coffee on the cork coaster on the end table and got up to answer it. It was his sister Karen.

"Jim," she said, "there's something I need to talk to you about." Her voice sounded controlled and even.

"Okay. I'm listening."

"Not over the phone," she said. "Have you had breakfast?"

"No," he said. "I was just having my first cup of coffee. Would you like to meet me somewhere?"

"How about Wanda's Waffle House over on Eastern, near Flamingo Road?"

"Okay. That sounds good. What time?"

"It's five after eight now," she said. "How about nine?"

Wanda's Waffle House was a mom-and-pop restaurant run by a middle-aged Norwegian couple from Bismarck named Eddie and Georgine. As far as Snow could tell, there had never been anyone named Wanda involved in the enterprise. He had asked Eddie about it one day when it came up in the conversation. Eddy had told him they had picked the name *Wanda* because it sounded good with *Waffle*. Sometimes the right name can make the difference between success and failure.

It was a pleasant place with lots of leafy indoor plants and large picture windows next to the booths so the customers could look out at the cars driving by on Eastern Avenue while they enjoyed their waffles.

Snow waited in his car, reading the morning paper while he waited for Karen. He learned that revenue was still sinking for casinos, especially those away from the Strip. Another chain of them had decided to file for bankruptcy over the weekend, the good news being that all of its casinos would remain open. Thousands of jobs would be safe for a while longer, and Snow wouldn't have to toss out any unused buffet coupons.

By the time Karen pulled up next to him in her silver Lexus, Snow had finished reading all of the paper except for the want ads and the obituaries. He seldom read those sections. The want ads seemed to list the same jobs every week, giving the impression they were never filled. The obituaries were depressing. Many of the deceased were younger than Snow, and they seldom listed the cause of death. It always gave him the feeling he was living on borrowed time. He gave Karen a wave, dropped the paper on the passenger seat, and got out of the car.

Karen gave him a smile as she approached. "Sorry I'm late, Jim."

Snow shrugged. "It wasn't so bad. Half an hour."

She came up to him and gave him a tight hug, then wrapped her hand around his arm, and they went inside. The bags under her eyes had shrunk somewhat, and she seemed nearly on the verge of being happy.

The waitress seated them in a booth and brought them coffee, and they sat looking through the large, plastic-covered menus.

"What are you having?" Karen asked. "Waffles?"

"I don't know," Snow replied. "I haven't run in two days; I'd feel guilty pumping all those calories into my system. But I need something to give me a rush. I'm experiencing an endorphin deficit that's making me feel like a zombie."

Karen put her menu down and looked at him. "What's that?"

"Walking dead."

"No. Endorphin."

Snow sighed. "Endorphins are natural painkillers created by the body when humans run. Running, to the mind, is supposed to mean danger; i.e., a predator must be chasing me, which could mean serious injury and pain. So the body pumps anesthetics to prepare for it. After you finish running, the endorphins stay in your system and make you feel good. That's how you get addicted to running. You actually become addicted to the endorphins. I think they must be something like heroin."

"Where did you read that?"

"I didn't," Snow said. "I figured it out for myself."

The waitress reappeared and took their order. When she left, Snow turned his head and stared out the window, watching a young Hispanic man with a bushy mustache trimming the grass around the bushes with a weed whacker.

"What are you grinning about?" Karen asked.

He shifted his gaze to her. "I didn't realize I was…just thinking about the only time I ever saw you run. Remember that?"

She shook her head. "When was that?"

"We were at Deebs Lake, camping for the weekend, when we were kids. The family next to us had finished cranking their camper down, putting everything away, rushing around to leave. But they forgot about the dog tied to the back bumper of the camper. They drove off and nobody noticed until after they had turned onto the road that led to the highway.

"Then you saw the dog trotting along behind the camper and pointed it out to us. And Dad said, 'Well, you'd better catch 'em.'"

Snow lifted his coffee cup, took a sip, and then continued. "At the time, I was working my way toward becoming a track star. I think by then I could run a mile in under six minutes. And your biggest athletic accomplishment was hula hoop.

"But I just stood there, and so did Dad. And you took off like a streak. I couldn't believe how fast you ran. Luckily, they turned left, and you got to them just as they were starting to accelerate for the open highway. Waved your arms at them, and they stopped and put the dog in the car."

She smiled. "I'd forgotten about that."

"Do you remember the time you saved *my* life?"

She shook her head.

"We were in the old Mercury. Dad was driving, you were in the middle, and I was sitting next to the door. We went around a curve, and my door flew open. And you immediately flung both arms around me. Kept me from flying out into the ditch."

"I remember that," she said. "That was the car that had the hole in the floorboard, and you could sit there and watch the road go by underneath, until it got going so fast it became just a blur."

Snow chuckled. "Then Dad took it in to the body shop and had a plate welded on underneath, so after that we had to throw our gum wrappers out through the window instead."

"I never did that," she said.

"Yeah, right." Snow took another sip of coffee. "What was it you wanted to talk to me about?"

Karen drank some of her coffee and put her hands together in her lap. She let out a heavy sigh. "Well, I gave it a lot of thought yesterday after you left, and I came to a decision and called that Detective Harris who is in charge of the case. I told him I want to take a polygraph test." She pressed her lips together and looked into Snow's face. "What do you think?"

Snow looked down at his silverware and considered this bit of news. "I don't know." He brought his eyes back up. "Do you think it's a good idea?"

"That's what I'm asking you," she said.

Snow scratched the side of his neck. "It can't be used in a trial, in any way, so I'm not sure what good it would do. And it's not completely accurate. Why do you want to take it?"

"I've gotten to a point where I'm getting desperate for something, anything, to help show that I'm innocent. If I can pass this test, then I'll have something in my corner. It might give those detectives a reason to think that it is possible that I had nothing to do with Bob's death."

Snow sighed. "I guess. What about Steve? Does he want to take it?"

She looked down at her hands. "I don't know. And I don't care. I stopped talking to Steve. This only concerns me."

"So...what did Detective Harris say?"

"It's all set," she said. "Two o'clock this afternoon at the area command over on Harmon."

"You want me to go with you?" Snow asked.

"Thanks, but I'm a big girl," she said. "I can handle this test. All I have to do is tell the truth."

Snow rubbed his chin with his fingers. "Yeah. I guess stranger things have happened. What if they ask you, as a preliminary question, if you ever stole anything?"

She tilted her head up. "I'll tell them no."

Snow nodded. "What about that tube of Clearasil you snuck into your purse at the little store up on the corner that time?"

"Oh." Her face began to flush. "That's different. I never considered that stealing..."

"What would you call it?"

She shrugged. "Hormones?"

CHAPTER 22

It was ten thirty when Snow arrived at the Sunrise Inn to pick up Willie for his first day on the job. As late as it was, Snow figured he should have had enough time for breakfast and a trip across the street to Walmart to pick up some new clothes and toiletries.

But Willie wasn't in his room. At least he wasn't answering the door. Snow entertained a sudden feeling of dread. Maybe he had skipped out. Taken a taxi down to the train yard and climbed into an open boxcar.

Five doors down, Snow noticed a cart with a dark-skinned cleaning woman beside it, sorting through the stack of clean towels. He walked toward her and asked her if she could open the door to his room and let him in.

She shook her head. "I cannot do that. You go to the office. They will let you in. I cannot."

Suddenly he remembered the extra key in his pocket. He pulled it out and showed it to her. "Never mind," he said, grinning. "I forgot to look in my pocket." *She must think I'm an idiot,* Snow thought.

She nodded and laughed.

146

He went back to Willie's door, opened it with the key, and went in.

The room had been cleaned and made up. Willie's two garbage bags were next to the bed. In the bathroom, on the counter next to the sink, was a disposable razor, a can of shaving gel, a bottle of Aqua Velva, some deodorant, and a small pair of scissors. In the closet, he found a new gym bag with several T-shirts of various colors, two pairs of blue jeans, two three-packs of underwear, and three pairs of white socks.

He was definitely around somewhere. No way he would have left without his possessions. He went back out to the foot of the bed and looked on the dresser, the desk, and the nightstand for a note. There was none.

Snow took his notebook out of his back pocket, ripped a page out, and wrote out a note for Willie; he put it on the dresser and left.

He walked down the stairs and along the sidewalk to room 138. The blue truck was gone.

At the motel office, there was a different clerk on duty. He was skinny, with short black hair, a white shirt open at the collar, and black slacks. He looked to be in his early thirties. He asked Snow if he could help him.

"Yes," Snow said. He walked up to the counter and hooked his thumbs into his back pockets. "I was supposed to meet a fellow here about a truck he put up for sale on eBay. I was the highest bidder, and I drove down here from Carson City to pick up the truck. But the problem is that I lost the slip of paper I had everything written down on. He said he would be in room 138 or 238 or something close to that. It's a blue Ford truck. I have the license plate number. Fortunately, I wrote that down on a separate piece of paper." Snow read it off to him. "Can you check and see if he's registered here?"

The clerk went to his computer and punched a few buttons. "What's his name?"

"I don't remember," Snow said. "I had that written down on the same piece of paper as the other information—and somehow I lost it." He grinned.

The clerk shifted his eyes to Snow, his eyes narrowing. "You don't remember his name? Not even his first name?"

Snow shrugged. "I forgot it."

The clerk punched more buttons and looked at the screen. Then he looked through some receipts next to the computer. "Here it is," he said. "His name is Daniel Guardino. Room 238. Upstairs."

Snow brightened. "Yeah, that's it. When did he check in?"

"Saturday."

Back in Willie's room, the note was still on the dresser. He balled it up and tossed it in the wastebasket. He turned the television on, pulled the desk chair out, and put it in front of the TV next to the bed. For the next fifteen minutes he flipped aimlessly through the channels, his mind poring over the information he'd collected, which didn't seem to amount to anything worthwhile. His flow of logic always worked its way back to the same point: Bob had known the killer and felt comfortable squatting down in front of that tire, working on it, with that person standing behind him in a dark, isolated area. Snow was at a dead end. Any digging around he might do now would just be busywork. If he were still on the job with Metro and this wasn't his sister, he knew he'd be going after her—and Steve.

He was mulling this over when he heard a car pull up outside the window. He heard the door open, then Willie's voice.

Snow got up and went to the window. Down in the parking area, a cab had stopped. A man in a navy-blue pin-striped suit stood on the passenger side facing the open cab door, with his back turned to Snow. He had gray hair, cut short and combed back.

Strange, he thought. He was sure it had been Willie's voice.

He went back to the chair and sat down.

The car door slammed shut, followed by the drone of the engine growing faint as the cab pulled away. There were footsteps ascending the stairway. Then continuing along the walkway past the window and stopping at the door to the room. It opened.

Snow didn't recognize him at first, even from the front. The beard was gone, the gray hair trimmed evenly. Under the suit, he wore a crisp white shirt, with a red-and-white striped silk tie knotted firmly at his neck.

Willie closed the door, took two steps, thrust out his arms at his sides to straighten his sleeves, and gave a single nod to Snow. "What do you think?"

"Don't tell me they're having a news show host convention down on the Strip. Who'd you steal that from? Keith Olbermann?"

"They're having a sale at Macy's," he said. "This was half off."

"But why?"

"If I'm going to be on the job, I need to look like I know what I'm doing. Look sharp, be sharp. That's my motto."

"Did you dress like that when you taught history?"

"You bet. That's one of the aspects of tramp life that's unbecoming to me—not having a decent suit for formal occasions."

"You consider this a formal occasion?"

"Compared to riding in boxcars and sleeping in hobo jungles it is. In the east, everything is formal. In California, CEOs wear T-shirts and sneakers; hardly anything's formal there. Who's to say." Then he clapped his hands together and rubbed them. "Okay. What's the plan of the day? Bring me up to speed on what I missed so far."

"You haven't missed anything. I went over to the office and asked about the guy with the Ford pickup while I was waiting for you."

"And?"

"His name is Daniel Guardino. And he checked in Saturday."

"The day after the murder."

"Yes."

Willie took a step back and leaned his rear against the dresser. "What does that tell us?"

Snow thought for a moment and then raised his palms in front of him. He shrugged. "I guess it tells us that he had moved out from wherever he had been living and was probably planning to take his RV out that day. But the murder ruined his plans. And his trailer got taped into the crime scene, so he got a motel room instead."

"And how does that tie him to the murder?"

Snow thought some more. "I'm drawing a blank."

"Me too," Willie said. "So why was it important to find out when he checked into this motel?"

Snow stared at Willie, his mouth hanging half-open. "I'm not sure. It seemed like a good move at the time. During any investigation, I always assemble a lot of information—which usually turns out to be worthless. But I've learned over the years that it's best to accumulate any clues you can pick up while they're fresh. Because further down the road, you may realize that you needed those facts and find that they're no longer available."

"Okay. So what other potentially useless information will we be gathering today?" Willie chuckled at his own joke.

"There's the towing company, down the street from the storage lot. We need to talk to them and find out if anyone saw anything. Then there's the brick hammer the police have in evidence, which may point to the possibility of the perpetrator being a bricklayer."

Willie nodded. "Good thinking."

"We can drive over to the local union headquarters and possibly get a list of names, addresses, and phone numbers of members who live around here. Then compare that with a list of names of people who rent storage spaces at the RV storage lot. If we can find a bricklayer with an RV stored in that lot, we could have a suspect. But first we need to stop off at a drugstore."

Willie's eyes narrowed. "You feeling ill?"

Snow shook his head. "I need to get you a dog collar so I can get in touch with you when I need you. I'll get you a temporary cell phone. Then I can call you whenever I want."

(HAPTER 23

Detectives Harris and James were waiting for Karen Williams outside the front door to the police station when she arrived. They shook hands, asked how she was doing, and then accompanied her past the front desk and down a series of hallways to the open doorway of a windowless room that appeared to be twice the size of a utility closet. The walls and ceiling were painted off-white. There were no pictures. Recessed in the center of the ceiling, a fluorescent fixture filled the room with light. Directly below the fixture stood a small wooden table with two chairs, the first of which was occupied by a white male in his mid-thirties with a butch haircut, white shirt, green paisley tie, and black slacks. The other chair sat alongside the end of the table. On the table, in front of the man with the tie, was an open notebook computer, connected to an electronic box. And attached to that was a blood pressure cuff and various cables and straps.

Karen took two steps into the room, followed by the detectives, and stared at the equipment. Her eyes grew large, her pulse quickening. "It feels kind of hot in here," she said, her voice wavering. She could feel her cheeks glowing.

"I don't think it's hot at all," said Detective Harris. "If anything, I'd say it's cold in here."

"Are you feeling alright?" asked Alice.

"I'm fine. I'm just hot." She looked around the room and up
at the ceiling. In the corner nearest the door, about a foot from
the ceiling, a video camera was mounted to a metal bracket,
bolted to the wall. It was aimed at the table. "Are you going to
be recording this?"

Harris nodded. "Detective James and I will be in another
room while you're taking the test. So there won't be any
distractions."

Karen looked at Harris and then Alice. Alice smiled and
reached out and touched her forearm with her hand. "It will
be okay," she said.

"So I'll be, like, under a microscope," Karen said. "Just me
and him." She flipped her hand toward the technician. She took
a shallow breath and held it. "I'd like you in here with me," she
said to Alice.

Alice's voice was calm, reassuring. "That will be okay."

"No, it's not okay," Harris snapped. "I don't want anybody
in this room except her and the technician. No distractions."

"How will that be a distraction if I'm just sitting here without
talking?" Alice protested.

Harris glared at Alice. "This is the way we always do it. Just
her and the technician."

"I feel like I'm going to the electric chair," Karen said. "I
don't think I can do this."

"You don't have to do it if you don't want to," Alice said.
"It's your decision."

"Wait a minute," Harris said. He pointed his finger at Karen,
jabbing the air as he talked. "You were the one who asked for this

polygraph test, Mrs. Williams. Not us. We didn't even suggest it. But we went to the trouble of setting it up for you, and you damn well better take it!"

Karen stared at Harris, her eyes large, her face losing color. It seemed as though the room was tilting a little, the walls closing in. She stepped over to the doorway and put her hand on the doorjamb to steady her balance. She shifted her eyes to Alice. "I'm not going to take it. I changed my mind. I can't do it."

"That is your choice," Alice said. She stepped toward her.

Harris shook his head. He pointed to the chair. "Get in that chair and get hooked up. You're not leaving until you do."

Karen looked at Harris, her eyes bulging, her lips firmly pressed together. "*I'm not taking any fucking test!*" she screamed at him. She began to tremble. "If you want to arrest me, go ahead! Lock me up! Torture me! I don't care anymore! I just want to go home!" Her face contorted into a mask of pain, her eyes squeezed shut, her lips pressing against the front of her teeth. Her hands balled up into fists. She began to sob uncontrollably, falling against the doorjamb.

Alice went to her and put her arm around her.

"Goddammit, just calm down!" Harris demanded. "There is no reason for this behavior. We haven't done anything to you, Mrs. Williams. Now you'd better calm down!"

"*Don't tell me to calm down, you fucking asshole!*" Karen screamed. "*I don't have to do anything you tell me! I'm not under arrest!*"

"It's alright, Mrs. Williams," Alice said evenly, her voice soothing. "You don't have to do what anyone tells you. You're free to go home whenever you want. There is nothing wrong with changing your mind. Everyone does it all the time, including me. I don't blame you for not wanting to take the test. I wouldn't want all that stuff hooked up to me either. Would you like to go outside?"

With tears running down her face and still sobbing, Karen straightened up away from the doorjamb. She threw her purse strap over her shoulder. "Yes, I'd like to get out of here."

Alice stepped back and motioned toward the doorway with her hand. "Alight, let's go outside and get some air. Would you like some coffee or some water?"

Karen sniffled and forced a smile at Alice. She shook her head. "I don't want anything. Thank you, Detective James. But I'd like to leave now."

"Will you be okay to drive?" Alice asked. "I can drive you home if you like. Your brother can bring you back later to pick up your car."

She shook her head and held up her hand. "I'm fine now, really. Thank you." She wiped her eyes with the back of her hand.

Alice opened her purse and took out several tissues. She offered them to Karen. Karen took them, opened one up, folded it in half, and wiped her eyes with it, then her nose. "I'm alright now." She touched Alice's hand, smiled at her, and then turned and walked out of the room.

A few steps down the hallway, Karen's pace quickened. And then she began to run. As fast as she could manage on the slick tile floor in her leather-soled shoes, she sprinted to the end of the hall, made a controlled sliding turn, and disappeared behind the corner of the wall.

Standing out in the middle of the hallway, his legs wide, Detective Harris crossed his arms, staring after Karen Williams. "She's as guilty as hell," he declared. "Her and her boyfriend Steve Helm. She's cracking under the pressure of guilt. It won't be long now until we get a confession out of her."

Detective James looked at Harris. "I think she's already cracked," she said. "But I'm not so sure it's from guilt."

Harris turned his head to Alice. "What are you talking about?"

"You dumb jerk," Alice said. "She's going through menopause."

CHAPTER 24

With his new partner riding shotgun, Jim Snow and Willie Hoffman interviewed the owner of the towing company that occupied the second lot over from Hollywood RV Storage. He hadn't seen anything. He told them two of his employees had been taking a smoke break out on the edge of the road and saw Bob Williams in his truck parked outside the gate two nights ago, presumably just before he was murdered. But that was all they saw. And nobody else, that he knew of, saw anything.

They broke for lunch after that, taking advantage of a two-for-one coupon at the Boulder Nugget buffet on Boulder Highway, using Snow's casino player's card.

At the bricklayer's local union headquarters, Snow and Willie talked to the office manager about the state of the economy in Southern Nevada, the shortage of jobs for trained workers in the trades, and hope for the future. She called her boss and got permission to print out all of the names of union members in the Southern Nevada area, but no phone numbers or other personal information. Snow told her that was fine. That was all the information he needed. She offered her heartfelt condolences for the death of his brother-in-law and the grief and pain his sister must be enduring, "Especially," she said, "with the cops trying to blame it on her."

Returning from the union headquarters on the way to the RV storage lot, Snow and Willie were eastbound on Tropicana near Maryland Parkway when Snow's cell phone chirped. He pulled the Sonata to the side of the road and fished the phone out of his pocket.

It was his sister Karen.

Her voice was calm and low. Almost serene. "I'm back home from the police station, Jimmy," she said.

"How did it go?"

"Not well, I'm afraid."

"You flunked the polygraph test?" Snow looked at Willie, who turned his head and stared out the window.

"I didn't take it," she said. "I got to the interrogation room where the equipment was set up, and I freaked out. I started thinking, *What if I tense up and my heart starts racing every time they ask me a key question?* I have no control over that, and it could happen. I could panic and blow the whole test, and then they would really be convinced I'm guilty. After the way I reacted this afternoon, I'm afraid they're even more certain of my guilt than if I had flunked the test."

"It doesn't matter what the detectives think," Snow said. "It's only important what they can prove."

Willie opened his car door, got quietly out, shut it, and sauntered along the sidewalk, ahead of the car. He shoved his hands into the front pockets of his pants.

"It does matter," she said. "They're going to dig up every detail they can find that might be twisted around to make Steve and me look like we planned and executed this crime. And then present that to a jury. They'll shove so much convoluted information down their throats for months on end that all twelve of them will be completely brainwashed into coming back with a guilty verdict. That's the way the legal system works. Everybody knows that. If you're rich or famous, or both, you can get the best lawyers in the country to work for you, and they can get you off. If you're a common person like me—you get screwed."

"It doesn't always work that way, Sis," Snow said.

She sighed softly. "Well, it doesn't matter. I've had enough. I can't go on like this. It was driving me crazy. And I won't let it anymore. That's it. Simple as that." She paused for a moment. Then she said, "Jimmy, I love you very much...I have to go now...good-bye."

The line went silent.

"Karen."

No answer. Snow disconnected and speed-dialed her cell number. It went directly to voice mail after the first ring. He punched in her home number. Five rings, and it brought up her recorded greeting.

He snapped the phone shut and gripped it tightly in his right fist. Stared at the steering wheel.

Then he started the engine, pulled up alongside Willie, who was moving toward the car, and yelled at him, "Willie, take a cab back to your motel! I'll see you tomorrow!"

Willie backed up, nodded, and gave a wave.

The car skidded away from the curb, the engine winding up. Snow activated his emergency flashers and turned on his headlights. He kept his speed as high as possible, without push-ing beyond the edge of control. When the lights were red, he stopped and waited, looking at his watch, beating his thumbs nervously on the top of the steering wheel, watching the traffic pass endlessly in front of him. When the lights turned green, he floored it and raced ahead.

Nine minutes after hearing the final words from his sister, he skidded to a stop in her driveway. Jumped out of the car, leaving the door open, and ran to her front door.

He punched the doorbell four times in rapid succession. Then pounded on the door with his fist. He listened. No sound from inside.

"*Karen!*" he yelled into the closed door.

He rang the doorbell again. Hammered on the door with the side of his fist.

"Shit!" he muttered.

But no one came to the door.

He stepped back to the edge of the stoop, turned sideways, and threw himself at the door. He heard a slight crack, and he wasn't sure if the sound had come from the doorjamb or his shoulder. There was a dull ache in his shoulder, but he backed up to make another run at the door, when he heard his sister's small voice from behind the door, calling his name.

A click of the deadbolt sliding open, and then the door.

Karen stood in the open doorway, wearing a purple bathrobe. "Jimmy," she said. "What on earth are you doing?" Her face was pale, her eyes red.

Snow gasped and stepped toward her, putting his arms around her.

Then he stepped back and looked into her face. "What are *you* doing? That's what I'd like to know."

"Getting ready to take a bath."

"Why?"

"Because I felt like it."

"Why did you hang up on me?" Snow asked.

She said, "I was done talking."

"You turned off your phone."

"The battery was almost dead," she said. "It's recharging. Why don't you come in?"

She backed up a few steps, and he came inside, leaned his head down, and peered at the doorjamb where the striker plate was screwed into it. There was a vertical two-inch crack in the doorjamb on both sides of the striker plate.

"You broke my door frame," Karen said, shoving her hands into her pockets.

Snow straightened up and closed the door, sliding the deadbolt into the locked position. "I'll get a carpenter out here to fix it tomorrow."

He stepped toward Karen, took hold of her wrists, and pulled her hands out of her pockets.

"Now what?" she protested.

He let go of her wrists, put his hands deep into the pockets of her robe, and felt along the seams and into the corners. The pockets were empty.

"I don't have anything on under this, you know," she said. "You're getting a little personal." She stood looking up at him with her arms hanging bent and limp away from her sides, in the same position he had left them.

Snow removed his hands from her pockets, took her hand in his, and led her up the stairway into the hall bathroom.

The tub was half-filled with water. Three lit candles had been arranged along the flat rim of the tub. They were short and pink, their perfumed fragrance filling the room. On the bathroom counter, next to the sink, was a full glass of red wine.

He let go of her hand and began opening drawers in the vanity cabinet, pawing through the contents of each. He did the same with the medicine cabinet and the storage space behind the double doors of the cabinet. Satisfied, he stood up and turned to her.

She stood with her arms crossed, watching him. "If I were planning to kill myself," she said, "I wouldn't have bothered to recharge my phone, now would I?" She tipped her head in the direction of the master bedroom. "Go in there and look. It's plugged in."

Snow felt his throat tighten. He stepped toward her and hugged her. "I thought you were dead," he said. "I was sure of it."

He felt her shoulders shrug against him. She put her face against his shoulder.

"Would you like me to promise you that I won't kill myself?" she said.

"What good would that do?" he mumbled. "You lie like a rug."

Suddenly he felt the spasms from her as she shook with laughter. The reaction infected him, and he began to laugh too. This was followed by sporadic giggling fits, and when that had subsided, he stepped back from her, kissed her on her forehead, and left the room, closing the door behind him.

Descending the stairway, with the sound of water filling the bathtub, Snow went downstairs, crossed the living room, and went into the kitchen. He opened the refrigerator, hoping to find beer, but there was only food and an open bottle of merlot.

He closed the refrigerator door and searched the shelves of the walk-in pantry. On the top shelf, he found a bottle of vodka next to a bottle of virgin olive oil and an assortment of canned goods. He took the vodka down off the shelf, poured three ounces of it into a short glass, dropped in a few ice cubes from the tray in the freezer, and headed back into the living room.

Plopping down into the stuffed chair with his drink, Snow picked up the remote and turned on the television. The tail-end of an old movie starring Humphrey Bogart was playing. He sipped his vodka and leaned back into the comfort of the deep cushions of the chair. He began to relax, and after draining the last of the liquid from his glass, drowsiness tugged at his eyelids.

He couldn't remember the point in the movie at which he had finally dozed off, wasn't even sure that he had slept, until the sound of yelling and gunfire clawed his mind back to a half-conscious state.

His eyes opened to the sight of a uniformed cavalryman standing on the high wooden walkway at the top of a fort. Suddenly an arrow struck the cavalryman in the chest. Dropping his rifle, the cavalryman staggered around dramatically for a few seconds and then fell sideways out of the picture.

An arrow.

Gaining his full senses, Snow replayed in his mind the scene he had just witnessed. It was an old cowboy and Indian movie from the fifties, rife with the shooting of guns—and arrows.

Arrows. Why hadn't he thought of that? Never outside the box. Always wandering around, looking for the same thing everyone else was looking for. The coroner investigator says it was a pickaxe—everybody looks for a connection to a pickaxe. Or a rock hammer, or a brick hammer. But nobody looks for an arrow. That's too far outside the box. *How could I have been so stupid?* Snow asked himself.

But this put a new spin on things. Tomorrow, he would strike out in a new direction. It was a long shot, but it answered the burning question that had bothered him since the beginning: How could you murder someone with a pointed object without attacking them at close range?

An arrow, two of them. Both penetrating the heart probably from at least thirty feet away, maybe more. An expert marksman, possibly. This was a crazy idea, but it was possible.

When Karen came downstairs ten minutes later, dressed in gray sweatpants and a T-shirt, carrying her empty wine glass, Snow broached the subject of his new theory.

Her initial reaction was somewhat skeptical. "That's the dumbest thing I've ever heard," she said. Despite the relaxing bath, her face was still pale, her wet hair clinging to the sides of her face and neck. She looked like she had the flu.

"What's dumb about it?"

"Think about it," she said. "Bob's changing a tire in the middle of a secure storage lot, and some crazy guy comes along, who just happens to have a bow and arrow with him in case he happens across someone to rob, in a place where you probably wouldn't even find anyone. And he shoots him with it. I'm pretty sure if the guy was a thief, he would have had a gun, or maybe a knife, or even a brick hammer. But not a bow and arrow. During your years on the force, did you ever hear of anyone getting killed in Las Vegas with a bow and arrow?"

He shook his head. "Never."

Holding her wine glass in her right hand, she raised it and pointed toward the kitchen. "I'm getting another glass of wine. Would you like some?"

"No thanks," Snow said. "I'm not partial to wine. It makes me dizzy."

"I wonder why," she said. "It doesn't have that effect on me. Maybe you're allergic to it."

"I don't think so," Snow said. "It's probably a combination of the sugar and the fact that it's made from rotten fruit. But while you're in the kitchen, maybe you could pour me a little vodka." He raised his empty glass to her.

"Do you want anything in it?"

"Just vodka and ice," he replied. "I think it's the mixers that give you the hangover."

"Yes. Orange juice gives me a bad one," she said.

She took his glass into the kitchen with her and came back a few minutes later, handed him his drink, and sat down on the couch with her glass of wine. She pulled her feet up alongside her legs and tucked them under a pillow.

"What if the perpetrator didn't have a gun?" Snow said, picking up where they had left off. "If he used a knife, there would have been a struggle, a lot of evidence left behind. But a bow and arrows. That would be clean. Why do you think the Indians used it as their main weapon all those years? They didn't have guns until the white man started selling them to them. And they wouldn't think of riding up alongside a buffalo with just a hunting knife. That would be insane."

She took a drink of her wine, her eyes misting up. "I don't know," she said. "I really miss Bob. I don't want to talk about this. You do whatever you think is best. But I'm just going to resign myself to the inevitability of prison. It will probably take them six months or more to put a case together, consisting of circumstantial bullshit, and then maybe a couple more years until the trial is over. I'm planning to make the most of that time. I've had a good life up until now. It won't be such a tragedy to have it turn to shit at this late period of my existence."

Snow frowned at her. He didn't know what to say. The problem was that she was probably right. Most of what happens to people during their lives isn't fair, especially in court. Attorneys hand-select a jury they're confident they can manipulate. When the jury retires to deliberate, they pick out the juror among them that they deem to be the smartest—usually the one with the strongest personality. That person usually herds the other eleven jurors into his or her line of reasoning and does the decision-making for all twelve. Snow had always thought that for a verdict to be unbiased, all jurors should be separated from each other, never to know how the others viewed the evidence—or voted—until after the verdict was read. And maybe not even then.

He took a hearty gulp of his drink. "Alright," he said. "What about dinner? I don't think either of us feels like cooking. Want to resign yourself to a pizza?"

CHAPTER 25

"Are you sure you want to do this?" Karen asked.

She had brushed her teeth and changed into white flannel pajamas with teddy bears printed all over them. She stood next to the king-size bed, near the bedroom door. Snow had taken the cushions from the sofa, carried them up to the master bedroom, and laid them out in a row on the floor, between the bed and dresser. He had finished making up the cushions with a mattress pad, sheets, and thermal blanket that Karen had produced from the hall linen closet. And now he was fluffing his pillow. She had given Snow a pair of Bob's cotton pin-striped pajamas, which fit short in the arms and legs, but had plenty of room everywhere else.

"This will be fine," he said.

"Bob and I always planned to buy an extra bedroom set and turn one of the other rooms into a spare bedroom, but nobody ever stays over, so the idea seemed like a waste."

"Probably no one ever stays over because there's no place for them to sleep," Snow said.

"I never thought of it that way," Karen said. "But there is no reason for you to stay over. I'm perfectly fine."

"You think you're perfectly fine. That's your opinion. I don't think you're acting normal. You shouldn't be left alone in your current frame of mind. I'd never forgive myself if I let something happen to you."

She dismissed him with a wave of her hand, the other on her hip, as she looked about the room. "Okay. Do you want something to read, or would you rather just go right to sleep?"

"What do you have?"

She said, "I have *Woman's Day*, *Women's World*, and *Redbook*."

"I think I'll just go to sleep."

She narrowed her eyes and frowned. "How do you expect to learn about women if you don't read our literature?"

"If I learn much more than I already know, I'm going to end up in counseling." He dropped his pillow and lowered himself to the makeshift bed. "You can turn out the light when you're ready."

"Alright, Jimmy," she said. "I love you."

"Yeah," he mumbled.

Snow awoke with a start and looked at the glowing dial of his watch.

Three forty a.m. He'd been dreaming about a thirty-foot snake, wrapped around his torso, squeezing his rib cage, abdomen, and lower back.

The cushions had separated during the night, and his butt had slid down to the floor between them. His lower back ached.

Using his heels, he pulled the cushions back together and rolled over. This made the pain worse. Plus his ribs hurt. He rolled onto his back and sat up. Then turned his head and looked at his sister, sleeping soundly on the far side of the bed, her back turned toward him.

This is a big bed, he thought.

He considered the situation for a few moments and then eased himself up off the cushions and onto the bed. Hugging his side of the mattress, he turned his back to his sister and noticed the relief of the subsiding pain. He drifted off into a deep sleep.

A few hours later he awoke to the roar of a chain saw in his ear. He felt the warmth of a body against his back, an arm draped around his chest. He raised his head from the pillow and craned his neck. It was Karen.

She stopped snoring and opened her eyes. Wide. Then scrambled back to the far side of the bed, staring at him in horror.

"What are you doing in my bed?" she asked.

Snow climbed out and stood up, his mouth hanging open. "What where you doing on my side?"

"Your side? This entire bed is my side. Your side is the floor. What are you, some kind of pervert?"

"The cushions wouldn't stay together. My back was killing me."

"Bob slept on those cushions, a lot," she said. "He never complained about it."

Snow put his hands on his hips. "Yeah, he moved out instead."

"Don't change the subject," she snapped. "There is no excuse for you getting into my bed in the middle of the night. I'm not some woman you picked up in a nightclub. I'm your sister. What do you think Doctor Phil would say about this?"

"I don't think Doctor Phil would sleep on these cushions either," Snow muttered. He moved away from the bed and started for the door. "I'm getting out of here. Your suicidal tendency is obviously diminished. You're back to your old self."

CHAPTER 26

"The beauty of this new supposition," Snow said, "is that it eliminates the necessity for the perpetrator to be someone familiar to the victim. It could have been a stranger." This was the final statement of the epiphany Snow had been struck with the night before. To celebrate, he and Willie were having breakfast at Wanda's Waffle House, which would have been the first event of this Tuesday morning even if there was nothing to celebrate.

Willie sliced through his stack of waffles, stuck a fork into the newly liberated segment, and shoved it in his mouth. He looked out the window and chewed thoughtfully. After swallowing it, he took a slurp of coffee and jabbed the fork in Snow's direction. "This is a commendable idea you've come up with, Jim. I like it. But the odds-makers wouldn't go along with it. It's highly improbable. And I'm not saying it's not worth pursuing. But I think we need to continue on the path our investigation has taken." Today, with his new suit, Willie was sporting a light-blue dress shirt, along with a burgundy tie with giant, overlapping blue and yellow circles.

"Which path is that?" Snow stabbed a link sausage with his fork and popped it into his mouth.

"The links to the suspected murder weapon—the brick hammer. We have the names of the bricklayers local for this area. Now we should continue with the plan of obtaining a list of the tenants of the RV storage lot, and then compare the two for a possible match."

"Jesus," Snow declared. "Here I thought I had come up with a major breakthrough, and everybody thinks it's a dumb idea."

"It's not dumb," Willie insisted. "It's just farfetched. Plus, how would you explain the bleach-soaked brick hammer?"

"The perpetrator could have tossed that out of their vehicle to throw us off. If it were me, I would at least have driven a little farther from the murder scene before heaving it."

"Good point, Jim. I like the way your mind works." Willie carved a portion of steak, swabbed it through some egg yolk, and put it in his mouth.

"How's that rib eye?" Snow asked.

Willie finished chewing and swallowed. He nodded. "Tasty and tender. Hardly any gristle or fat to it. Grilled to perfection."

Snow nodded. "I think I'll give that a try tomorrow. By the way, I was wondering…?"

"What?"

"I thought homeless people all have rotten teeth. But yours look pretty healthy. How do you manage that?"

Willie drank some coffee. "First of all—like I said—I'm not homeless. But I can still take advantage of their benefits. They have a really nice homeless facility that I frequent down in Arizona. Free dental care, and even medical. There are a bunch of dentists and doctors who volunteer their services for free. Good people. It's worth the trip down there once a year or so to maintain your good health and dental hygiene."

While Willie was in the men's room, Snow paid the check and then stepped outside to make a call on his cell phone.

Alice picked it up on the first ring.

"Hi, Jim," she said. "How are you?"

"Not bad, under the circumstances," he replied. "I talked to Karen, and she told me what happened at the station."

"Yes," Alice said. "She's having a tough time of it under the circumstances. But it's perfectly normal."

"Yeah, for someone being investigated for murdering their husband."

"I was referring to menopause."

Snow's mouth dropped open. "She has menopause?"

"You didn't notice?"

Snow hesitated. "I know she's been acting crazy lately. I never considered that."

"Few men do, believe me. But it's different for everyone. Some women are hardly affected by it, and the duration is brief. For others it can be devastating. And then if you add to it the additional stress of her current situation, you can imagine…"

"I'll keep that in mind," Snow agreed. "The main reason I'm calling you, Alice, is a new idea that popped into my head that I wanted to run by you—to get your opinion." He went on to explain the entire hypothesis. When he had finished, he asked her what she thought.

There was silence for a few seconds, and he thought, for a moment, that they'd lost the connection.

"That's an interesting concept, Jim," she said. "I guess any-thing is possible."

"Yeah…even…aliens. Right?"

She laughed. "You want me to run it by Mel and get his opinion?"

"Good idea," Snow said. "I might as well have everyone laughing at me."

She laughed again. "Why don't we get together for dinner tonight and discuss it further. What do you think?"

"Best idea I've heard all day."

"Me too," she said, and laughed even harder.

Snow chuckled. "How about Silvey's Steakhouse on Flamingo? It's just down the street from Terrible's Casino. Have you ever been there?"

"No, I haven't. But I've heard it's nice."

"It is. Shall I pick you up, or meet you there?"

"Hmm," she said. "It's better that I meet you there. If it doesn't work out, I can always crawl out through the ladies' room window and make my escape."

CHAPTER 27

"Is there something wrong with your hamburger?" Alice said.

Detective Harris's shoulders sagged. He frowned at his half-eaten double-decker cheeseburger and the half-dozen french fries that lay scattered in front of it on the plate. "I was hoping this would do the trick. You know—comfort food. But I can't get my appetite going."

"Is there something wrong?"

He tilted his head up, leaving the rest of his posture unchanged. "Bad pain," he said. Then he raised a fist and thumped it against his chest two times.

"Heartburn?" Alice asked.

"Worse than that. Candy and I split up last night." He lowered his head back down to his unfinished meal.

"I was wondering why she hadn't called you today. What happened?"

Harris sighed, slipped his paper napkin out from under the silverware, and wiped his mouth with it. Then he dropped it on the cheeseburger. "She invited me over for dinner, which I was really looking forward to since she's always been telling me she's a gourmet cook. She made hot dogs and potato salad. To be fair, they were actually gourmet hot dogs. But I was expecting some sort of fancy casserole or something special like that.

"So I get there, and she takes me in the kitchen to show me the surprise she got for me. She opens the fridge and there's a six-pack of beer in there. Which, I'll admit, was a nice touch. Shows she's been paying attention.

"Well, I finish the first beer and get halfway through the second, when she starts to complain in a subtle way about my drinking."

"What did she say?"

"She gets in my face, and she says, 'You sure like to drink!' Well, of course I like to suck 'em down now and then. What red-blooded American male doesn't? Besides, she's the one who bought the beer for me. All I did was show my appreciation by drinking it."

"Did you tell her that?"

"Of course I did. We both agreed to an open, honest relationship, right from the beginning. She's the one always wanting to know what I'm thinking. So I told her—and she couldn't handle it. She wouldn't talk to me for ten minutes, until I agreed to apologize. I still don't have any idea what the hell I was apologizing for, but it was either that or get up and leave.

"So then she jumps up and goes to get a picture of this dog she's been telling me about that she used to own, which died of some sort of disease. She said the dog was called an Afaird, which is a cross between an Afghan hound and something else. She sits down next to me on the couch and shows me the picture. And I told her that was the ugliest dog I've ever seen. It looked like a mutt that was covered with a thick shag carpet. Sort of like it was half sheep.

"She starts crying and snapping at me, telling me how could I talk about that poor dog that way, being that it was dead. Hell. What difference does it make that the dog's dead? It was still ugly."

Alice put her fingers over her lips to keep from smiling.

Harris shook his head. "It all went downhill from there. And I go through this every time with women. At first, they have nothing but praise for everything you do, telling you, 'Oh, my ex would never do anything as wonderful as that.' And then, when the relationship starts heading south, it's nothing but, 'Oh, my ex would never do anything as rotten and horrible as that!'

"I don't know where it all came from. It's like she was storing up all this negative stuff inside her, waiting for the right opportunity to dump it all on me. Just like Pearl Harbor." He shook the ice around in his glass of iced tea and took a swallow. "That's it for me. I've had it with white women. They're all spoiled rotten. I've been thinking about trying some interracial dating. See how that works out." Harris looked into Alice's eyes and raised an eyebrow. "So how's your love life going?"

Alice shrugged. "I don't have one right now."

Harris nodded. "You just mainly hang out with the brothers?"

She smiled. "Are you asking whether I only date black men?"

"Yeah."

"I don't necessarily have a preference," she said.

Harris grinned. "You want to have dinner sometime?"

"I don't think so," she said.

The smile faded. "Why not?"

"You're not my type."

Harris put up his hands. "Alright. I can handle that. You can't blame me for trying."

"That's true," Alice said. "That's the one thing nobody can blame you for."

Harris interlocked his fingers and rested his chin on his knuckles. He put his elbows on the table. "I think what I need," he said, "is a good Oriental woman. I'd like to find one from the old country." He narrowed his eyes and nodded.

Alice pushed her empty plate aside and slid her water glass in front of her. She raised it and took a drink. "There's an idea concerning the Williams murder case I need to run by you. Jim Snow came up with it, and he wanted to know what you think."

"Alright, I'm listening" Harris said.

"Jim thinks it's possible the brick hammer may not be the murder weapon."

"It was scrubbed with bleach and tossed out in the desert, a quarter mile from the murder scene. It fits in with the puncture wounds. What else could it be?"

"Jim's thinking maybe a bow and arrows."

Harris squinted at her and raised his upper lip. "Huh? Arrows? So—we're talking an Indian attack? Renegades, maybe? That's the dumbest thing I've ever heard. I don't think a human has been killed in this state with a bow and arrow since before the end of the westward expansion."

"It struck me that way at first, too," she said. "But I thought further into it, did some searching on the Internet. It's not common, but there have been people convicted of murder using a bow and arrow."

"No way." Harris shook his head and snorted. "You've got a better chance of getting hit by lightning while riding a hog down Las Vegas Boulevard."

"It wouldn't hurt to look into it."

"The hell it wouldn't. It'll take time away from our investigation."

"What investigation?" Alice said. "All we're doing is interviewing acquaintances of the suspects. There is nothing left to do until the lab gets around to our case. And then what if they don't find anything?"

"Then we start grilling them," Harris said. "Put the heat on them. Make them think we have something. Besides, what evidence is there to substantiate this arrow scenario?"

"The puncture wounds. I talked to the coroner investigator who wrote the initial report, and he told me the wounds could be consistent with arrows. He thought it made sense."

"It doesn't make sense that Steve Helm used a bow and arrow. Why would he? He was standing right there. All he needed was that brick hammer, a bucket, and a jug of bleach to clean it with."

"But what if he didn't do it?"

"He did do it!" Harris snapped. "Who the hell else had the opportunity? Helm said himself that there was nobody else there!"

"He said he didn't see anybody."

Harris's eyes widened. "That's right. Because it was a ghost. A ghost with a bow and arrow. I think we need to call in a psychic. She can tell us who the ghost belongs to. Then we can drive to the cemetery, dig up the grave, find the bow and arrow, and put the cuffs on the stiff."

"Fuck you," Alice said.

Harris leaned toward her. "What did you just say to me?"

"I wasn't thinking," she said evenly. "I didn't mean that. What I meant to say is *go fuck yourself*. That would be more appropriate."

Harris's face began to flush, his eyebrows drawing together. He pointed at her. "Do you know who you're talking to?" he snarled.

"I sure do," Alice replied. "A complete waste of skin."

CHAPTER 28

Metro Homicide section chief Lieutenant Calvin Bradley was seated behind his double-pedestal oak desk sorting through a stack of reports when Detective James appeared in his doorway. He was a heavy man of six foot, with sloping shoulders and a thick neck that was nearly as wide as his large, square head. Combed straight back was a thick mat of black hair, streaked with gray. Wire-rimmed glasses accentuated his beady blue eyes, and his jowls hung like those of an aged bloodhound. His white shirt was open at the collar, the blue-and-black-print tie hanging loose, his gray suit jacket draped over the back of his executive leather chair.

He looked up from the paperwork and forced his thin lips into a half smile. "Detective James. Come in."

"Thank you," she said. Then she crossed to the wooden chair in front of his desk, lowered herself into it, and smoothed out her skirt.

Bradley stood up and shuffled to the door. He closed it quietly and then went back behind his desk and sat down.

He smoothed out his tie, adjusted himself in his chair, and then leaned forward, his forearms on his desk, his fingers interlocked. "I believe this is the first chance I've had to talk to you since I took over this position back in July."

Alice crossed her ankles and moved them back alongside the front leg of her chair. "That's correct."

"I haven't really been here long enough to get to know all of the detectives working in this section, but I'm getting there slowly." He turned his head to a thin stack of papers on his left, reached for the top sheet, and placed it in front of him. "I see you haven't been in Metro Homicide much longer than I have—six months." He looked up at her.

"That's correct," Alice said.

"How do you like it here so far?"

She clasped her hands together in her lap and shrugged. "I'd have to say it's a mixed bag."

"Can you give me a little more detail? What do you like about it?"

"When I passed the exam and got the promotion, I was excited about it. I thought it would give me a chance to work with some bright people and, at the same time, make a contribution of my own. I've noticed there are quite a few talented individuals working in this section, and I was hoping I'd get to work with one of them as an equal partner…" She paused.

"And the other parts of the bag?"

She sighed. "I got stuck with the bottom of the barrel."

Bradley straightened up, as much as his overhanging abdomen would allow. He narrowed his eyes. "I assume you're referring to Detective Harris."

"That is correct," Alice replied.

He took a deep breath and pressed his lips together. "I had a long talk with Detective Harris this afternoon. I don't know him as well as you do, but I have been impressed so far with his professionalism, especially in his procedures, his adherence to regulations, the code of conduct that defines a top-notch detective, and his passion for the job.

"Now, I can understand how frustrating it must be for you starting out as a junior detective, and having to learn all you can while dealing with the constant stress of your new position. And wanting to contribute more, even though you may not be too sure what it is you can contribute that would be worthwhile."

"Sir, I don't have any problem figuring out what to contribute, and I'm sure it's worthwhile."

Bradley grinned and nodded. "No doubt. Having raised two daughters, I can definitely understand."

Alice tipped her head slightly. "Understand what? That I'm a female, so I must be stupid?"

Bradley raised a hand. "I didn't say that."

"No, you inferred it."

"You seem to like to twist things around, Detective James." He folded his hands. "I just think that there are a lot of opportunities for women these days that didn't exist before, especially for minorities. And that's good. But there are opportunities in other bureaus such as Vice/Narcotics. In fact, the section chief in Vice is a woman. And I would think that you might excel in a field such as that."

"You mean working as a prostitute, or just posing as one?"

He chuckled. "I'm just saying that there are other areas of law enforcement that might be of more interest to you, in case you've discovered that Homicide isn't your cup of tea."

"I don't drink tea," Alice said. "And I prefer Homicide. I would just like to have the chance to do the job I'm being paid to perform. So far, that hasn't been the case. Instead, I've been dragged around like a pet on a leash to observe—never allowed to speak, but only to watch my partner make a complete fool of himself on a steady basis. And it's embarrassing."

Bradley scowled and shook his head. "Now, this is what I've been talking about with regard to code of conduct. We are a team of professionals that can only succeed at our mission to protect and serve if we operate with the utmost of mutual trust and respect for our fellow team members."

"No one should ever demand trust and respect," Alice said. "I was raised to believe that was something you earned over a long period of time. Not something that should be handed out along with a gun and a badge."

"From what I've seen, I would say Detective Harris has earned it. He may not be perfect, he may not be the best detective in my section, but he's alright in my book." He pointed a finger at her. "Now you, Detective, are another case. I'm afraid I'd have to put a few negative question marks next to your name—in my book. And that isn't a good way to start off with me.

"I want you to know that I didn't call you in here to issue a reprimand. The last thing I need is Jesse Jackson showing up here with the news media." He chuckled. "So I'm trying my best to handle this situation in the least explosive way possible.

"Like I said, I had a long talk with Detective Harris, and he told me what's been going on between you two for the last six months. The insubordination, the insults, the lack of respect for his guidance, experience, and the badge he wears so proudly on his belt..."

"What about that thing he wears so proudly below his belt—that he'd like to have going on between us—did he tell you about that?"

Bradley stiffened in his seat. His eyebrows rose. "Are you saying there have been unwelcome sexual advances toward you?"

"Nothing a stun gun couldn't deter. He hasn't done anything reportable, but I would describe it as a constant source of electrical sexual tension. Positive for him and negative for me. He has the libido of a teenager."

"Would you like me to talk to him about it?"

"What good would that do?" Alice demanded. "I've been talking to him about it since we started working together. A smack on the head with a two-by-four might be the only thing that'll get the message across."

Bradley smiled and nodded. "You are a very attractive lady," he said. "Maybe you should take it in a positive way."

Alice raised an eyebrow. "I'm not taking it any way. Especially not lying down."

Bradley licked his lips. "I see." Sweat had begun to pop up on his forehead. He wiped it with the back of his hand. "At any rate, Detective Harris suggested this, and I concur, that the best solution to this problem is to split the two of you up."

Alice breathed a sigh of relief. "Oh, thank you. I've been hoping for that. I can't tell you how happy that makes me." She smiled.

"Detective Stevens is still on maternity leave, which won't expire for another two and a half weeks. She has been teamed up with Detective Brewer. And ever since she left for her maternity leave, he has been moving around amongst the four teams, filling in and helping out wherever needed. So, starting tomorrow, I'll put him together with Detective Harris. And when Detective Stevens returns from leave, I'll team you up with her. How does that sound?"

Alice's jaw dropped. "Marcia Stevens?" she said.

"Yes. Do you have a problem with that assignment?"

"She has more kids than the old woman who lived in the shoe. All she talks about is kids. How to produce them, how to

183

raise them, how to put up with them. Couldn't you team me up with somebody else?"

"There's no one else available, unless I move people around, and that wouldn't be fair to anyone but you. It's beginning to look to me as though you have problems getting along with people."

"We have twenty-four detectives in Homicide," Alice said. "I would be happy to work with anyone—except Mel Harris and Marcia Stevens. Why don't you team them up together? Give them a van to work out of. One with really strong springs."

Bradley laughed. "At least you have a sense of humor about it. I have to admit that."

Alice shook her head and looked Bradley in the eye. "Yeah, and you're not such a bad guy after all. You can't always judge a person by appearances." She grinned.

Bradley chuckled again. "Always with the compliments."

"I try."

"That's all I'm asking. Now here's the deal. Why don't you take vacation time until Detective Stevens gets back. And give it a try with her. If that doesn't work out, then maybe, further down the road, we can do some further switching around. But I need you to try harder than you have been. Otherwise, there's always Vice."

"Uh-uh. I'm not much of a drinker," Alice said. "And drugs don't do it for me."

CHAPTER 29

Sitting at the bar in Silvey's Steakhouse, nursing a Stoli on the rocks, Jim Snow checked his brown corduroy jacket for lint. It had a notched lapel, four-button cuffs, and flap-patch waist pockets. Willie had picked it out for him at Macy's. The cost was three times what he usually spent for jackets, but this was a special occasion. Along with the jacket, he wore a maize-colored button-down shirt and pleated navy slacks.

When he saw her walking in, he stood up suddenly, almost spilling his drink. He'd forgotten that his hand was still attached to it. Complementing her lean, toned legs, she wore a black, wool miniskirt with three gold buttons along each of the angled pockets. Black heels and a white silk blouse, with layered ruffles cascading down the V-neckline, rounded out her ensemble.

Snow wondered where she carried her gun.

"I didn't wear a tie," he said as she approached. "I wasn't sure how formal I should dress."

"Perfect," she said. "I'm not wearing one either." She moved her face close enough to his that he thought she might be closing in for a kiss. But she stopped short, smiled, pulled her head back, and sat down at the bar before Snow could pull her stool out for her.

He sat down next to her, and she turned halfway, crossing her legs toward him.

"What would you like?" Snow asked.

"What are you having?" she said.

"Just vodka, straight, on the rocks."

"That sounds simple, yet enticing."

Snow signaled the water and ordered a round. He drained his. Setting his glass down, he asked how her day went.

"It could have been better," she said. "I thought I was going to get written up. But I didn't. At first the news was good, but then it got bad."

Snow winced. "What happened?"

"Detective Flash and I got into it at lunch, and it turned ugly. I told him to go have carnal activity with himself, and he complained to the lieutenant. I got called in. Now I'm off the case and on vacation until my new partner comes back from maternity leave."

"That sounds like good news."

"Except that my new partner is dumber than a sack of cement, and she thinks a good time is watching marathon reruns of *Romper Room*. I believe, with the latest addition, she has six kids now."

"Oh. That's too bad."

"I have another option," she said. "The lieutenant offered to move me over to Vice, where there are more women and he thinks I'd be happier. I got the impression he thinks I'd be good walking the streets, helping to bust prospective johns. I have two and a half weeks to think about it. I might quit."

"And do what?"

The bartender arrived with the drinks. Snow slid a twenty toward him and took a sip of his vodka.

Alice took her drink in her hand and turned it, watching the ice. "I don't know. I could go back to being a cocktail waitress. The pay was good, but I doubt anyone is hiring. The economy is so bad in Vegas right now, even the hookers are getting laid off." She took a sip of her drink and winced. "Uh. This tastes like rubbing alcohol."

"It's like brussels sprouts," Snow said. "It'll grow on you."

"I don't need anything growing on me," she said. She took another sip. "Have you ever thought about using your experience on the force to start your own business?"

"You mean security or investigations?" Snow shook his head. "That doesn't sound appealing."

"Are you planning to keep playing poker all your life?"

"Not if I keep losing," he said.

"Well, what's your backup plan? I'm sure you've thought about it."

"I have. And it's depressing. I was really excited when I decided to quit the force and play poker full time. And then, after I had been doing it for more than a year, it started to feel like any other job. Only poker's not like a real job where you contribute something. You sit there for hours on end, trying to extract money from people who are inexperienced, drunk, and strung out on their emotions. After you take their money and they get up and leave the table, it doesn't make you feel good. I started feeling like a leech. And then I started losing, and...I just got to the point where I'm not sure I could ever have a winning month again.

"So it's been a month now since I've played. And all I've thought about is what now? Do I go back and tough it out until my bankroll is gone?"

"You might be able to get back on the force," she suggested.

"I thought about that," Snow said. "I'm not sure I'd want that. And the section chief transferred out shortly after I quit. So it's not like I'm a known quantity there anymore. It's amazing. The lieutenants move in and out of that position like it's a temp job. I think the longest anyone stayed was three years."

"I wonder why."

"It's a tough job. They get called in at all hours of the night on these cases and have to put on a suit and tie and go in front of the media. I wouldn't want that job for anything."

He took a sip of his drink. "How is the new guy—what's his name?"

"Calvin Bradley," she said. "He moved here from Cleveland. I thought he was a jerk at first, but he seems alright."

"I'll give him a year," Snow said.

Alice smiled. "You know, when I was in high school, I got into tennis. I had this dream of being a professional. I read all I could about it, played every chance I got. Back then, I thought all I needed to do was practice more than anyone else, and I could make it. I thought I could be like the Williams sisters are now. Then when I got older, I realized it takes more than working your butt off. It takes an extreme amount of natural ability. You can't just go out there day after day, stumbling around over your feet, and think you've got what it takes."

"You still play?"

"All the time," Alice said. "Do you ever play?"

"Off and on. Twenty years ago I was dating a woman who was an avid tennis player, so I bought a book. This book was so old it said you should always dress completely in white. So I did. Now, whenever I play, I have to get that book out to brush up."

"We should play sometime," Alice offered.

"Sounds good," Snow said. "I'll get the book out and dust it off."

He moved his head toward her. "Tell me—what are you planning to do on your vacation?"

"I don't know," she said. "I might fly back home to Detroit and visit some family. Or I could just stay here and hang out."

"I could use your help," Snow said. "My team is pretty ragged right now. I could use a good detective."

"What team?" she asked.

Snow told her about Willie.

"You hired a tramp to work with you? Whatever for?"

"I want to keep him around," Snow said. "I think he may know something. Maybe he saw something. I don't know, but if I didn't offer him money, I'm sure he would have caught a train out of here by now. Besides, I feel sorry for the guy. He's been through hell. He could use a break. On top of that, he reminds me of my old high school basketball coach."

"But what will become of him when you don't need him anymore? He'll just go back to sleeping in the bushes?"

"I've been thinking about that," Snow said. "Maybe I could help get him a job."

"Doing what? And how will he explain the nine-year gap in his resume?"

Snow nodded. He lifted his drink, swirled the ice around, and set it back down. "That's a tough one, alright. I'm pretty sure if he got his driver's license up to date, if nothing else, he could call one of those over-the-road trucking companies that always needs drivers. If it were me, I'd much rather sleep in a truck every night instead of the hard ground. But if he doesn't want any help, at least he'll have a small bankroll to head down the road with."

Alice smiled. She put her hand on his. "You're a pushover," she said. "That soft heart could get you in trouble someday."

"You'll help me?"

"Of course I'll help you," she said. "I told you I would the day I met you. Besides, you don't have a badge or a private investigator's license. You probably don't even carry a gun."

Snow tilted his head and shrugged.

CHAPTER 30

It was eight forty a.m. when Alice walked into the Waffle House. Wearing black, boot-cut jeans, hiking shoes, and a teal, scoop-neck blouse, this was the most casual Snow had ever seen her. He and Willie were seated across from each other at a table, drinking coffee and staring out the window. Snow wore his usual jeans and polo shirt, with Willie sporting a new yellow power tie to highlight his suit.

The two men stood up in unison. Snow introduced Willie, and he shook Alice's hand.

Alice stepped back and examined the suit. "Nice," she said. "You didn't tell me we would be having breakfast with an executive." She looked at Snow. "Where is this tramp you've been telling me about?"

Willie beamed. "I'm the tramp."

Alice chuckled. "And the best dressed I've ever seen. Jim has told me all about you; I understand you've been camping out in the Las Vegas Wash."

"Among other places."

"Aren't you concerned about flash flooding? It is a canal, after all."

Willie shook his head. "Nah. It almost never rains here. Most of the time there's just a trickle that runs through it. Sort of like a small creek. And those bushes that grow all over the place soak the water up pretty good and keep the ground dry. The only time I need to worry is when it starts raining. And when that happens, I get out of there fast and find a dry spot."

"Like somebody's boat," Snow said.

Willie arched his eyebrows and shrugged. "You do what you have to in order to survive in this world. Whatever it takes. That's my strategy—besides, I'll bet ninety percent of those boats in that storage lot never get used. They're all covered with dust, and the tires are almost flat. Might as well get some use out of them before they're completely rotted out with corrosion and hauled off to the scrap yard. People don't seem to realize, it's not always using something that wears it out. If you've got moving parts that sit idle long enough, those parts will just fuse together. Then you'll never get them moving again. You got to move that oil and grease around, keep everything lubricated. Just like the human body. That's why I get out and keep on the move." He shifted his gaze from Alice to Snow and back again. "Well, I better not get too far into that subject or I'll never shut up. I think we should eat."

The waitress showed up with a cup for Alice and a pot of coffee. She filled Alice's cup, and the three of them sat down to study the menu.

Small talk dominated the conversation during breakfast. When everyone had finished eating and the plates and silverware were taken away, Snow took out his pocket-size spiral notebook and began thumbing through it. He closed it and set it in front of him.

"I can summarize the status of this investigation very simply. Beginning with the possible murder weapons, we can presume that if a pickaxe or any sort of hammer with a pointed head that could have been used at close range was the actual murder weapon, then the perpetrator would have to have been very well known by the victim. Because there was no sign of a struggle, and evidence shows that he was caught by complete surprise, with his head facing forward—I don't think it's likely that a stranger or casual acquaintance committed this act with a handheld tool. But Willie and I followed up on the brick hammer possibility. We got a list of all of the members of the local union who have a Las Vegas address. Then we got a listing of the tenants of Hollywood RV Storage. Willie and I compared the two lists. No matches at all. Of course, you don't have to be a bricklayer to own a brick hammer. But there is no way to find out who those people are, since you don't need a license to own one.

"Moving on to the next possible murder weapon: If he was shot from a distance with two arrows, then of course it could have been anyone who was inside the storage lot at the time of the murder and who had access to an archery set. A likely scenario for that could be an archery enthusiast who has a space rented inside the lot and happened to overhear the transaction taking place. Someone who had an archery set handy, and decided, on the spur of the moment, that eight thousand dollars was enough money to kill for. I know from my own experience that a lot of people have been killed for quite a bit less."

"What about a javelin?" Willie said.

Snow squinted at him. "A javelin."

"If an arrow could be the murder weapon, so could a javelin."

"Willie, you thought the possibility of two arrows was unlikely, and now you're suggesting two javelins?"

"I'm just trying to explore all of the possibilities," he insisted.

"Yeah, right." Snow shook his head.

Alice smiled. "I did some research on the Internet after I got home last night."

Snow raised an eyebrow. "At two a.m.? What time did you go to bed?"

Her smile broadened. "I found a Web site that lists all of the archery clubs in the United States. There is only one in this area: Southern Nevada Bowmen. They have a Web site, which lists the officers and their phone numbers. I called the president, Jack Keller, this morning and talked to him. He said they have ninety-seven members, and if we stop by his home before noon, he could give us a printout with all of the names, phone numbers, and addresses of the current members, along with those who have become inactive during the last five years. We could compare that list of names with the storage lot listing and see where that takes us. One good bit of news is that archery isn't all that popular. He thinks there probably aren't many enthusiasts in the area who aren't members of that club."

"Why would that be?" Snow asked.

"He said the yearly dues are pretty cheap, forty bucks. But the benefits include weekly shoots at various ranges, with discounted fees, tournaments, and outings. There is a national organization, and one for the state of Nevada, but neither of them have any get-togethers, other than tournaments."

Snow nodded. "Good work, Alice," Snow said. "All I did was go to bed when I got home."

Jack Keller was an average-size man, in his early forties, with slicked-back hair, graying around the edges. He had an open face with a prominent nose and an easy smile. Dressed in a gray T-shirt and blue jeans, he answered his front door, shook hands all around, and invited the investigative team into his living room.

There were no trophies in sight, or framed awards, or even photos of archery events or contests. Most of the pictures that covered the walls were of family, mainly Jack, his wife, and their two daughters at various ages.

"I take it," Snow said, "that you must be quite accomplished to be elected president."

Keller slid his hands into his back pockets and grinned. "I've won my share of tournaments over time. But I've been at it for thirty years. And I've been a member of the Bowmen since I first got interested in it."

"How old were you?" Alice asked.

"Twelve," he said. "My dad was a member, and he taught me how to shoot and bought me my first bow. I really enjoyed it. Most people think there isn't much to the sport, just standing around shooting at targets, like you would a handgun. But the club has a target shooting range on public land the Forest Service lets us use. It's on Highway 160 between Vegas and Pahrump up on Saddleback Mountain. We built a clubhouse, a storage shed, and a big garage unit. It's got over fifty field and hunter targets, and twenty-five animal targets, plus a large outdoor target practice shooting range.

"It's really nice. There are a lot of trees up there, and we allow dry camping on the facility. A lot of the members go up there for the weekend with their RVs and stay. All of the members have full access to the range whenever they want. Of course they all have to help maintain it. And we have scheduled shoots up there occasionally." He paused and pulled his hands out of his pockets and then motioned toward the sofa and chairs. "Why don't you sit down. Would you like some coffee?"

Everyone declined the coffee. Alice and Snow took the couch, Willie and Keller the two chairs.

Willie smoothed out his tie. "That sounds like interesting stuff. If you don't mind my asking, I'm just curious what you do for a living. You own a sporting goods store or something like that?"

Keller smiled at Willie. "No, Lieutenant, nothing like that. I wish." He leaned forward and interlocked his fingers, his elbows resting on his knees. "I'm a structural engineer. Used to be, anyway. I got laid off three years ago when the construction boom started hitting the skids. I couldn't find a job anywhere. So when my unemployment ran out, I got a job driving a cab. I thought it would pay better than it does. I work sixty hours a week or more, and hardly make enough to get by. My wife makes more than me, and she's an accounting clerk for the water department."

Willie stuck out his chin, basking in the glory of his newly awarded rank. "What seems to be the problem?"

"The Taxicab Authority keeps putting more cabs and more drivers on the streets. They're worried that there aren't enough during the peak times, holidays and such. But the rest of the time, none of us get enough fares to make any money. I spend most of my shifts sitting in my cab, waiting in line. It's terrible. Now, I feel like I'm stuck in this job. I can't very well go back to school and get a different degree. I'm still paying off my school loan for my engineering degree—which seems to be completely worthless now."

"These are tough times alright," Willie said. "For everybody. Nine years ago, I myself fell upon hard times. I was—"

"Mr. Keller," Alice interrupted, "we don't want to take too much of your time. And we sincerely appreciate your willingness to talk to us on such short notice. You said that you could print out a list of members belonging to your club?"

"Oh yes. Let me get that." He got up, crossed to the stairway, and went upstairs.

After he was gone, Snow turned to Willie and snapped at him. "Stop asking impertinent questions. Keep your mouth shut. Now this guy thinks you're the section chief, and you're going off about your life on the street."

Willie shrugged and put up his hands. "I'm just trying to contribute to the conversation. It's an interesting topic. I got caught up in it."

Snow pointed at him. "If you open your mouth one more time, I'm going to send you out to sit in the car. And that's where you'll stay from now on."

He held up a palm facing Snow. "Alright. You're the boss. No problem."

Keller came back downstairs with four sheets of printer paper, stapled together. He walked over to Willie, handed it to him, and then sat down.

Willie looked through the three sheets, his face pinched in concentration. He nodded and handed the list to Alice.

"Is there anyone on this list who, in your opinion, exhibits aggressive or antisocial behavior of any sort?" Alice asked.

"Antisocial?" Keller asked.

"Mischievous," Snow said. "Possibly in a criminal way."

Keller's eyebrows shot up. "Oh, definitely. We have a member who spent twelve years in a Wyoming prison for manslaughter.

His name is Mike Mayfield. He was bowhunting deer out in the woods with his buddy. They got into an argument about money. The way Mayfield tells it, you'd think it was a shoot-out, face-to-face. He says he shot the guy through the chest with an arrow. But the truth is, the guy was walking out in front of Mayfield when he pulled an arrow out of his quiver and shot him in the back with it. Everybody he's met in this club—he's told that story to. He tells it a different way each time. He acts like he's proud of it."

Keller shifted his gaze to Willie. "You said that guy who got shot with the arrows—it happened at Hollywood RV Storage?"

Willie raised an eyebrow and looked at Snow.

"That's right," Snow said.

"This Mike Mayfield has a pickup camper. He was always hauling it up to the range with his girlfriend and her dog. I'm pretty sure I overheard him telling somebody he kept that camper at Hollywood RV Storage. Just my opinion, and I'd definitely appreciate it if you don't tell him I said so, but that guy gives me the impression he'd kill somebody for little or no reason—if he thought he could get away with it. Hell, he's already done it once."

CHAPTER 31

Lunch was at Sandwich Express on South Pecos Road. Snow laid out the printed sheets of names, and they scanned through them. There were two matches, other than Mike Mayfield, which wasn't surprising since many of the archery club members were bowhunters with recreational vehicles. But Mike Mayfield drew the focus of Snow's interest.

With lunch out of the way, the three of them piled into Snow's Sonata, Willie in the backseat, Alice in the front. She entered the address into the GPS, and Snow followed the turns announced by the computerized voice to the home off of South Lamb Boulevard.

The woman who answered the door, appearing to be in her late thirties, bore a striking resemblance to Judy Garland. She was petite, with brown hair, parted down the middle and combed into pigtails. They were held in place with strips of cotton, tied in bows. Her brown eyes were smaller, her nose slightly larger than the former star this woman was apparently trying to impersonate. But her blue cotton dress with the billowing sleeves brought the resemblance to a convincing match.

"Can I help you?" she asked.

Alice produced her badge, and the woman's eyes grew large. "Don't worry," Alice said. "There's nothing wrong. We'd like to talk to Mike Mayfield for a few minutes. Is he home?" "No," she said. "He moved out two weeks ago. What's this about?" "Do you mind if we come in?" Snow asked.

"Oh, I'm sorry," she said. She stepped back out of the doorway. "Have a seat."

Everyone sat down. A black Labrador lumbered into the room from the kitchen and sat down next to the woman. She reached her hand out to the dog and ran her fingers through the fur along the side of his neck.

"I'm Detective Alice James. And these are my associates, Jim Snow and William Hoffman."

She moved her red, leather slip-ons together under her chair and nodded at each of them. "My name is Melanie Larson." She looked at the dog. "This is Munchkin."

"That Munchkin got pretty big," Willie observed.

Alice and Snow shot him a look. Then Alice turned her gaze back to Melanie. "I like your dress. Did you make that yourself?"

Melanie looked at it and smiled. "Oh, this," she said. "You're probably wondering why I'm made up to look like Dorothy from *The Wizard of Oz*." Returning her gaze to Alice, she said, "This is what I wear at my job. I work at the Royal Palace Casino on the Strip. I'm a blackjack dealer. And some of us take turns getting up to sing and impersonate famous artists. I do Judy Garland. There's a guy who does Elvis, there's a Michael Jackson, Frank Sinatra, Paul McCartney, Cher, Dolly Parton, Madonna, Neil Diamond, and Betty Boop."

"Someone impersonates a cartoon character?" Snow said.

"She's pretty convincing," Melanie said. "Oh, and I also do Liza Minnelli sometimes. She was Judy Garland's daughter, so it's an easy transition for me."

"That's something I'd like to see," Willie said. "I wonder. If it wouldn't be any trouble, maybe you could give us a quick sample? I'd love to see that."

Alice put a hand up. "Oh no. That's not necessary."

Smiling, her fingers interlaced at her abdomen, Melanie rose out of her chair. "Why—it isn't any trouble at all," she said. "I enjoy performing, otherwise I wouldn't do it. Because I certainly don't make any money at it. What would you like to hear?"

"'Over the Rainbow,' of course," Willie said, beaming. "That's one of my all-time favorites."

With a serene expression slipping over her features, she looked up at the ceiling as though she could see through it, all the way to the land of Oz. She began slowly, working her way through the song, rooted to the same spot in front of her chair, her hands waving around, her eyes shifting between the three in her audience.

When she finished, the living room filled with applause.

"That was incredible," Snow said. "Have you ever considered singing professionally?"

Melanie sat back down. "I went to quite a few auditions, but nothing ever came of any of them. So I just go on performing at the casino. That's enough for me. I enjoy it and it gives me pleasure to see the reaction I get from the people who gather around to watch me. I don't think it's good to expect too much from whatever talent we have."

"That's a sensible goal," Alice said. "I don't think there are many people, once they discover they have talent, who can find it in themselves to limit their ambitions to any level below stardom. But then, I would imagine, there are probably a lot of people who never realize their talents at all."

"You're a poet, but don't know it," Willie said. "I guess that old saying sums it up nicely."

Alice and Snow stared at Willie for a moment. Melanie continued to pet her dog.

Turning her attention back to Melanie, Alice said, "Now, concerning the reason for our stopping by—this Mike Mayfield. Was he your roommate, or…?"

"He was my boyfriend. He was a bartender at the Royal Palace. We started dating three years ago, bought this house, and moved in together. Two weeks ago he got laid off and suddenly moved out."

"Do you know where he went?" Snow asked.

She shook her head and began petting Munchkin. "He wouldn't say. He just told me he was getting out of here. He said he'd had it with Las Vegas."

"If you don't mind my asking, did he offer to take you with him?" Alice said.

"No. Not really," she said. "But I wouldn't have gone. They've cut back on my hours, but at least I have a job. I'd be crazy to leave that. And that would be the end of my singing." She looked down at the floor, her eyes tearing up. "The problem now is this house." Her voice took on a slight quiver. "We both had pay cuts because of the reduced hours, and we started getting behind on the mortgage payments. This house is going into foreclosure pretty soon, and I don't know what to do. I suppose I could rent a small apartment somewhere, but what would happen to Munchkin? They don't allow large dogs, and he's twelve years old. Nobody would want to adopt him. They'll put him to sleep." She began to weep.

"I don't think it's quite that bad," Alice said, her voice low. "The rental market is in bad shape right now. There's a lot of property sitting empty. I'm sure you wouldn't have any problem negotiating with a desperate landlord. In fact, I happen to have a three-bedroom home available over near Horseman Park, close to where Flamingo Road ends. It's been empty for four months now. I've been having a terrible time with tenants. I've been forced to evict some of them; others move out in the middle of the night, after getting behind in their rent. It's been costing me thousands on constant renovations from the damage they cause. I think you'd like it. Munchkin would love the back yard. There's grass. I could let you move in with a small deposit—say three fifty—and let you have it for seven hundred per month."

Melanie brightened. "You're kidding. That would be wonderful."

Alice dug through her purse, came out with a business card, and handed it to her. "Think about it and give me a call if you decide you're interested. Now, about Mike Mayfield. We were told he has a pickup camper."

Melanie looked at the card and then set it on the arm of her chair. "Yes, it's kind of old. He's had it for more than ten years. We used it quite a bit on our days off—but what's this all about?"

Snow explained about the murder and his theory concerning the feasibility of a bow and arrows being used.

"You think Mike had something to do with it?" Melanie asked.

"Not much chance of it," Snow said. "But we're exploring all possibilities at this point."

"For one thing," she argued, "Mike wouldn't do anything like that. I mean, shoot somebody in the back for eight thousand dollars? No way. And for another, he wasn't even here. He left two weeks ago."

"But you don't know that he left the area for sure," Alice said.

"He said he was sick of Las Vegas, that he was getting out of here. If he were planning to stay in the area, he wouldn't have moved out."

"You were getting along alright?" Snow asked.

She looked down at her hands. "Well, you know, we were having a few minor problems. Everybody does. But I don't think he was leaving *me*. He was leaving because of the job situation. It sucks."

Willie nodded. "It sucks everywhere."

"Do you know if he took his camper with him when he left?" Snow asked.

"I don't know," she said. "He threw his clothes, and whatever else would fit, into his truck and left."

"His camper wasn't on the bed of his truck when he loaded up?"

"No."

"He took all of his archery equipment?" Snow asked.

"Yes. He has two bows, a bunch of different arrows, and a quiver. He wouldn't leave that behind."

"What does he use them for?"

"Target practice. Hunting rabbits."

Snow looked down at his hands, thought for a moment, and then brought his gaze back up to Melanie. "Did you know that he served time for killing a man with a bow and arrow?"

"Of course," she said. "He wasn't the sort of person to hide anything. He told me all about it. But it was self-defense. The other guy threatened him. The guy was threading an arrow to shoot him with. But Mike beat him to it. He's really fast."

Alice and Snow exchanged a knowing look. Munchkin gave Melanie a bored look and then lay down on the carpet.

"Is there anyone who might know how to get in touch with Mr. Mayfield?" Alice asked.

"If I don't have that information, I doubt anyone would," she said. "But he has a close friend that he was always hanging out with. His name is Frank Hale. I have his address and phone number, if you'd like to talk to him."

CHAPTER 32

Frank Hale's phone rang for half a minute with no answer. Alice tried his cell number. He came on the line after three rings. She identified herself, explained about the murder investigation, and asked if they could stop by and spend a few minutes of his time. He was on the east side of the man-made lake at Sunset Park, he told them. He was fishing for trout, but they were welcome to stop by and chat for as long as they wanted. He told them to look for a fifty-five-year-old man with a black cowboy hat, white handlebar mustache, blue jeans, long-sleeve green shirt, and brown cowboy boots. He said he was sitting in a lawn chair with a fishing rod in his hand, and they couldn't miss him.

They found him, as he had described, sitting in a folding lawn chair positioned in the shade of a pine tree, near the edge of the cement bank. Behind him, there was a jogging path that continued on around the border of the tiny lake. In front of him, rising up out of the middle of the water, an oval-shaped concrete island spewed streams of water into the air in every direction. Covered with gravel, an assortment of small trees growing up out of it, a variety of ducks, geese, and other birds waddled around squawking and screeching at each other. Hale sat with his legs crossed, a fishing pole resting on his lap. He gave them a wave. Introductions were made.

"Had any luck?" Willie asked.

Hale shook his head. "Nah, it's usually pretty slow. You can't expect much from a man-made lake in a county park. I just come here mostly to get some fresh air and relax."

Snow looked around the lake and noticed other fishermen scattered about, on both sides of the lake, equipped with coolers, tackle boxes, and rod-holders, screwed into the ground. "I didn't know they stocked this pond."

Hale gripped his cowboy hat by the front of the brim and lifted it off his head. He smoothed his silver hair back and set it back down. His voice was deep and gravelly. His words came slow and easy. "Oh yeah. They put trout in here during the cooler months. Catfish in the summer. You can do pretty good right after they stock it, but it slows down gradually until they dump in another load. You can't beat the price, though—it's free." He chuckled. "I've lived here since 1980, and I didn't discover this park until five years ago. I'll bet you most of the people who live in Las Vegas have never even been here. People get all wrapped up in their day-to-day lives; they don't even take the time to explore their environment. You go to work, come home, cook dinner, do the dishes and some laundry, watch the television, go to bed. Same thing every day. I'll bet there are a lot of people who know more about this city than the ones who live here. And I'm not talking about the usual tourists who go straight to the Strip and stay there until they leave. Or if they do decide to take a little side trip, they go to the Hoover Dam, and that's it." He looked up at Snow. "You ever been to Valley of Fire?"

Snow shook his head.

"It's fifty miles north of here, not far from the interstate. I go up there several times each year to do some hiking, or just drive around. Beautiful formations. It reminds me a lot of Red Rock Canyon, but it's different. There's hardly ever anyone there. I'll bet you if you stopped people along the Strip and asked them if they've heard of it, nine times out of ten, they'll ask you if it's a casino." He chuckled again.

"What brought you out here?" Alice asked.

Hale leaned back in his lawn chair. "That's a bit of a long story," he said. I grew up in Omaha. Used to play the horses at the local bush tracks all over Nebraska. I did alright at it, but I started reading up on blackjack. Bought a couple of books on it. Card counting books. I thought maybe I could do that for a living. Others have, so I figured I could if I worked at it. So I studied the strategies. Memorized them and practiced counting. After a few weeks, I got to where I could keep an accurate count running in my head without losing it.

"So I took a week off from my bartending job and flew out here. I was betting ten bucks when the deck was bad, and worked up to forty when it was good. I made over a thousand dollars during that week. That convinced me I could do it for a living. So I moved out here, got an apartment, started playing. And it all went to hell.

"The pit bosses all got to know me in no time, and they'd get the dealers to shuffle every time I bet high. Some of them told me to leave the casino. I lasted five months at it, and then went back to bartending."

"Is that where you met Mike Mayfield?" Snow asked.

Keller nodded. "We worked a lot of shifts together. Started hanging out together after work, shooting pool or just sitting around watching football, drinking beer."

"What about archery?" Alice asked.

"Yeah, a little. I have my own bow. And we'd go shoot once in a while. But I'm not into it like Mike is, with the tournaments, the rabbit hunting, all of that. I can understand why there isn't much interest in it as a sport. It's pretty boring."

"When's the last time you saw Mr. Mayfield?" Snow asked.

"Two weeks ago. They were cutting back at the casino. Used to be two of us working the bar each shift. They cut it back to one. Mike never got along very well with management, so he was an easy choice for them.

"They gave him his check and he went home, packed up, and left. He didn't even stop by to say adios. He called me and said he was leaving town."

"Did he say where he was going?" Alice asked.

Keller shook his head. "He said he was heading northwest. Said he'd know where to stop when he got there." He gave Alice a sidelong look. "Even if he were still here, I don't think he's the sort to murder someone in cold blood for money."

"He did it before," Snow said.

Keller swung his head to Snow. "He didn't kill that guy because of money. That was just a sudden burst of uncontrolled rage. It's pretty easy to do something like that when you've got a lethal weapon in your hand and you stop thinking for a few seconds. And that's all it takes. You know what I mean?"

Snow nodded.

Keller turned back around. "There's a guy I know who I think you might want to check into, though."

"Who is that?" Snow said.

"There's a small neighborhood bar on Nellis, just south of Charleston Boulevard. It's called the Wishing Well. Mike and I have always hung out there. They've got two regulation-size pool tables. The regulars go there to shoot pool for money. They don't charge for the tables.

"One of the regulars there is a guy by the name of Danny. Young guy, late twenties. He's always talking about bowhunting to anybody who'll listen. Mike and he would sit there for hours talking technique, bragging, what-not. This guy was always bragging about poaching deer. He said he was cited for it a few years ago in Montana."

"Why would we be interested in talking to him about this investigation?" Alice said.

"Nothing specific," Keller said. "He's just a creepy sort of guy—gave me the impression he'd do anything for money. And I know he's got a travel trailer parked at that Hollywood RV Storage. He's mentioned that a few times."

"Do you know what his last name is?" Alice said.

Keller shook his head. "Just Danny. That's all I can tell you. You know how it is in a neighborhood bar. Everybody knows everybody. But nobody cares about your last name."

Back in the car, Snow pulled out the printout from Hollywood RV Storage and looked through the list of over eight hundred names. There were fourteen with first names of Dan or Daniel. Those were a lot of people to contact. It could take days to interview all of them. A visit to Danny's favorite watering hole would be the shorter route that might lead to the man.

Snow fired up the Sonata and pulled out of the parking lot, heading east on Sunset Road.

CHAPTER 33

The Wishing Well was an appropriate name for Snow's current destination. It's easy to get discouraged when you're chasing leads that take you to dead ends, or crossroads, where you can chose to turn or continue on, knowing that, no matter which direction you chose, you'll probably have to turn around sooner or later. Conducting a murder investigation can be like being lost, wandering around a strange city without a map.

Now that Jim Snow was navigating outside the box with the assistance of a talented investigator, who had a badge and a gun, the dynamics had changed dramatically. Though she was no longer assigned to the case, the citizens of Las Vegas didn't know that. Her position as a member of Metro's Homicide Section provided access to information that would otherwise require wrangling, cajoling, and begging to collect. Snow realized her use of authority was unauthorized and subject to scrutiny by her supervisors. No doubt she knew this as well—yet she took the risk because it was a small risk. And the payoff far outweighed it. This was the basic principle a good poker player adhered to. Snow's only hope, however, was that his luck with this case would be better than his recent luck with the cards.

The Wishing Well was a comfortable tavern with a hardwood floor and a dark wooden bar, with nicks and scrapes that appeared to have been varnished over and polished many times. A full-length mirror filled most of the wall behind the bar. The walls were covered with cedar paneling, on which were mounted an assortment of neon beer signs.

Along the wall, opposite the bar, stood two regulation pool tables, with the balls racked up, ready to break. Adjacent to those were a jukebox and a row of three pinball machines. Besides the seating available on the stools in front of the bar, there were two booths and a scattering of small tables.

It was a few minutes after four p.m. on a Wednesday when Jim Snow, the lady, and the tramp strode in through the front door. Two men wearing dark blue work pants and long-sleeve gray shirts sporting white name patches sat at the far end of the bar. Three stools down from them, perched with her legs wide, her forearms resting on the bar, a middle-aged woman took a drink from the cocktail glass she held between her hands. With disheveled platinum-blonde hair and droopy eyes, she appeared to have just crawled out of bed.

Snow and his associates approached the bartender. He was a tall, lanky man with short brown hair, bald on top. He wore a white dress shirt with the sleeves rolled up and a short, black apron. He nodded and smiled.

Alice flashed her badge. "I'm Detective Alice James, and these are my associates, Jim Snow and Will Hoffman. We need to ask you a few questions concerning one of your patrons," she said. Snow noticed her introduction of Willie's name was getting shorter each time. He wondered if it would be long before she referred to him as W.H.

The bartender produced his hand. "I'm Larry Wilcox, owner and proprietor." Hands were shaken all around. "Would you like anything to drink?"

The three of them exchanged glances.

"What the hell, it's cocktail hour," Snow said. "I'll have a Wild Turkey on the rocks."

Alice ordered a gin and tonic, and Willie a Tom Collins. They slid their barstools back from the bar and sat down as Wilcox busied himself behind the bar with their drinks.

"Nice place you've got here," Willie said, his eyes surveying the row of liquor bottles arranged in front of the mirror. "It has a homey feel to it. How long have you owned the place?"

"Twelve years," Wilcox said. "I used to shoot pool for a living when I was younger. I spent almost ten years traveling the tournament circuits. I had high hopes for that profession when I first started out. You know how it is when you're twenty-three and you think you can conquer the world. But I peaked three years into it. Never finished in the top five in any tournament, ever, and I barely made enough money to scrape by on. The constant traveling around, living in hotel rooms—it was a lonely, miserable life. But I kept at it because I was convinced it would get better." He shook his head.

"I had an uncle on my mother's side," he continued, "who used to own this bar. He started having heart problems and couldn't handle the long hours anymore. So he wanted to sell it. It was pretty run-down and grungy. It had a single seven-foot, coin-operated pool table that had seen better days. So he gave me a good deal on the place. I took over the payments, and he floated the rest. I gutted it, put in new paneling, those two full-size pool tables, refinished the bar, and here I am." He nodded. "And, I have to admit, it's not a bad way to make a living."

He set the drinks on the bar. Snow slid a twenty toward him, and he waved it off.

Alice took a sip of her gin and tonic. "Do you still shoot pool?"

Wiping his hands on a towel, Wilcox shook his head. "Not much anymore. When I opened the place, I was playing all the time. Everybody who came in here wanted to challenge me. I'd give them ten-to-one odds. If they won, they'd get ten bucks; if I won, I'd get a buck. I think it helped to bring in new customers for a while. They seemed to like the idea of trying to beat a former pro, when all it would cost them was a dollar.

"But it took away too much of my time from serving drinks. I hired an extra bartender to help out, but that wasn't cost-effective. So I quit playing, and now I just stay behind the bar where I belong."

"We talked to a fellow by the name of Frank Hale, who comes in here a lot," Snow began.

Wilcox propped his arms up against the bar. "Sure. Frank. Good guy."

Snow explained about the murder. "We're grabbing at straws, chasing down any possibilities that might turn out to bear fruit. Mr. Hale mentioned a regular who comes in here, said his name is Danny..."

"Oh yeah, sure, Danny," Wilcox said. "Good guy."

Snow wondered idly if there were any regulars of this bar who weren't considered "good guys."

The peroxide blonde on the middle stool perked up suddenly. "Larry," she croaked. "I'm ready for another one."

He scooped some ice into a glass, positioned two plastic drink dispensers over it, and filled it with the mixture. He grabbed a fresh napkin and set the drink in front of her.

"Put it on my tab, honey," she cooed, using the sexiest voice she could muster. Then, stirring her drink, she went back to admiring the reflection staring back at her in the mirror, probably wondering how many more drinks it would take until she would see the face of a princess.

The bartender came back to his former position in front of Snow. Willy picked up his drink and walked over to the nearest pool table, set his glass on the rail, and selected a cue from the rack on the wall. He straightened the balls, removed the rack, and drove the cue ball into them, scattering them and sinking two of them.

Alice and Snow had turned to watch, wondering what he was up to. Willie worked his way around the table, lining up shots and sinking them, one after another.

They turned their heads back to Wilcox.

"He gets bored easy," Snow commented.

Wilcox shrugged. "Hey, when you're the boss, you can do whatever you want. Right?"

"I guess so," Alice said.

Snow took a drink of whiskey, swirled the ice around in the glass, and set it down. "So this guy Danny…do you happen to know what his last name is?"

Wilcox shook his head. "I don't know what anybody's last name is, except, maybe, for our nation's president. Last I remember, it was Johnson. Is he still in office?"

Alice and Snow chuckled. Behind them, billiard balls cracked and caromed off the cushions.

Alice asked, "What can you tell us about him?"

Wilcox sighed. "He's in his late twenties, about my height, slender build. Brown hair. Some sort of mechanic, because most of the time he comes in here wearing a mechanic's uniform with a name patch that says *Danny* on it. Or he used to. He said he got laid off. I need a little help around here, so I've been slipping him a few bucks to stock the bar and the coolers, unpack boxes, clean up now and then. You know. It helps him, and it keeps me from having to hire somebody part time."

"Anything else?"

Wilcox looked over at Willie and thought for a moment. "He's into bowhunting big time. Always talking about that. Hunting elk, deer, rabbits. Mostly up in the northwest. You won't find many deer around here." He laughed. "He used to live up there, Wyoming, Montana. He seems to me to be a survivalist sort of guy. Always talking about living out in the wilds in his trailer. Hunting for food, the way the Indians used to. He didn't put much stock in game ordinances. I got the impression he did a lot of poaching, when he could get away with it. He's a pretty smart guy. I think he could get along just about anywhere, using his wits."

Snow took another drink. Then he threw the question out there: "You think he might be the sort to kill somebody for money? Say eight thousand dollars?"

Wilcox pondered the idea. Nodded. "I don't like to speak badly of anybody, especially one of my customers. But to be honest, I believe he would. In fact, I don't think it would take that much. In fact, he's the kind of guy that had he been born a hundred and fifty years ago, they'd have been writing dime novels about him. That's what I think."

"Do you know where he lives?"

"Not exactly. He did mention, more than once, an apartment he said he was living in. I'm pretty sure he said it was in a complex on the corner of Sahara and Winkelman Avenue. That's all I can tell you. Sorry."

Snow finished his drink and stood up. "That's okay. You've been a help, and we appreciate the drinks. I think I may have to stop in here sometime and see if I can refurbish my billiard-playing ability. It's been twenty years."

"It's like riding a bicycle. It comes back pretty quick," Wilcox said.

Alice finished her drink, got up, and looked at Snow, smiling. "I'll give you three-to-one I can beat you, Mr. Snow," she said.

"I didn't know you shot pool," Snow said.

"Every now and then," she said. "I have a table in my family room. Since I'm the only family living in my home, other than Stripes the cat, I decided to make my own use of it. I'll have to invite you over some night to show you how the game is played." She touched his arm with her fingertips.

Snow felt an electrical charge run up his spine. An image of her sitting on the rail of her pool table began to form in his mind. He shoved it aside before it could play forward.

He asked Alice for a business card. She pulled one out of her purse. Snow printed his name and cell phone number on the back of it. Then he handed it to Larry Wilcox. "If Danny comes in here, could you do me a favor and give me a call?"

Wilcox smiled and nodded. "Will do. Good luck to you folks, and don't be strangers. Stop in again sometime, when it isn't business-related."

"Looking forward to it," Snow said.

They shook the bartender's hand again.

"W.H.," Snow said over his shoulder. Then he snapped a finger next to his left ear and pointed at the door. "Rack 'em up and put the cue away. Let's go."

"Shit," Willie muttered. "I was on the road to victory. Just a few balls shy of kicking my own butt."

CHAPTER 34

There were two apartment complexes across the street from each other at the corner of Sahara and Winkelman Avenue. Desert Springs was on the south side, and Mountain View Apartments was on the north side of Sahara Avenue.

Snow turned the Sonata into the driveway leading to the rental office of Mountain View Apartments. He pulled into a space designated for future residents and shut off the engine.

He looked at his watch. "It's four fifty-five," he said. "What time do these rental offices usually close?"

"I don't know," Alice said. "It varies. Usually five or six."

"We don't have much time left today, and I don't want to have to wait until tomorrow morning." He turned his head toward Alice. "Why don't we split up? You check this complex. Willie and I will try the one across the street."

He leaned forward and pulled his notebook out of his back pocket and flipped though the notes until he came to the page listing the fourteen names beginning with Dan or Daniel who were listed on the printout from the RV storage lot.

He handed the notebook to Alice. "Write these names down, and have the apartment manager check them against their list of tenants. If you get a match, then he's the guy."

"Then what?" Willie asked from the backseat.

"Then we move forward from there," Snow said. "Let's go. We can leave the car here. Willie and I can walk over to the Desert Springs."

Alice took a notepad and a pen out from her purse and started scribbling names.

The rental office of Desert Springs was busy. A young Middle Eastern couple sat in front of the manager's desk, looking over brochures and floor plans. At another desk, a few feet away, two Chinese women in their early twenties sat patiently waiting their turn.

With a head of auburn hair streaming down to her shoulders and a face covered with freckles, the apartment manager was leaning over the scattered literature covering her desk, a pen in her right hand, the other waving around in the air, helping to accentuate her sales pitch.

"So there is no storage on any of the balconies belonging to the two bedrooms," the male half of the Middle Eastern couple said.

"That's right," the manager replied. "Only the one bedrooms have storage on the balconies."

"I don't understand why this is so," the man said. "Why do not they both have storage? This does not sound fair to me, that the smaller apartment would have it, and we will be paying more for the two bedroom, yet will have no storage on the balcony."

"The two bedrooms have a pantry," the manager explained. "The single bedrooms don't. That's the reason."

"That doesn't sound like a very good reason to me," the man insisted. "They are two completely different things. One is for storing canned goods and other items that are used in the kitchen. The other is used for storing things that will be used on the patio and out of doors."

"Look," she said, her words growing sharper. "These apartments are the way they are. They're already built. There is nothing I can do to change them to suit your needs. If you rent a one bedroom, you'll get the storage space that comes with the balcony. If you rent the two bedroom, you don't."

"But the one bedroom will be too small for us," he said. "Because it only has one closet in which to put both of our clothes and other things. And when we are having a child, then the child will need its own bedroom."

The manager suddenly became aware of the two new additions to the office. She looked up at Willie and Snow. "I'm sorry," she said. "We're closed. It's after five, and we close at five. You'll have to come back tomorrow."

Snow started to open his mouth, but before he could say anything, Willie pulled back the lower right half of his suit coat. Snow looked down to see what looked like a toy silver sheriff's badge, shaped like a star. It was pinned to a slab of leather, which appeared to have been cut from the outer portion of a cheap wallet, folded in half and tucked into his suit pants. From a distance it looked somewhat impressive.

The manager's eyes widened. "Oh. Can you wait just a minute, and I'll be right with you?"

"No problem, ma'am," Willie said. He let his suit jacket fall over the badge and folded his arms.

Snow rolled his eyes and shook his head.

The manager continued to argue with the prospective tenants seated at her desk, finally convincing them to try another complex, perhaps the one across the street, which she was pretty sure didn't close their rental office until six. They got up and left.

Rushing back and forth between desks, she then produced some paperwork for the two Chinese women, check-marked the spaces requiring a signature, and left them to read everything over.

Back at her own desk, blowing out a breath of air, she fell into her chair, interlocked her fingers on her desk, and looked up at Willie. "Okay. Sorry to make you wait. What can I help you with?"

"We're sorry to bother you so late in the day," Snow blurted out, in order to cut Willie off. "This should only take a minute. Then we'll get out of your hair."

"That's alright," she said. Then she motioned toward the two seats in front of her desk. "Why don't you make yourselves comfortable."

They crossed to the empty chairs and sat down.

"It looks like you're having a rough day," Snow said.

"You don't know the half of it," the woman said. "It's hectic enough in here as it is. But on top of that, the leasing agent called in sick this morning, and there's no one to take her place, so I have to handle all of the prospective renters who come in here, along with everything else that requires my attention during the day. And people are supposed to make an appointment to see the apartments, but they just ignore that and come in here from out of the blue, expecting to be given a tour. Well, it's just not going to happen. You know?"

They both nodded.

"You know," she continued, "what frustrates me the most is that I didn't come to Las Vegas to work as an apartment manager. I could have done that in Wichita."

Sensing she needed to hear the question, Snow offered it: "What was it that brought you to our fine city?"

"I wanted to be a dancer," she said. "A professional. I was involved in ballet when I was living in Wichita. We had a small local ballet company that put on performances periodically. It was nonprofit, and we mainly did it for fun, performing for a few hundred people, sometimes more. Well, everybody told me I had too much talent to waste in a place like Wichita. They all said I should move to Las Vegas and become a dancer. I thought, what the heck. You only live once—so I did it. I quit my job at the bank, sold all my furniture and anything that wouldn't fit in my minivan, and just moved here.

"I went to a dance school. Finished that. Then I started going to auditions, but could never make the cut. I can't believe how good these dancers are here in Las Vegas. There are thousands of them. And that makes for a lot of competition. I mean, there are a lot of really good dancers, like me, who aren't even working as dancers. We're all doing other things, like working as a waitress, clerk, or apartment manager." She raised her eyebrows and pointed to herself with both hands.

"That's too bad," Snow said.

"Yeah, but I'm not giving up," she insisted. "The ones who succeed eventually are the ones who never give up. Never say die. Uh-uh. Not this girl."

"Good for you," Willie said. "Hang in there. You'll make it."

She put her hands on the desk and sighed. "But enough about me. What can I do for you?" Her voice seemed a little brighter.

Snow handed her the notebook, open to the page with the fourteen names listed. "Can you tell me if any of these people reside here?"

"Sure. No problem." She took the notebook and started punching commands into her computer.

A few minutes later, she looked up at Snow. "Nope. None of these people are current residents here." She started to hand the notebook back, but then she stopped. "Wait a minute." She looked at the list again.

She pointed at one of the names. "This guy. Daniel Guardino." She punched more keys and studied the monitor. "Yes, he's the one..."

"The one what?" Snow asked.

"Daniel Guardino. He moved out a little over three weeks ago. No notice. He just suddenly packed up and moved out. Plus he was a month behind in his rent. He put his apartment keys in an envelope and dropped them in the mail slot after the office was closed."

"Did he leave a note in the envelope with a forwarding address or anything?"

She shook her head. "No, just the keys. But he wrote something on the envelope."

"What was that?" Snow asked.

"It was pretty brief," she said. "It read, *Apartment 326. I'm out of here. Kiss my ass. Best wishes for a bright future.*"

Snow winced. "Not much information there," he said.

Outside the office, walking toward the entrance to the complex, Willie turned to Snow. "You ever notice, Jim—it seems like everybody has an interesting story to tell?"

"I noticed," Snow agreed. "Somebody ought to write a book."

"Somebody did," Willie said. "Studs Terkel. Back in the early seventies. The title is *Working*. It's almost six hundred pages of people in all lines of working, talking about their jobs and the effects their chosen professions have on their lives. He wrote other books too. One about the Depression, World War II—all of them written the same way—from the perspective of the common man."

He shook his head. "You won't find anything like that published these days. Nobody wants to read about the common man today. If you aren't a prominent entertainer of some sort or a politician, nobody cares. If you ask me, the average person leads a hell of a lot more interesting life than some bureaucrat in Washington. But those guys are all writing their memoirs. I think most of what they write is fiction—just an attempt to glorify their existence. Bunch of greedy, narcissistic assholes, if you ask me."

Snow had no response. He'd stopped listening to Willie's rambling.

His mind was deep in thought.

CHAPTER 35

Alice was sitting inside the car when Willie and Snow returned.

"No luck," she said.

"That's okay," Snow said. "We got him." He slid into the driver seat and slammed the car door. He turned to Alice, smiling. "In fact, not only do we have the guy's last name—I think we could have the perpetrator."

Alice arched her eyebrows and turned toward Snow. "I must be missing something. What have you got?"

"You are missing something," Snow said. He opened the notebook and flipped a few pages. "Here it is: Daniel Guardino. Checked into the Sunrise Inn the day after the murder. His apartment manager, across the street, told us he moved out of his apartment more than three weeks ago. His travel trailer is two spaces over from the scene of the murder. He has the battery on his trailer hooked up to a solar panel to keep it charged. He has a generator. You want to know where he's been living for the last three weeks? In that trailer. I think he was in his trailer the night Bob was killed. He heard the transaction taking place, heard Steve Helm counting out the money. Helm told me the door to Bob's trailer was wide open."

"Maybe he was living with a girlfriend or someone else during that time," Alice said.

"Then why move into the motel the day after the murder?"

"It could be a coincidence," Alice said. "He could have had an argument with the person he was staying with and moved to the motel."

Snow considered this. "That's possible," he said. "But I have more."

"I'm listening," Alice said.

"The crime scene analyst said that Bob Williams's rear tire was punctured with a small screwdriver or an ice pick. Well, I don't think a screwdriver, no matter how small, would puncture a tire that isn't moving along at a good speed. And what would an ice pick be doing on the ground inside an RV storage lot?

"This Danny Guardino is an auto mechanic. I'll bet his tools are inside his trailer, and that he has a pretty good assortment of screwdrivers, being that he's a mechanic."

Alice thought for a moment. "But you said you didn't think it was a screwdriver that punctured the tire."

Snow's heart was racing now. "I don't. But do you know what is usually included in large set of screwdrivers?"

"I've never purchased a large set of screwdrivers," she said.

"Well, I have," Snow said. "I have a set in one of my tool-boxes at home."

"So what is it?" Alice said.

"An awl."

"You mean the thing you use to punch holes in leather?"

"That's one type. This is called a scratch awl. It looks like an ice pick, only thicker. And it has a handle like a screwdriver. Guardino probably wedged that under the rear tire so Bob would have to change it after Helm left with the trailer."

"But what if Steve Helm hadn't left? What if he had stayed to help with the tire?"

"Then, I suppose, Bob wouldn't be dead. And Danny Guardino would be out an awl."

Alice worked this over in her mind.

"Okay," she said. "That all sounds plausible. But if Danny was living in his trailer on the storage lot, how did he get in and out through the gate without his entry code showing up on the computer in the manager's office?"

Snow's heart rate slowed. He sighed. "Yeah," he said. "That's a big fly in the ointment. I didn't think of that."

He turned his head to Willie in the backseat. "Willie, you sure you didn't see anybody coming or going while you were there?"

"No," Willie said. "I told you. I come in, go straight to that boat, crawl in it, and go to sleep. But I couldn't hear the gate opening and closing from there. It's too far away. So I can't tell you anything about that."

"But what about that corner of the fence with the bungee cords?" Snow pressed. "You could have heard somebody screwing around with that fence, right?"

"Sure, that boat was close enough to hear that, but I never heard anyone coming in through there while I was there. But like I told you, I wasn't there that night. I was in the wash on the night of the murder."

"What about that fence, Willie?" Snow said. "Were you the one who took it apart and put it back together with those bungee cords? I need to know."

Willie hesitated and then answered. "Alright, I'll admit it. I was the one who did that. I found a whole bag of them in that boat. I seriously doubt anybody but me has ever gone through that section of fence. And that's the truth."

CHAPTER 36

Danny Guardino's pickup was nowhere to be seen in the parking area of the Sunrise Inn. Alice and Snow went into the motel office to see if he was still registered. The Korean woman working the counter checked and confirmed it.

"Now what?" Alice asked.

Snow pondered this for a moment. "No sense all three of us waiting around for this guy to show up. We'll leave Willie here to watch for him. I want to take a look at the opener for that gate at the storage lot."

Snow drove with a sense of urgency, yet keeping his speed no more than ten miles over the speed limit. They were losing daylight fast.

Arriving at Hollywood RV Storage at shortly after six p.m., Snow entered the police code for the gate and drove inside. The office was locked. Norma Hecker had gone home at five. Snow parked the Hyundai, and they got out and walked over to the gate opener. They stood looking at it.

There wasn't much to see. The chain drive unit was completely enclosed by a green rectangular cover, the front surface of which had a slot. There was a hasp sticking through the slot.

And a new padlock was attached to the hasp, preventing the cover from being removed. On each side of the cover, a large opening provided access for the chain to run freely through it as the gate opened and closed. The chain was covered with grease and grime.

Snow looked at Alice. "You see what I see?"

"Not much to look at," she said. "It's completely covered and secure. But this thing looks like it must be at least twenty years old, and it's got a brand-new padlock."

"Indeed," Snow said. "Why would they put a new padlock on the cover?"

"Maybe the old one corroded so bad, it wouldn't open. So they replaced it. Or maybe they lost the keys."

"Could be," Snow said. "I'm going to find out." He slipped Norma Hecker's business card out of his wallet, opened his cell phone, and called the pager number printed on the card. He entered his cell number and snapped the phone shut, waiting.

A minute later his phone chirped. He opened it and pushed the connect button.

"Norma," he said. "This is Jim Snow. I'm here at the storage lot with Detective Alice James. I'm sorry to bother you, but I was wondering if you could stop by here for a few minutes and help us out with something."

Ten minutes later, Norma Hecker pulled into the lot. She got out of her car and ambled over to the gate opener.

Snow pointed at the padlock. "Do you have the key to that lock? We'd like to take the cover off and have a look inside."

"Oh sure. No problem," she said. "It's in the office. Let me go get that for you."

She came back with two small keys held together on a wire key ring. She handed them to Snow. He looked at them. They were both stamped with the name of the lock company, which matched the name printed on the padlock.

He squatted down in front of the padlock, slid the key in, and wiggled it. But it wouldn't turn. He tried the other key. It was an exact duplicate of the first key, and it wouldn't turn in the lock either.

Snow stood up. "Are you sure these are the keys to this lock?"

Norma looked up at Snow. "Yes. Those are the only ones in the desk," she said. "I don't understand why they don't work."

"They don't go with this padlock," Snow said. "Did somebody change this lock that you know of? Maybe they put the keys someplace and didn't tell you."

"The only person who would do that would be the owner," she said. "I can ask him."

Snow put his hand on her arm. "Would you please?"

"No problem," she said.

She got out her cell phone, punched some buttons, and held it to her ear.

"Hello, Al?" she said. "This is Norma, and I'm at the lot with the detectives who are investigating the murder. We're standing in front of that green box that opens the gate. And it has what looks like a brand-new padlock on it. I got the keys out of the desk in the office, and they won't open the lock. The detectives would like to know if we replaced the padlock recently...no... no...okay..." She took the phone away from her ear and looked at Snow. "He said he never replaced that lock. He said the last time he had the cover off this thing was two years ago. And the padlock is more than twenty years old."

Snow nodded. "Ask him if he would mind if we remove this padlock so we can have a look inside the cover."

She put the phone back to her ear and asked him, and then she turned back toward Snow. "He said go ahead. He wants to know if you want him to come out here."

"No, that won't be necessary," Snow said.

Norma relayed the message and closed her phone.

"How will we get the lock off?" Alice asked.

"Usually these cheaper padlocks will pop open when you give them a good whack with a hammer, but I don't want to damage the hasp. We could drive to Home Depot and get a bolt cutter, but the thing is…" Snow paused. He rubbed his chin with his fingertips. "The thing is, Guardino would need a way to actuate the opener, without taking the cover off, when he's outside the gate. How would he do that?"

Snow stepped around to the side of the cover that faced away from the gate. He squatted down and peered into the chain opening. He reached inside and pulled out a small toggle switch, attached to two thin wires.

Standing up, he pulled the switch toward the chain-link fence, pulling it all the way through an opening between the wires of the fence.

Snow flipped the switch, and the gate began to open.

He looked at Alice and grinned. "This is how he got in and out of here without entering his code. He broke the padlock off and replaced it with his own lock of the same brand. Then he wired this bypass switch to the terminal block inside there. He keeps the switch and wiring stuffed inside the cover so nobody will notice it. He's probably got some sort of flexible, claw-type grabber tool to reach in through the fence and pull the wiring and switch out from inside the cover."

"You don't think that switch could have come with the gate opener?" Alice said.

"No way. Look at it. The switch is brand-new. This is jury-rigged to the terminal block."

"But how would he know how to hook it up?"

"Easy," Snow said. "Once you take the cover off, you'll no doubt find the manufacturer's name and model number. I'll bet you can go to their Web site and download the owner's manual and installation instructions for this thing. I expect there are two control wires that come from the keypad, and that circuit would normally be open. He connected this bypass switch to the same terminals as those two wires. Hit the switch, it closes the circuit. The gate opens. And you'll probably find Danny Guardino's fingerprints all over this thing."

"That won't prove he murdered anybody," Alice said.

"No, it won't," Snow agreed. "But I'll bet the evidence is inside his trailer. I'll bet the awl and the bow and arrows are in that trailer. Possibly even most, if not all, of the money. And there should be trace evidence from the tire on the awl, and possibly Bob's DNA on two of the arrows."

"Okay," Alice said. "Now we find Danny and get a search warrant for the trailer. That means we'll need to get Mel involved. And he might not cooperate."

"That's not a problem," Snow said. "That's why he has a supervisor."

CHAPTER 37

At the Sunrise Inn, Alice and Snow found Willie sauntering back and forth on the sidewalk in front of Danny Guardino's motel room. Snow told him to get in the car.

They parked a short distance away in the motel parking lot, facing forward, and waited.

A little over an hour passed. Then Snow's cell phone chirped. He pulled it out and answered it. The call was from Larry Wilcox at the Wishing Well. Danny had just walked in.

Snow started the car and pulled out of the motel lot.

Business at the Wishing Well had picked up. Half the stools at the bar were occupied, along with three of the tables and one of the booths. Both pool tables were going full steam.

They found him sitting at the bar nursing a draft beer. Wearing a wrinkled shirt and blue jeans, he turned his shaggy head toward Snow as they drew near.

His eyes widened, and he smiled. "Hey. How's it going?" he said to Snow.

Larry Wilcox moved along the bar toward them. "What'll you guys have?" he asked.

"I think we're good," Snow said.

Wilcox smiled and nodded, and then he went to the far end of the bar.

Snow turned his attention back to Guardino. "It's going pretty good, Danny," he said.

Guardino narrowed his eyes. "How do you know my name?"

"Danny Guardino. Right?" Snow said.

He nodded and stared at Snow with his mouth open. "Yeah." He shifted his gaze to Alice, then Willie and back to Snow. He said nothing else, just waited.

A few of the customers at the bar had turned their attention to the conversation, and they sat watching with interest.

"Would you mind if we step outside for a minute? We're still working on that investigation at the storage lot, and we just need you to help clear up a few things for us."

"Oh. Sure. Not a problem," he said.

The four of them walked outside and stood illuminated in the glow of the streetlight above them. It was completely dark out now. But it was still warm, the lingering effects of an Indian summer holding the evening temperature above seventy degrees.

Snow shoved his hands deep into the front pockets of his jeans. Looking down at his loafers, he said, "Danny, it looks to us as though you may have been living in your travel trailer at Hollywood RV Storage. Is that true?"

His eyes larger now, his mouth still hanging open, Guardino looked at Alice, then Willie. "Who are you guys?" he asked.

"Oh, I'm sorry," Snow said. He pulled a hand out of his pocket and pointed it at Alice. "This is Detective Alice James, Metro Homicide."

She pulled her badge out of her purse and displayed it in front of Guardino's face.

Then Guardino looked at Willie.

"Don't worry about me," Willie said. "I'm nobody. I just came from church."

Guardino turned his head back toward Snow. "What makes you think I've been living in my trailer? It's against the rules. They don't allow it. I'm living in a motel right now."

Snow shoved his free hand back into his pocket and looked at Guardino. "We know, Danny. You moved into the motel the day after the murder. You moved out of your apartment three weeks ago. And you've been living in your RV on that storage lot during the time in between. You rigged the gate opener to let yourself in and out with a switch so the manager wouldn't know. You probably kept your truck parked down the street so no one would be suspicious. Is that true?"

Guardino's eyebrows moved together, forming two creases between them. He glared at Snow and seemed to have stopped breathing. Finally he spoke. "You can't prove that."

"That should be easy," Alice said. "We can get the lab people out to pull your prints off the gate opener."

His eyebrows lifted. "Alright. So what? Why would that concern you? That's not against the law. It's between me and the manager."

"Danny, were you inside your RV last Friday night around nine p.m.?" Alice said.

Guardino stared at her, his mind working.

"That would be the night Bob Williams was murdered," she said.

"I don't think so," Guardino said. "I probably got in late that night. Yeah, in fact, I remember noticing his trailer was gone."

"Then you would have also noticed his body lying there in the gravel, next to his truck," Snow reasoned.

"Not necessarily," Guardino said. "It's pretty dark in there at night. I wasn't paying much attention when I walked by."

Snow shook his head and chuckled to himself. "I don't think it's that dark in there, Danny, that you could walk right past a body and miss it."

Guardino considered this. "Well, yeah, alright. I might have been asleep in the trailer when it happened. I didn't hear anything."

"Do you sleep with your windows open in there at night? And the roof vents? It's been pretty warm lately, even at night."

"Look." Guardino's voice rose an octave. "I didn't hear anything. I was asleep."

"Are you sure, Danny?" Snow pressed. "Two guys with booming voices in the dead of night, slamming car doors two spaces over from yours, and that didn't wake you up?"

Guardino said nothing.

"A loud voice," Snow continued, "through an open doorway, counting out hundred-dollar bills. That must have sounded pretty enticing to an unemployed auto mechanic, forced to live in a trailer in an RV storage lot. I know that would definitely wake me up."

"I was asleep," Guardino said. "I didn't hear anything. That's all I have to say."

Snow studied the man's face for a moment. Then nodded. "Okay, Danny." He turned to Alice. "Better call Mel and see about the search warrant."

Guardino's eyes opened wide. He stared at Snow in horror. But he said nothing more.

Alice got her phone out of her purse and speed-dialed Mel Harris's cell number. It rang through to his voice mail. She left a message and disconnected the call.

"That's strange," she said. "He always answers his phone, unless it's turned off—even when he's on the john."

"What do you think?" Snow asked her.

"I'm going to call the lieutenant," she said. Then she punched in his home number.

He answered after a few rings.

"Lieutenant Bradley, this is Detective James."

"Oh yes, how are you?" Bradley asked.

"I'm fine," Alice said. "I'm trying to get in touch with Detective Harris, but he's not answering his cell phone—"

"You haven't heard the news, I take it," Bradley said. "Oh yes, you're on vacation. Well, Detective Harris is in the hospital, I'm afraid."

Alice looked at Snow, her mouth open. "What happened?"

"Well, apparently," Bradley began, "he was in Red Rock Canyon this morning, running on one of the hiking trails. I guess he had some bad Mexican food last night, and during his run, he was overpowered by a bad case of the backdoor trots. So he darted behind a large mesquite bush to take care of the problem, and he was in such a hurry that he wasn't paying any attention to his surroundings. He landed right in front of a rattler. Almost stepped right on it.

"Of course the snake bit him in the calf, and that, in turn, caused a secondary reaction, which alleviated the initial problem, but complicated things.

"So he got back on the trail. And being that it was so early in the morning, there wasn't anyone around. He didn't have his cell phone with him, so he ran back to the road and tried to flag down a motorist. A few cars came past, but no one would stop for him because of…well, you know, his appearance. Finally a park ranger happened by and reluctantly took him to the hospital."

"Oh, that's terrible," Alice said. "Is he alright?"

"Yes, they got him there in time. The Mojave rattlesnake, I guess, is a very deadly snake. He could have died. Except that, by the description Detective Harris gave, they think it was a Western Diamondback instead. Luckily, they had the antivenin right there at the hospital, so there shouldn't be any permanent damage. Although the doctor said he would have probably been fine if he just went home to bed—they think the snake only injected a small amount of venom. His symptoms were pretty mild. But he'll be in the hospital for a couple of days at the most. And after that he'll have to take it easy at home for a while longer."

"That's good news at least," Alice said.

"Yes," Bradley said. "And everyone in the bureau got together to get him a gift, which has already been delivered to Detective Harris at the hospital."

"What was that?" Alice asked.

"A large box of adult Pampers." Bradley chuckled. "A sensitive, caring group there at the Robbery/Homicide Bureau." He laughed again. "I'm afraid Detective Harris will never hear the end of this."

Alice smiled. "Who is handling the Williams murder investigation?"

"Well," Bradley said, "Detective Brewer, who was to be Detective Harris's new partner, has been tied up with other investigations, so he hasn't transitioned over yet. Right now, I guess that falls onto my plate for the time being. Why do you ask?"

Alice explained about the information they had implicating Danny Guardino as a suspect, and the existence, in her opinion, of probable cause.

"I'd like to get a warrant to search Mr. Guardino's travel trailer."

Guardino was staring down at the sidewalk, his teeth clenched, shaking his head.

"You say the trailer is taped inside the crime scene?" Bradley said. "If that's the case, we may not need a search warrant. I can check on it."

Guardino suddenly raised his head, his eyebrows arched. He waved his hands next to his face. "It's okay!" he blurted. "You don't need a warrant! I'll let you in. I don't have anything to hide."

"Oh," Alice said into the phone. "We won't need the warrant after all. The suspect is granting us entry."

"Good," Bradley said. "I guess I'd better meet you there since you're no longer assigned to the case. By the way, Detective, aren't you supposed to be on vacation?"

"This *is* my vacation, Lieutenant," Alice said. "If I want to spend it in an RV storage lot, that's my business."

"That's true," Bradley said. "I guess I'll see you in, say, fifteen minutes at the crime scene?"

"Yes sir."

"By the way, Detective..."

"Yes sir?"

"Nice detective work."

"Thank you, Lieutenant." She disconnected the call.

Snow gave her a curious look. "What happened to Mel?"

Alice sighed. "The short version of the story is that he went out for a run, got bit by a snake, and shit his pants."

CHAPTER 38

The crime scene tape was still in place, with a black-and-white squad car guarding the scene. Danny Guardino parked his Ford truck next to the front door of his trailer and swung out of the driver seat. Snow parked behind him.

Everyone stood around, each with a flashlight, by the side of the trailer, avoiding conversation. Guardino was clearly nervous, continually kicking at the gravel with his hiking boots.

Five minutes later, Lieutenant Bradley drove up in an unmarked Crown Victoria. Wearing a pair of tan slacks and a green golf shirt, his nine-millimeter and badge clipped to his belt, he got out of his car. He walked over to Snow, holding his Mag flashlight in his left hand, and introduced himself. They shook hands. It was a three-pump, a fairly positive sign.

"I've heard quite a bit about you," Bradley said. "I heard you did a lot of good work for the section. Sorry you left. We could use a good man like you on the team."

Snow nodded. "Thank you."

"I heard you quit the force to play poker for a living."

"That's true," Snow said.

"That's something I've always wanted to try," Bradley said. "I watch it on television quite a bit. It doesn't look that tough, but I imagine it's a lot more difficult when you don't know everyone's hole cards."

"That does make a difference," Snow said.

Bradley turned to Willie. "And who is this gentleman?"

"That's Willie Hoffman," Snow said. "He's a friend of mine."

Willie and Bradley shook hands.

"Nice suit," Bradley said.

Willie nodded. "I just came from a job interview."

Bradley smiled and nodded. Snow rolled his eyes.

Producing a pocketknife from his trousers, Bradley walked over to the trailer and cut the yellow tape. Holding the left end tight, he wrapped it around the rear bumper of the trailer. Snow grabbed the other end and tied it around the hitch coupler in front.

Danny Guardino unlocked the door and opened it. He lowered the step and climbed inside the trailer, flipping on the ceiling lights. Alice and Snow followed close behind, and then Bradley. Willie remained outside, standing next to the door. With the four of them inside the trailer, it was a fairly tight fit.

"Alright. What are we looking for?" Bradley said.

Snow surveyed the inside of the trailer. He stepped around Bradley into the tiny bedroom area. He stood at the corner of the bed. "You mind if I look under here?"

Guardino had moved over in front of the refrigerator. He had his hand on the refrigerator door, leaning against it. "Be my guest," he said.

Snow reached down, gripped the sheet of plywood under the mattress, and pulled up on it. Aided by two gas springs, the entire end of the bed rose up at an angle. He looked inside the storage compartment below it. Nothing but the fresh water tank, a small vacuum cleaner, and an empty luggage bag. He lowered the bed to its frame.

"We're looking for a bow and some arrows, Lieutenant," Snow said. "And possibly a stack of hundred-dollar bills."

Between Alice, Snow, and Lieutenant Bradley, they searched every cabinet and storage space inside and out of the trailer. No sign of anything archery-related, and no money.

Snow had begun to sweat. It was warm inside the small trailer. He looked down at the three red toolboxes arranged on the floor under the kitchen table.

"Do you have a set of screwdrivers in one of those?" Snow asked.

Guardino narrowed his eyes. "Of course. Why?"

"You mind if I take a look?"

"Okay. Sure." Guardino crossed to the table, leaned over, and lifted one of the toolboxes out from under the table. He flipped the clasps open, lifted the lid, and pulled out the middle drawer of the toolbox. It was full of various screwdrivers. Slotted and Phillips, large and small.

Snow pulled a rubber glove out of his pocket, turned it inside out, and stretched it over his hand. He reached into the assortment of screwdrivers and shoved a few of them out of the way.

He stood up and pointed to it. "You see that pointed tool?"

Everybody leaned over and looked into the drawer of the toolbox.

"That's an awl. I think Mr. Guardino wedged that under the victim's tire. When the victim tried to drive forward in his truck, it was driven into the tire. Steve Helm then left with the victim's trailer. And then Mr. Guardino snuck around behind the victim, at a safe distance so as not to disturb him while he was changing the tire, and shot him in the back with two arrows."

"*I did not!*" Guardino protested, his eyes wide, his face losing color. "*No way!*"

"Alright," Alice said. "Lieutenant, I'd like to get a CSA out here to bag this awl and have it sent back to the lab to check for trace evidence from the victim's tire."

Guardino was livid, his face slick with sweat. "You're not gonna put that murder on me! I didn't do it!"

"If that's the case, then this awl should be clear of any particles or fibers from the tire, and you have nothing to worry about."

Guardino held his hands open in front of him, as though he were trying to ward off an attack. "Alright. Alright. Look. I'll tell you the whole story. Every detail. But you have to believe me—I didn't kill that guy. I swear. I never planned to kill him!"

Bradley looked at Alice. "Do you have a Miranda card with you?"

Alice took it out of her purse and read it to him. Guardino, his shoulders sagging, said he understood his rights.

Then he started in at the beginning: "I got laid off from my job about a month ago. I was living paycheck to paycheck and couldn't get by on unemployment, so I got the idea to move into my trailer here. I already had a generator, and I hooked up the solar panel to keep the battery charged. I broke the lock off the gate opener and rigged a switch so I could come and go without the manager noticing that I was living here. Most of the time, I parked on the street and walked in so nobody would get suspicious seeing a truck parked in front of my trailer at night.

"Last Friday night I was sitting in here, watching a movie on my portable DVD player. All my windows were open a little, and I could hear them over there talking about the trailer. They were really loud. And then they started talking about the eight thousand in cash. And I began thinking that money would really help out. I could just get out of here and head up north. Just travel around, boondocking for a while.

"I heard that Steve guy go out to his truck to get the cash, and then he came back inside the trailer with Bob. And he started counting out the money in thousand-dollar stacks. That's when I decided I was going to do it. And it suddenly came to me how I could do it.

"I thought if this guy Bob discovered that he had a flat, he'd probably get left behind to change it by himself. You know, most people are basically assholes. Nobody wants to help anybody, if they can avoid it. So I figured Steve would just drive off with the trailer and leave Bob alone to deal with the flat tire by himself. And Bob would have the cash. It was perfect.

"So I got the awl out of my toolbox and snuck around in a wide circle so they wouldn't hear me. While they were still in the trailer, counting out the money and filling out the title, I crept up to Bob's truck and angled the awl up under his tire. I pressed the point of it into the rubber a little to get it started. And it worked.

"I was back in my trailer, waiting and listening. They hooked the trailer up, and Steve pulled ahead with it. Then Bob drove ahead in his truck and the awl penetrated the tire. They both got out and looked at it. Like I figured, Steve made a lot of noise about sticking around to help, and then he just left. But actually, you know, how many people does it take to change a tire anyway? One person watches, the other does the work.

"So Steve left, and Bob was out there changing that tire—all alone. I was planning to put a paper bag over my head, with cutouts for the eyes. But there was just one problem. I couldn't get myself to do it. I figured out right then that I don't have it in me to rob somebody. So I said the hell with it and went back to watching my DVD player.

"But then a few minutes later, I heard two thuds and the sound of Bob falling over onto the gravel. I was scared out of my wits. I wasn't sure what happened out there. But it didn't sound good, so I turned off my DVD player and just sat here without moving a hair.

"I heard footsteps in the gravel, like somebody walking up to him, then some rustling like he was moving the body around on the gravel. I knew then that somebody else was robbing the poor bastard. Only they had decided to just go ahead and kill him along with it.

"After that I heard the footsteps going back in the same direction they had come from. And then it got quiet again. I sat here for over an hour without moving. I knew I had to get that awl out of the tire, or the cops would figure I did it. So I went outside real quiet, crept around to the front of my trailer, and saw that nobody was around. Just Bob laying there dead next to his pickup.

"I went over and pulled my awl out of the tire, came back, and put it away in the toolbox. Then I threw some clothes and stuff in an overnight bag and got the hell out of here. I slept in my truck in a parking lot that night. I was so upset I didn't even feel like checking into a motel, just wanted to park and go to sleep."

"Did you sleep?" Snow asked.

"No," Guardino said. "Just lay there all night with my eyes wide open. I don't know, maybe I slept for an hour or two. Sometimes it's hard to tell if you really slept."

No one said anything for more than a minute. The three of them just stood there, staring at Danny Guardino.

Finally Guardino broke the silence. "I know you think I killed Bob with my bow. But when you think about it, that makes no sense at all. Why would I use a bow and arrows when I have a gun?"

With that, he reached into his front pocket and brought out a chrome-plated derringer with wooden grips. He held it in his palm, with the barrel pointed toward the roof of the trailer.

Bradley reacted immediately, flipping off the strap to his handgun with his thumb and drawing in one quick motion. He aimed the gun at Guardino's chest and ordered him to lay the weapon on the table and step back from it.

"Take it easy, man," Guardino said, his eyes wide. He eased forward and laid the derringer on the kitchen table and stepped back.

"You have a concealed weapons permit for that thing?" Bradley demanded.

Guardino dug into his back pocket and pulled out his wallet. He slipped a laminated card out and tossed it on the table next to the gun.

Bradley picked it up and examined it front and back. "Alright." He dropped the card back on the table and then pointed a finger at Guardino. "But in the future, don't be pulling that thing out like that unless you intend to use it. That's a good way to get yourself shot."

Snow spoke up. "What happened to your archery set?"

"A couple of weeks ago I was taking target practice with it along the back fence," he began.

This was all Jim Snow needed to hear. He knew where this was going. A sudden chill crawled up his spine. How could he have been so stupid?

"I had a small bag target that I set out next to the fence. So I was shooting at it and drinking a beer. I needed to take a leak and grab a fresh beer, so I left everything out there, even my quill full of arrows. I was only gone five minutes or less. When I came back out with the beer, everything was gone—even the bag target!"

Snow shot a glance at Alice. She stared back at him, her eyes wide.

"Willie," Snow muttered under his breath.

He stepped over to the door and hurled himself down the step to the gravel, nearly falling. He stood, turning in half circles, looking in every direction. There was no one in sight.

The tramp was gone.

CHAPTER 39

With the beam of his three-cell aluminum flashlight showing the way, Jim Snow ran toward the back corner of the fence. When he got there, the last bit of doubt filtered away. The bungee cords had been unhooked, and the section of fence was hanging back at an angle, the end of it almost touching the ground.

He climbed through and then stopped to listen, playing the circle of light along the feathery arms of the tamarisk bushes down in the wash, the shadows behind them shifting along the ground like black phantoms.

A crunching of footsteps, rushing toward him from behind, captured his attention, and he turned quickly, swinging his light toward the sound.

Alice was running toward him, a Mag flashlight in one hand and a nine-millimeter automatic in the other.

"Wait for me, you dumb shit," she snapped. "You don't even have a gun."

They scrambled down the sloping gravel bank together, working their lights over the bushes. They followed the trail between the reeds, dodging hanging limbs, Snow out in front and Alice close behind.

When they got to the small clearing, Snow stopped abruptly. "Jesus," he muttered.

He aimed the beam of light at it.

Spread out over fifteen feet, in a thick, tubular mass of brown blotches, a Burmese python lay resting on top of Willie's cardboard mat.

Snow stood frozen, unable to move.

Alice came up beside him. "What is that?" she whispered.

"What the hell does it look like?" Snow whispered back. "It's a big-ass snake. And it's lying on top of the money."

"How do you know the money is there?"

"Because that's where Willie sleeps down here, and I doubt that he would hide something valuable anywhere else but underneath where he sleeps. And now that I see that snake there, I'm sure of it."

"You think he dragged that snake over there?" Alice whispered.

"I'm sure of it," Snow insisted.

"Well, then let's just move it off the cardboard. What could be so hard about that?"

Snow tilted his head toward her slowly, his eyes nearly bulging out of his head.

"Don't tell me you're afraid of snakes. A big tough guy like you?"

Snow took a deep breath and let it out. "Alright, let's go. How do we do it? You have any idea?"

"This was probably somebody's pet," Alice explained, "so just move casually up to his head. Pet him a few times to show that you're friendly. Then slip your left hand around his neck, with your right hand further back, and lift him up. I'll lift up the middle, and we'll drag him off the cardboard and set him down." She returned her weapon to her ankle holster and propped her flashlight up against the trunk a tree, the beam of light pointing upward.

Snow shivered. "How do you know all this?"

"I saw it on a documentary," she said. "They show little kids in the Amazon, with big smiles on their faces, carrying snakes bigger than this one around."

Snow crouched down slightly and shuffled along the length of the snake to the head. Its head rose up off the cardboard, the forked tongue darting in and out of its mouth. Snow laid his flashlight on the ground next to his left foot. He reached into his pocket and pulled out a small penknife, opened it, and stabbed it through the cardboard into the ground.

"If he sinks his fangs into my leg, I'll cut his head off," Snow snarled. He reached out with his left hand and grabbed the snake's neck. It felt like smooth leather. The snake's mouth opened.

"His mouth is opening—what does that mean?" Snow asked. "You think I might be holding him by the neck too tight? Maybe I'm choking him."

"I think he's laughing at your knife," Alice said.

"I think he's getting ready to bite," Snow said. Then he glanced back at Alice. "This is all wrong. You've got the heavy part and my end is light. I'm a lot stronger than you. I should be lifting the heaviest section."

Alice rolled her eyes. "Alright. Let's switch then."

They changed places, lifted, and then dragged the snake a foot to the left of the edge of the cardboard mat, and set it down. Snow hurried to the other side, lifted the cardboard, and tossed it off between two bushes. The ground underneath near the center of where the mat had been was soft and loose. With Alice shining her flashlight, Snow squatted down and dug with both hands until he worked his way down to a white plastic grocery bag. He pulled it up from the loose soil and shook the dirt off from it. Then he set it on the ground and opened it.

Inside was a thick wad of hundred-dollar bills, held together with a single rubber band.

"Got it," Snow said.

"You got it alright." Willie's voice came from behind Alice.

He stood ten feet behind her, the bow in his left hand, an arrow threaded and ready to fire in his right. He was still wearing the suit and tie.

Snow stood up.

Alice reached down to her ankle slowly, brought the nine-millimeter up, and aimed it at Willie with both arms extended.

"Now this is how this is going to work," Willie said. "Jim, you'll toss the bag of money over to my feet. Alice, you'll put the gun down and kick it over here next to the money. Then both of you will back away. And I'll be out of your hair. Otherwise Jim's going to have this arrow sticking out of his chest."

Nobody moved.

"So you've been practicing with that thing, I take it," Snow said.

"Yep. Two weeks now. I thought this would be useful for hunting rabbits down here in the wash. Never thought I'd get the opportunity that presented itself last Friday night."

"I thought you said you weren't up there Friday night."

"I lied," Willie said. "I could hear those guys talking about that money from more than a hundred feet away. They were talking so loud I bet they could hear them over on the other side of the wash. I had the archery stuff stored in another boat a few spaces over. You didn't think to look anywhere but the boat I was sleeping in, did you, Jim? You know what your problem is, Jim?"

"What's that, Willie?"

"Most of time, you actually believed your own sister had the guy killed. Your own sister. Yet here I am, somebody you had never met, and you trusted every word that came out of my mouth."

"But I talked to your lifelong buddy from your childhood days. He should know you better than anybody."

"One subjective opinion," Willie said. "You should have gotten a consensus from more people. Ah hell, I don't know. If I had it to do over again, I wouldn't have shot that guy. But I didn't have time to sleep on it. I never would have planned anything like that. The opportunity was there, and I took it. Afterward, I began to regret it. But from the back, the guy looked like a politician, so that made it a little easier."

"If it's any comfort to you," Snow said, "he looked like one from the front, too."

"I'm not seeing any movement from either of you to comply with my wishes," Willie said. "Alice, if you'd like, you can go first."

"If I go first, your guts will be splattered all over that tree behind you," she said.

"That's not what I had in mind," Willie said. "And my arm is starting to get tired."

"She won't give up her gun, Willie," Snow said. "She's an experienced police detective. She's trained to never give up her weapon under any circumstances. And if you shoot me with that arrow, the only way it will kill me right away is if it punctures my heart. Failing that, and if Alice doesn't shoot you, I'll come running over there with this arrow sticking out of me and rip your eyeballs out."

"Huh," Willie said. "That doesn't sound good. Maybe this isn't such a good plan after all."

"Tell me something," Snow said. "You soaked that brick hammer in bleach and threw it out there alongside the road and then called it in—didn't you?"

Willie chuckled. "That had everybody running around for a while. Didn't it?"

"Yeah." Snow looked over at the snake. It appeared to be sleeping. "Did you drag that snake over here?"

"He didn't mind," Willie said. "He's a good boy."

"I noticed." He looked back at Willie. "I think you and that snake have more in common than you know. Here's what's going to happen. And you'd better put some thought into this. I'm walking out of here with this bag of money. If you want to shoot me, go ahead. Otherwise, you can put the bow and arrow down. Take the money and the murder weapon up to the lieutenant and turn yourself in. Alice and I won't say anything about what happened down here tonight. Right, Alice?"

"Speak for yourself, Jim," Alice said. "I'm getting ready to blow his ass into those bushes."

"Well, hell," Willie said. "I'm sixty-one. I probably should start thinking about retirement. I'm too old to be riding the rails, sleeping in the bushes, and eating canned food. Not many options to choose from at this point. It's a little late to start saving. With prison, I'll get free health care, three squares a day. Work toward my doctorate. I guess that doesn't sound too awfully bad. I'll just ask one favor of you."

"What's that?" Snow said.

"That you and Alice will find it in your hearts to grace my stay at the penitentiary with your periodic visits."

"Forget it," Snow said.

"Alright. How about just Thanksgiving and Christmas?" Willie said.

"I can't speak for Alice," Snow said, "but I'll give it some thought."

Willie lowered the bow. He looked at the snake. "I'd appreciate it if you would see to it that Arnold gets a good home. Poor fella. He didn't do anything to deserve living in a cage."

CHAPTER 40

What a difference forty-eight hours makes. Karen came to the door full of bounce, grinning from ear to ear, her eyes clear and sparkling. Steve Helm was standing right behind her, gripping a bottle of Tsingtao like it was rooted to his hand. Some things never change.

Alice James and Jim Snow walked into the entryway, Alice holding a bottle of sauvignon blanc, Snow holding Alice's hand. Alice offered the wine to Karen, which was followed by lots of hugging. Except for Helm and Snow, who partook of the customary male ritual. It was a firm five-pumper. A lot can be conveyed in a single handshake.

"Cold beer?" Helm asked.

"Well, I was hoping to get into some of that wine." Snow nodded at the bottle in Karen's hand.

Helm laughed. "What'll it be? I'm fully stocked. I brought my cooler over."

"Good man," Snow said. "Let me have a Foster's. I'm feeling down under today."

Alice and Karen went into the kitchen. Helm and Snow headed out to the back yard. It was nearly six p.m., and the sun was setting, casting a wide shadow from Karen's desert willow tree near the edge of the cement patio.

Helm dug around in the plastic cooler and brought out a dripping bottle of Foster's. He popped the cap off and handed it to Snow.

They settled back in two of the lawn chairs.

Helm took a slug of beer and sighed. "There is nothing like the resolution of adversity to calm the soul. That and a few brewskies."

"Isn't that the truth," Snow said.

They clinked their bottles together and drank.

"You did a hell of a job, you know," Helm said. "And I sincerely appreciate it."

Snow cradled his beer in his lap. He resisted the temptation to confess that for most of the investigation he was convinced Helm was the culprit. "We just lucked into it," he said. "But I wouldn't have gotten anywhere without Alice. She's good."

"She's not so bad looking, either," Helm observed. "You think the two of you might make a go of it?"

Snow shrugged. "She does seem to be a refreshing change to my usual selection of women. Usually, I just pick the first one that comes along who looks like she still might fit into her high school cheerleader outfit. By the way, I still have your rock hammer in the trunk of my car. You'll probably want that back."

"Nah, keep it," Helm said. "I won't be doing anymore rock hunting, if you get my drift."

"You mean because Karen knows about Linda Maltby?"

"Ah. Not just that. It was getting kind of old with her, anyway. The thrill wears off pretty quick when there's nothing between the ears."

Snow nodded. "That's for sure."

"By the way, I have your check."

Snow turned his head to Helm. "What check?"

"Two thousand dollars. Made out to the Salvation Army. You still want to go that route?"

Snow took a swallow of beer. "I'd forgotten about that."

"You want me to give it to you? It's in my wallet."

Snow shook his head. "Just send it in."

They drank more beer and stared at the willow tree.

"What are you going to do now?" Helm asked.

"About what?"

"Your livelihood."

Snow shrugged. "I've been thinking about that for over a month. Still don't have a sense of direction. I may be finished with poker. I seem to have developed a genuine phobia for cards—worse than my fear of snakes."

"What about getting back on the force? Any chance they'll take you back?"

"Possibly, but I'm not so sure I want to go back to that. I don't know what I want to do. But I better figure it out before my money runs out."

Helm nodded. "By the way, what happened to that python you and Alice ran into down in the wash?"

"I don't know," Snow said. "I called animal control. They went down there and looked all up and down the wash. They couldn't find it. So they gave up and left."

The patio door slid open. Karen and Alice came through the doorway, each holding a glass of wine. Alice walked over to Snow and began to run her fingers through the hair on the back of his head.

"Steve!" Karen protested. "You haven't even started the barbeque, and it's going to be dark soon. What are you waiting for?"

Helm stood up. "Just waiting for you to come out here and get me motivated."

"Well—get your lazy ass in gear!"

Helm looked down at Snow. "I wonder how much longer this is going to last," he muttered.

Snow nodded. "You'd better get that grill fired up before she gets the pickaxe out of the garage."

With evening settling over the various plants and wildlife thriving in the overgrown jungle of the Las Vegas Wash, a fifteen-foot Burmese python lay curled up with his mate, hidden in a thick stand of reeds.

Fully rested, he stretched and slithered toward the open area at the edge of the reeds.

It was time to think about dinner.

END

ABOUT THE AUTHOR

Rex Kusler was born in Missouri and raised in a small town in Iowa. Thanks to a lifelong fascination with mathematical probability and gambling, he enjoys spending his free time in Las Vegas and looks forward to retiring there. For now, he lives and works in the Bay Area of northern California, seeking humor and fun in whatever he does.